THE
SCOUNDREL
AND THE
OPTIMIST

Maggie,
I was so wonderful seeing you
after all these years. Thank
you for your support!
        Let's please keep in
        touch.
    With affection,
        Mallo
            7/21/11

Bilingual Press/Editorial Bilingüe

Publisher
Gary D. Keller

Executive Editor
Karen S. Van Hooft

Associate Editors
Adriana M. Brady
Brian Ellis Cassity
Amy K. Phillips
Linda K. St. George

Address
Bilingual Press
Hispanic Research Center
Arizona State University
PO Box 875303
Tempe, Arizona 85287-5303
(480) 965-3867

THE
SCOUNDREL
AND THE
OPTIMIST

Maceo Montoya

Bilingual Press/Editorial Bilingüe

Tempe, Arizona

Library of Congress Cataloging-in-Publication Data

Montoya, Maceo.
    The scoundrel and the optimist / Maceo Montoya.
        p. cm.
    ISBN 978-1-931010-65-8 (hc. : alk. paper) — ISBN 978-1-931010-67-2 (pbk.
: alk. paper)
    1. Fathers and sons—Fiction.   2. Domestic fiction.   I. Title.
    PS3613.O54945S36 2009
    813'.6—dc22

                                           2009010401

Front cover art: The Scoundrel and the Optimist *(2008) by Maceo Montoya*
Cover and interior design by Aerocraft Charter Art Service

Para mi hermano Andrés.

Hace años, en el invierno más solitario que recuerdo,
se me ocurrió que tal vez me dejaste tus palabras
por estos campos verdes y mojados y fui en busca.
Sigo buscando.

PART.

f Filastro Agustín's seven children, the only one he couldn't bear to beat was his youngest son, Edmund. There were, to be exact, three reasons for this. First of all, Edmund was a very fragile boy. His head seemed much too large for his puny body, his limbs merely an assortment of sticks. Filastro firmly believed in good solid beatings, not just for his own children, but also for his nephews and the neighborhood riffraff, not to mention his wife (and when drunk, just about anyone). But Filastro also firmly believed in one's right to live, and he had reason to worry that his sickly-looking child might very well die if dealt too serious a blow.

The second reason follows the first. Filastro, worrying about his son's fragility, took him to the doctor and asked point-blank: "Doctor, I'm worried that if I beat him I might kill him! What is your opinion? Is it safe?" The doctor examined the boy from head to toe, checked his pulse, peered into his tonsils, and hit his knee with a small mallet. "I think this boy would be perfectly fine with a good beating from time to time," said the doctor in his final analysis. "Well, that's fantastic!" Filastro exclaimed, his face radiant. "But," continued the doctor, "there's something you should be careful about."

"And what is that?" Filastro asked.

"His psychological state," replied the doctor.

"His what? Just what in the hell are you talking about?"

"It means that bones and flesh heal, but feelings do not."

"What do you take me for, a sissy, doctor? Don't give me that schoolgirl shit. What do I care about feelings?"

"You *must* care," the doctor implored. "If his psychological state is damaged, you never know what might happen. Dreadful consequences! Remember, Filastro, you won't always be a young man; in fact, you'll soon be an old man. And what will happen when you're half-blind and feeble, dependent on your children to feed you, to house you, to fiddle with the antenna when the television gets fuzzy? You'll be all alone if you damage your children's psychological state! Who knows, maybe you'll damage it too much, and you won't even make it to old age. I've heard stories of patricide that you wouldn't believe!" The doctor discreetly winked at Edmund. "Just the other day I read in the paper that three sons killed their father over a lousy ten pesos!"

On their walk home, Filastro asked Edmund if he believed his siblings' psychological states had been damaged.

"Yes, I think so."

"What about yours?"

"I'm fine, Papá," Edmund responded, smiling. "But I'd feel better, maybe, if I had a guitar."

So Filastro resolved that although his son was strong enough to be dealt a few swift kicks from time to time, he needed at least one of his children to possess a sound psychological state. "You will tell me if your brothers are plotting against me, right?" he asked Edmund frequently.

"Yes, Papá," Edmund would say, strumming a chord on his new guitar.

The third reason doesn't closely follow the first or second, as often Filastro forgot about his son's fragile body and psychological state. He forgot because he was drunk, which was more often than not. He'd come home from the bar, reeking of liquor, stumbling across the cobblestones, talking to imaginary friends, and he'd slam on the front door. "Open up! Open up!" he'd scream, until usually the neighbor would open the window and say, "Next door, damn it!" Filastro would find his way to his own house, where his wife would be waiting for him, water, aspirin, and midnight snack in hand.

If he was up to it, he'd slap her across the cheek. On a good night, he'd merely call her names. On a bad night, he'd wake up all his children—five boys and two girls—and have them stand at attention while he ate his meal. If they didn't wake up, he'd take out his belt and whip them. If they nodded off while standing at attention, he'd rise from the table and pinch their ears. If they stood at attention perfectly, he'd pick one who stood all too perfectly and beat him for thinking he was better than everyone else. The only one exempt from this late-night roll call was Edmund. He was required to play the guitar while his father sang.

Filastro would request a song and Edmund would strum the chords, the same combination over and over—C, F, G7, C, F, G7—but his father didn't know the difference. He would belt out the lyrics in between bites, meat and tortilla flying from his mouth, *I am just a man, a rock on the road, living out my sad destiny*, and Edmund would stand there, guitar in hand, smiling blissfully at the sleepy-eyed roomful gathered to watch his performance.

"I can't bear to beat my little guitarrista!" Filastro would say before collapsing on the table.

His other brothers and sisters, understandably, despised Edmund. So whereas he was safe from his father's blows, he received his fair share from Abel, Ezekiel, Tomy, Gandolfo, and his twin sisters, Agnes and Alfonsa.

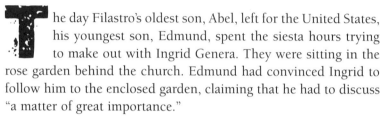

The day Filastro's oldest son, Abel, left for the United States, his youngest son, Edmund, spent the siesta hours trying to make out with Ingrid Genera. They were sitting in the rose garden behind the church. Edmund had convinced Ingrid to follow him to the enclosed garden, claiming that he had to discuss "a matter of great importance."

"What are you talking about?" she asked.

"Well, listen, Ingrid, it's a matter of great importance."

"Why can't you tell me here in front of my house?"

"Because what I'm about to tell you is not for others to hear."

"What is it, then?" she inquired, her curiosity piqued.

It was the club-footed Jorge el Gato, Edmund's half brother and cousin (a result of Filastro's philandering with his wife's sister Lupe), who told him that in order to conquer a woman you must surround yourself with an aura of mystery.

"How do I do that, Jorge?"

"Well, usually you tell them something like 'I must talk to you about a matter of great importance.' "

"Just like that?"

"Just like that."

So Ingrid followed Edmund to the peaceful garden behind the church and when he was sure no one could see them, he leaned in and kissed Ingrid on the lips. She backed away, startled.

"You're just a little boy!" she cried.

"I'm thirteen and you're only fourteen," he argued.

"But, Edmund, you look like you're eight."

"And you look like a horse!"

"A horse?" she exclaimed.

"Yes, a horse because you have skinny bowlegs."

It wasn't Jorge el Gato, but his father who told Edmund that in order to conquer a woman you must be mean to her, insult her if need be, reduce her to tears.

"Reduce her to tears?" Edmund had asked inquisitively.

"Yes, to tears! And then you comfort her, pat the top of her head, wrap your arm around her shoulders, and she's yours because now she's afraid she's too ugly to get anyone else."

"But Ingrid isn't ugly. She's the prettiest girl in all of La Prudencia."

"Well, mijo, you must make her feel ugly."

"Like how?"

"Tell her, for example, she looks like a horse."

"But horses aren't ugly."

"Damn it, Edmund, women who *look* like horses are! You ask too many questions! Leave me in peace!"

So Edmund told Ingrid she looked like a horse and then added the part about bowlegs because Ingrid did indeed have knees that traveled outward. But Ingrid wasn't so easily fazed.

"Well, you look like a troll," she retorted.

"A troll? What the hell is a troll?"

"Something that looks like you and lives under a bridge."

"But I don't live under a bridge."

"So what? You have a big head like a troll, and red hair like a troll, and you have a scraggly mustache just like a troll, and you—"

"My mustache isn't scraggly!"

"Yes it is. You have three hairs on your lip and you think it's a mustache."

Edmund wasn't prepared for such harsh insults. He was so taken aback that he couldn't think of anything to say in return, and if he could have thought of anything, he feared his voice would crack with emotion. So he opted for a different tactic. He reached out and tried to touch Ingrid's breasts.

"You little piece of goat shit!" she cried. "I'm going to tell Rafa and he's going to beat you!"

"Beat me?"

"Yes, beat your skinny eight-year-old-looking troll butt!"

"Why are you being so mean to me, Ingrid?" he cried.

"You were mean to me first!"

"I was only trying—"

"Trying to do what?"

"Well, if you must know the truth . . . I love you!"

It was his sisters, Agnes and Alfonsa, who taught him that saying "I love you" got men out of many a damaging situation.

"Yes, it's true," Agnes was telling Alfonsa, "I saw Beto looking at another woman, making eyes at the whore, so I threw my drink at him and walked out of the bar."

"And what did he do?" asked Alfonsa.

"He ran after me, of course."

"And what did you do?"

"I told him that I hated him, that he treated me worse than a dog, and that he was going to be worse than my father."

"And what did he do?"

"He got down on his knees in the street in front of everyone, and said, 'But Agnes, I love you!' "

"Oh that's so romantic!" Alfonsa squealed with delight.

But unfortunately, Ingrid Genera wasn't so easily won over. "You love me, huh?" she said.

"Yes, I do."

"OK, then, prove it."

"Just tell me how."

"Go to confession and tell the priest that not only did you lie to me and insult me, but you also tried to touch me in private places."

"I can't tell the priest that! Please, something else!" Edmund pleaded.

"Well, I guess you don't love me," Ingrid said, a mocking smile on her face.

Edmund walked home dejected, cursing the woes of the heart. He wished he had never met Ingrid Genera. He wished he had never met any women at all, except for his mother and his grandmother and his tía Lupe, because without her there'd be no Jorge el Gato, his best friend, favorite cousin, and favorite half-brother (although he only had one, as far as he knew).

When Edmund arrived home, he found his mother sobbing in the kitchen while his father was tearing the bedroom apart in a blind rage.

"What happened?" he asked Ezekiel, his second eldest brother.

"Abel is gone."

"Where'd he go?"

"To Nebraska."

"Where the hell is that?"

"In the United States."

"Why'd he go there for?"

Agnes and Alfonsa were crying as well, both of them holding a letter in their hands, emitting muffled sobs as they read its contents.

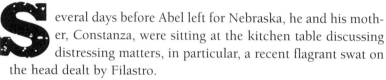
Several days before Abel left for Nebraska, he and his mother, Constanza, were sitting at the kitchen table discussing distressing matters, in particular, a recent flagrant swat on the head dealt by Filastro.

"Why are you so upset?" she asked.

"Why? Why? How can you ask why? Amá, look at me, I've just been beaten for the second time in as many days."

"But, mijito, this is nothing new; you must have gotten used to it."

"To my father beating me? How can I ever get used to it? He saves his worst blows for me!"

"I beg to differ," said his mother with her brow raised. "He saves his worst for me."

"Maybe so, and you're telling me you've gotten used to it?"

"Numb to it, more likely."

"Well, I don't believe it, I really don't. He's beaten me for the last time! I'm leaving!"

"But Abel, where will you go?"

"Where? Where else?"

"But, mijito, you have a good job here in La Prudencia. You're willing to give that up—"

"I deliver pizzas, two a night at best!"

"We depend on the little you bring in."

"My father does. He drinks it away, all of our money! And don't tell me that's not true."

It was true. Filastro required all his children, except Edmund, who was too fragile to work, to hand their earnings over to him. Then he doled out a few pesos to each of them, some pesos for his wife's domestic concerns, and the rest for himself. He always told them, "I'm off to the bank!" And he did intend to head to a certain financial institution, a gambling house to be exact, hoping to augment the week's collection. But he was invariably sidetracked by one or two or all three of his compadres, Big Gaspar, Mendigo, and Jerry, commencing a night of drinking and carousing, which *ended* at the gambling house where he subsequently lost the remaining pesos in his possession.

"Amá, I have to go," Abel continued, his voice firm. "In the next couple of days, but first I want to let Papá know just how much I hate him."

"And how will you do that?" his mother inquired hesitantly.

"I'm going to write him a letter."

"A letter?"

"Yes, a letter."

"But what can you say in a letter? My son, let's be honest with ourselves, we are not educated people."

"I'll have Ricardo do it, he's a friend of mine."

"Ricardo? The notary?"

"Yes, we went to school together before Papá made me drop out to deliver pizzas."

Ricardo the Notary sat at a wobbly little table under the overhang in front of the municipal building. His typewriter was official government property, meaning that when his hours finished he had to lock it away in the secretary's office. He had accepted the position *only* because he thought the typewriter would be his to take wherever he wanted. His limited mobility was a source of bitterness.

He wore a white visor, which complemented his starched white shirt. He wore thin wire-rimmed glasses and had a perfectly trimmed mustache. He fancied himself an intellectual, and modeled his appearance after José Vasconcelos, the long-ago former minister of education.

He had wanted to attend the university in Guadalajara, but his father had made him stay in La Prudencia to find a respectable job instead of becoming a marijuana-smoking homosexual. This was also a source of bitterness.

Thus, when Abel approached him about writing a letter spewing nothing but pure hatred toward his father, Ricardo was ready for the challenge.

"I think you should take a more diplomatic approach," the notary advised.

"How do you mean?"

"I mean, instead of telling Filastro you hate him, you hate him, you hate him, tell him the many reasons why, complete with irrefutable examples."

"How do you mean?"

"I mean, for instance, tell me one reason why you hate your father."

"Because he beats me."

"Because he beats you—good. And why does he beat you?"

"For no reason."

"For no reason at all?"

"Sometimes a little reason, like if I make too much noise when I get up in the morning."

"That's not a very good reason to beat your son."

"You're telling me."

"OK, well, that's something to work with. Let me start. How about something to the effect of 'Papá, you are a despicable tyrant, a troglodyte incapable of reason.' How does that sound for a beginning?"

"Good, but what's a tro—— whatever that word you said?"

"It's a man who beats his children for no reason at all. It's an appropriate word, cuts to the chase, leaves no room for interpretation."

"But how is my dad supposed to know that word?"

"What matters is that everything's said as articulately as possible. Who cares what your father understands? What matters is posterity."

"Posterity?"

"Yes, one day when you've made your fortune in the United States, you'll come across this letter and show your sons, 'Look, this is the kind of man I was.'"

"But that's a hard word to remember. What if my sons ask me what it means and I no longer know?"

"Well, then write it on a flashcard and keep it in your wallet. That's what I do."

By the time Ricardo the Notary finished Abel's letter, the majority of it was clearly borne from his empathy for the subject. It went as follows:

Dear Father (or do you even deserve the title?),

You're a despicable tyrant, a troglodyte incapable of reason. Over my short lifetime, I've suffered your countless blows, both physical and psychological; how can I say which has been worse? You have looked upon me with scorn ever since I was a child and I liked to play capture the flag, and you said to me after one particularly grueling game, "You come home like a sweaty hog. You disgust me!" How does a child feel after such venomous, disdainful remarks? Obviously I've never forgotten them. And then there was the time you found me reading a book about owls, and you said, "Owls? Owls? Owls are for sissies!" Why did you have to say that to me? What is it about owls that make them for sissies? Nothing, I conclude. You merely pick something I like and choose to deride it, to make fun of it, to hold it up for ridicule. But no more, Father! No more because I'm leaving your home, your den of brutality, your prison where you preside as merciless warden. With this letter in your hand, you know I am gone, off to Nebraska where I'll find work with Gregorio, my cousin's cousin's friend, the nephew of your compadre Gaspar, the son of the neighbor of my tía Lety. You'll never see me again, I promise you that because I'll only return to La Prudencia to spit on your grave. And that's a promise!

Your eldest son,

Abel

When Ricardo finished reading the letter aloud, he asked Abel his thoughts. Abel responded, "I like it . . . except I don't think I ever had a book on owls."

"Then see it as a metaphor."

"What?"

Ricardo sighed. "Listen, Abel, we are old friends, ever since the fourth grade, and even though we haven't spoken since then, we are kindred spirits, more or less. I am a Man of Letters; you must trust me, trust my intellectual impulse. Do you understand?"

"No."

"Take this letter to your father. I promise he'll rip apart his bedroom in a blind rage."

"OK, how much do I owe you?"

"There is no price on a man's art."

"How much?"

"Five pesos."

ot long after Abel departed, Filastro's second oldest son, Ezekiel, also left for the United States. His youngest son, Edmund, played no small role in escalating matters. That day Filastro and Edmund were sitting in the backyard doling out seed to the chickens. Filastro asked him if he had known beforehand about Abel's departure. When Edmund shook his head, Filastro flicked his son's ear and demanded the truth.

Edmund backed away and looked at his father in disbelief. "Why'd you do that for?"

"Because you're lying!"

"Me? How do you think I can lie to you about a situation I know nothing about? I came home the other day, same as you, found Abel gone, same as you, and saw nothing but that letter, same as you. What do you want me to say?"

Filastro brooded for a moment and then said, "Tell me which of your brothers helped him plan his trip and I'll beat the living shit out of him."

Edmund knitted his brow. "What do you take me for, Papá? You remember what the doctor warned—how many years ago was it? I still haven't forgotten. You think I'd contribute to the damage of my brothers' psychological state? If you want to beat up *Ezekiel* and have him resent you, harm you in your old age, then that's your problem. The blood won't be on my hands!"

"Ezekiel, you say," said his father through clenched teeth.

*　　*　　*

Ezekiel didn't know any more about Abel's departure than Edmund. He was merely in the forefront of Edmund's mind, the result of a troubling conversation they had shared that morning.

"Why are you so moody, you little shit?" Ezekiel had asked him.

"Because Ingrid Genera hates me."

"Why would Ingrid even talk to your ugly face?"

"Maybe because I play the guitar and Jorge el Gato says that musicians get all the women."

"That's stupid, you hear? And Jorge's a retard."

"No, what Jorge says is true. I saw Benni Terraza and his Banda del Fuego at the fiesta and all the girls were following him around, so you see, you don't know what you're talking about!"

Ezekiel laughed. "The difference between you and Benni Terraza is that he can actually play the guitar, and not only that, Benni Terraza doesn't look like a red-headed monkey."

"Well, I don't look like a red-headed monkey either," Edmund said, discouraged.

Ezekiel, sensing his younger brother's dilemma, decided to help. "Edmund, listen to me. I have some advice regarding Ingrid."

Edmund looked up expectantly.

"Forget her, you understand? A few weeks ago I saw her dancing with Rafa Fontana at the disco and he had his hands all over her ass."

"That's not true!"

"And what's more, after seeing that, *I* decided to dance with her, and *I* put my hands all over her ass."

"Not true!"

"And what's more, she—"

Edmund rushed at his brother, barreling his head into Ezekiel's stomach. Ezekiel grunted, took a moment to catch his breath, then promptly lifted his brother over his head, carried him outside, and threw him into the mud.

For this reason, hours later, Ezekiel's name was on the tip of Edmund's tongue.

"So that ungrateful shit knows something?" Filastro asked without waiting for confirmation.

While his father chased Ezekiel around the house, swinging his fists wildly, yelling at the top of his lungs, demanding to know all those involved in Abel's departure, Edmund decided to climb over the side fence and go find his best friend and favorite half brother, the club-footed Jorge el Gato. He needed advice, and Jorge was extremely knowledgeable when it came to women.

Jorge was called "the cat" because—rumor had it—he had forced himself upon a cat when he was twelve years old. In truth, Jorge had only been dared to force himself upon a cat—Doña Flabia's cat to be precise—and, thinking he would impress his friends and younger half brothers who always treated him cruelly, he decided to tell them he had done it. Needless to say, his friends and half brothers were not impressed. But Edmund, only a toddler at the time, believed Jorge's revisionist explanation of his nickname.

"I'm called el Gato because I look like a cat."

"No, you don't."

"I mean, I don't think I do, either, but some say I do. Maybe when I was littler."

Jorge el Gato's job was pushing a popsicle cart around town, calling out, "Ice cream, popsicles, and treats for the kiddies!" Edmund had to comb the streets listening for his friend's distinctive cry. When he found Jorge he explained his predicament.

"What kind of indecent girl have I fallen for?" Edmund asked.

Jorge el Gato mulled over this for a moment and then said, "Seems to me like you should ask her before coming to any conclusions."

"Ask her what?"

"Ask her if anyone has tried to touch her in places they shouldn't have."

Edmund sighed. "I can't."

"Why not?"

"Well, because just the other day I tried to touch her in a place I shouldn't have."

"Hmmm . . . did she let you?"

"No, in fact, she told me to confess to the priest what I had done."

"See, it seems to me like she's a respectable girl. Now, why didn't you listen to me and play her a song? Women love serenades."

Having his jealous torment somewhat assuaged, Edmund headed home thinking of the song he was going to sing for Ingrid.

His good spirits ended, however, when he arrived and found his mother and sisters on the couch trying to console Ezekiel, whose left eye was swollen shut.

"I'm leaving, I swear it!" his brother cried.

"Now, mijito," his mother said, holding ice to his head. "We can't have all of you abandoning us here. We need you. Your father, he has his ways, but you mustn't—"

"You're always defending him, Amá—why? Why?" Ezekiel rose from the couch. "All of you, listen to me. If you stay, it's your own fault! Enough is enough."

He went to his dresser drawer, removed his clothing, and threw it into a bag. In a matter of minutes he had moved out. He kissed his mother and sisters on the forehead, told Edmund that he was a "lousy shit for a brother" and that he had better not squeal on him, and promptly left.

That night Filastro didn't come home, so the next morning Edmund went looking for him. He found his father sleeping on the street, his head resting on the curb. Edmund roused his father. He was still half-drunk and rose from the ground with difficulty.

"What's that in your belt?" Edmund asked.

Filastro looked down and found an envelope stuffed into his pants. "What the hell is this?" he grumbled as he pulled it out.

It was yet another letter.

This time Ricardo the Notary had gone too far, leaving his all-too-personal stamp on a father-hating letter that wasn't to his father, creative license notwithstanding, metaphors aside. Filastro read the letter laboriously, muttering the words aloud, while Edmund peered over his forearm, occasionally peering up to monitor his father's reaction. It went as follows:

Dear Filastro the Fascist,

I'm your son, yes, but what does that mean, exactly? You gave birth to me, nothing more. I don't look like you, I don't talk like you, I don't believe we share one thing in common. Except, of course, our love of classic Westerns. But forget that! You have beaten me for the last time. You are an odious drunkard, an obsolete macho in a time when sensitivity is finally in fashion. You deny me my education, my growth, my quest for spiritual advancement, and why? Because you're an old man of the old school, meaning you treasure only old things like mescal and horses and nights spent sleeping on sacks of grain. I curse you! Beating after beating after beating, and finally I can take no more. I am leaving for the United States, a land of opportunity, a land free from your wretched grasp. There I shall find a people thirsting for knowledge, accepting, generous—they know not what despots exist in this world! I remember clearly your words to me the other day when you said, "Son, of all my children, you are the one I'm most ashamed of." And when I asked why, you simply said, "Because you look like a fruitcake."

19

I say you are a fruitcake, a coward just like Benancio Peletoso in The Gunfight in San Pedro! Yes, I know you remember that film; I bought it for your birthday and what thanks did you give me? So, Father, expect this: I'll return to La Prudencia only when you're dead and then I'll piss on your grave, just like Sancho Sifuentes in the same said film (he was not a coward!).

Your "son,"

Ezekiel

When Filastro finished reading the letter he looked at Edmund and asked, "What is he talking about?"

Edmund scanned the letter. "What are classic Westerns, Papá?"

"I don't know . . . and I never told Ezekiel he looked like a fruitcake. In fact, I've never called anyone a fruitcake!"

"Why did he write that, then?"

"Beats me," Filastro grumbled as he wiped the sleep from his eyes. "Let's go home. I'm going to pummel someone until they tell me the truth."

When they arrived home, Tomy, Gandolfo, Agnes, and Alfonsa had already left, sensing that hell would have to be paid once their father returned. Constanza had encouraged them to leave, telling them she would handle Filastro. By that she meant she'd stand in the way of his blows and maybe, just maybe, he'd tucker out. But Filastro was in no mood for beating his wife; that would come later. He opened a cabinet door and pulled out a bottle of ponche. He poured the alcohol straight into his mouth, then poured himself a sizeable glass and sat down at the table.

"Make me breakfast," he screamed at his wife. Constanza heated up the stove, her hands shaking. Filastro took another gulp of ponche and rested his forehead on the table.

"What a damned hangover I got," he mumbled into the glass top, fogging it up. "And now two of my ungrateful sons have abandoned me, abandoned their family. All my life I try so hard, work so hard, giving everything to this family and this is the thanks I get . . ." His voice trailed off.

"Papá," Edmund said, "Can I see that letter you got?"

Filastro removed the letter from his pocket and handed it to Edmund, who was holding Abel's letter from days before. "Look at this, Papá, the same person wrote both letters." Edmund placed the two letters side by side so Filastro could examine the similar typescript and matching off-white paper with tan flecks.

"Son of a bitch," Filastro exclaimed. "Who could it be?"

"The notary, Papá, who else writes letters for other people?"

Constanza dropped two eggs on the floor.

"What's your damned problem, woman?" Filastro yelled.

His wife apologized and wiped up the mess.

Ricardo the Notary sat at his wobbly little table typing a letter for an old woman who wanted her grandsons in the United States to know that she was healthy after her long sickness and that they shouldn't worry. Ricardo was uninspired.

"That's probably enough," he kept saying.

"No, just one line more," the old woman pleaded.

"Five pesos a line."

The old woman looked in her purse and counted her change.

"OK, maybe that's good for now."

Ricardo pulled the paper out of the typewriter, folded it, and stuffed it into an envelope. When he looked up, two figures stood in front of him. He recognized them as Filastro Agustín and his son Edmund. The former held two letters and did not look happy. The old woman, sensing an oncoming confrontation, grabbed her letter, left the payment on the desk, and quickly departed.

"What's the meaning of this, you shit-faced goat?" Filastro yelled.

"I don't know what you're talking about," Ricardo said, his brow raised in exaggerated surprise.

"You wrote this garbage, didn't you?"

"I'm not disposed to discuss private matters, Don Filastro. Think of me as a messenger, an innocent vessel—"

"Shut up, you damn sissy! Now tell me who helped my sons leave for the United States!"

"Once again, Don Filastro, I'm not disposed to discuss private matters. It is a matter of occupational honor, you must understand—"

Filastro raised his hand to slap him, the movement alone enough to knock the notary off his stool. Ricardo began to shriek, "No, no, no, don't hurt me!"

Filastro picked up the typewriter and held it over his head. "Now tell me who helped my sons leave. Who fronted them the money? I'll drop this, I swear it."

"Please, no, no, please," Ricardo whimpered, hiding his face. "I swear on my mother's grave I don't know a thing!"

Filastro sighed and placed the typewriter back on the small table. "Goddamn coward," he said, and walked away.

Edmund lingered for a moment and bent down to help Ricardo rise to his feet. The notary continued to whimper, his hands shaking, his face as pale as the stack of papers on his table.

"Can I ask you a question?" Edmund asked.

The notary nodded numbly.

"By any chance do you write love letters?"

CHAPTER 6

Ingrid Genera was immediately skeptical when Edmund presented her with the love letter written by Ricardo the Notary. He had waited outside of her door for almost an hour, sitting in the burning sun, sweating profusely, until finally she took pity on him and opened the door. He placed the letter in Ingrid's hands and backed away unsurely. He watched her face, monitoring her reaction: she mostly frowned.

"Who wrote this, Edmund?" she asked upon finishing.

"What do you mean? I wrote it, of course!"

She read through the letter again and paused at a line. "So you really wrote that I'm 'more beautiful than dew-covered peacocks' feathers glistening in the morning light of spring'?"

"Well, yes."

"And you really wrote that your 'heart sings for love such as mine, heart-wrenching ballads full of longing and lament'?"

"Of course I wrote it. I give you a letter from *me*, for *you*, and you ask me whether or not I wrote it? What kind of nonsense is that?"

"Nonsense is getting someone else to write a love letter for you!"

Edmund's face turned red, even redder than the hour-long stay in the sun had made it. "Why do you say that?" His voice began to tremble. "Here I go and spend time writing a letter to you expressing myself and you accuse me of such a thing."

"Yes, that's exactly what I think," Ingrid said, unmoved. "OK, Edmund . . . if you did write it, what is the last line?"

Edmund knew this because he himself had chosen the last line from a list of options. "Warmest regards."

"Not that last line, stupid. The last sentence."

Edmund thought a moment. He remembered vaguely what Ricardo had written. "Something about the sun setting on the streets of Ciudad Juárez, and a gunfight or something in some movie."

"Yes, and what about the sun setting in Ciudad Juárez, a place you've never even been to, and this movie you've never seen?"

"I don't remember."

"How can you not remember what you wrote?"

"Because I wrote from my heart and that's easy to forget. You try writing a love letter." He placed his hand over his heart.

Ricardo the Notary had advised Edmund to answer thus if Ingrid pressed him too hard for details. "Just tell her that when one writes from the heart there is no telling what poetry may spring forth: words not from the mind, but from here," he said, putting his hand to his heart.

"Oh, you are such a little lying troll, Edmund," Ingrid said laughing. "You are full of it!"

"I'm not full of it. And I'm not a troll, you—you—" He tried thinking of an insult other than bowlegged horse, but his frustration got the best of him. So he stomped away, furious, once again cursing the woes of the heart and wishing he had never met Ingrid Genera. "She brings me nothing but trouble, damn it," he said aloud. "All she ever does is call me a troll. Well, *she's* a troll, that's what I say!"

An old man peeked his head out his window and told Edmund to shut up.

"You shut up!" Edmund screamed back on the verge of tears. "You deserve to be treated so badly!"

The old man laughed. "It only gets worse, young man."

Edmund decided to go home and strum his guitar. As he lay on his bed, brooding over Ingrid, he played a few chords from a song one of the plaza troubadours had taught him. He sang a few lines quietly to himself. His mother walked into the room and said to him, "Edmund, that sounds very nice, sing louder for your mamá."

So Edmund sang louder, and when his sisters Agnes and Alfonsa came home they heard him singing the same song and said, "Hey, little brother, that actually sounds nice." He continued playing until Agnes asked him, "How about you play outside now?"

"Why? You said it sounded nice."

"Yeah, but all you play is one song."

"So what?"

"So what? So it gets boring after twenty times. Now go outside and play!"

Edmund decided to head to the town square, strumming his guitar along the way. It was almost dark, and dim houselights illuminated the broken cobblestone streets. When he arrived he saw the silhouettes of his father and three compadres, Big Gaspar, Mendigo, and Jerry, sitting at the open cantina. He watched them curiously for a moment, wondering what the cause was of their boisterous laughter. Every now and then different women—fat ones with dresses too small, skinny ones with dresses too big— would approach the men and touch their shoulders and whisper in their ears. The compadres would put their arms around the woman and pet her hair, and once Edmund saw his father grab a woman's behind. She turned around and slapped him playfully.

"Ay, Filastro, you owe me!"

"Yes, I know," his father responded, ordering another round of drinks for his friends.

Edmund sat down on the curb. He sighed heavily and felt a lump in his throat. "Ingrid," he whispered, "why don't you like me? All I want is to be nice to you and for you to be nice to me, but it never works out like that." He watched the bar scene for another half hour, fingering the chords but not strumming them, afraid his father would hear. After a while he tired and set the guitar down. He watched passersby for a few more minutes, then rose to leave.

He saw his brother Tomy approaching with his girlfriend, Paty. They had been dating for several years despite the forbiddance of their relationship. Her father had said at the beginning of their courtship that Tomy was destined to become a low-down scoundrel like his father, and word had gotten back to Filastro, who then forbade his son to date the daughter of man who had so flagrantly affronted him. Adding insult to injury, Filastro proceeded to make catcalls at Paty's mother on her way to the market.

"What do you want, Tomy?"

"Go home. Mamá is looking for you."

Edmund noticed that both Tomy and Paty were holding suitcases.

"Where are you going?" he asked.

"We're taking the bus to Guadalajara, then we're going to the United States."

"You too? Wha—what—but why?"

"To get away from here," Tomy said coldly. "We're going to get married, and Papá won't let us, so this way we'll go and both get work and be able to live on our own."

"Are you going to Nebraska?"

"No, Paty has family in a place called Wyoming."

"Where's that?"

"In the United States, stupid."

"I know that . . . is it close to Nebraska?"

"I don't know. Look, we have to go—"

Suddenly they heard Filastro's slurred voice behind them. "Tomy, you shit for a son, what are you doing with that slut?"

Tomy turned around slowly, his head bowed. "Father, don't call her that. Paty and I are getting married. We are leaving."

Filastro stepped toward Tomy, his face inches from his son's. "I'll kill you first!"

"No, you won't. You've hit me for the last time." Tomy grabbed Paty's hand and they walked away from Filastro, who staggered backward, almost falling. He continued screaming insults, but was too sloppily drunk to pose a physical threat.

Edmund watched his brother board the bus, then picked up the guitar and walked home, listening as his father banged his fists against the bus's side, demanding Tomy fight him like a man. Edmund walked with his head down, but out the corners of his eyes he saw people enjoying the spectacle, pointing their fingers and laughing.

Abel had only been gone a month when he sent 300 dollars to Constanza by way of her sister, Lunasa. He sent the money with a postcard of the St. Louis arch and instructions on how to handle his monthly remittances. "I'll send money to Tía Lunasa She cash it and hold it for you Don't buy expensive things or Papá will notice Use this money to pay back Tres Pasos Then save for Tomy and Gandolfo and Ezekiel They should all come when there's enough." He ended the postcard with "I love it here!"

When Gandolfo heard the news, he nodded silently at the empty place settings on the kitchen table. He understood that he would be making the journey alone. He was only sixteen but big for his age; he prided himself on his muscular arms and wore tank tops to display them. Of all his brothers, he may have been the one to overpower Filastro, but he always took his beatings with an eerie silence. In fact, he took all of life in much the same way.

When Agnes and Alfonsa arrived home, they read Abel's note and pouted in unison. "We want to go, too, and of course he forgets about us! We just get to stay in La Prudencia and have nothing to do except work at Tía Lunasa's store. Pleeease, Mamá, let us go, too!"

Constanza asked them about their boyfriends.

"Oh, they'll follow us," Alfonsa said.

"And if they don't, then we'll find others," Agnes followed, giggling, then snorting.

When Edmund woke up from his afternoon nap and heard the news, he asked the first thing that came to mind. "Do you think Abel has gone to visit Disneyland?"

"You're so stupid, Edmund," Agnes said.

"Why am I stupid? I heard it's a lot of fun there. That's the only reason why I'd go to the United States."

"He's working too hard for fun," Constanza interrupted, her voice stern. "Now daughters, you're not going to the United States alone. Only Gandolfo will go, and only because he's mature enough to find work like his brothers. Who would take care of you?"

"Our brothers will watch over us," they pleaded, "and if we go with Gandolfo he wouldn't let anything happen to us on the way, isn't that right, Gandi?"

Gandolfo considered them silently, staring for several seconds, first at Agnes, then at Alfonsa, then at his mother, and then—skipping over Edmund—he stared at the calendar, not uttering a word in response.

"You're so weird, Gandi." Alfonsa said, "Why do you look at everybody so creepy like that?"

"Leave your brother alone," Constanza said.

Just then Filastro stumbled through the door accompanied by his compadre Mendigo, an elfish-looking man who had followed the latter around like a puppy since grammar school.

"Woman, make us some food for the road!" Filastro cried just before entering the kitchen. When he walked in and found the five of them all seated silently around the table, their faces sharing the same guilty look, he stopped short, his bloodshot eyes narrowing.

"You see that, Mendigo," Filastro said, snickering with malice, "my family lies to me, keeps secrets from their father, the man who puts the food on the table, the clothes on their back. They think I won't find out what they're up to, but I will!"

Constanza rose from the table. "We have no secrets from you. Now you and your compadre just sit down at the table and I'll heat up some food. What would you like?"

Filastro stumbled forward and grabbed his wife's arm. He squeezed her wrist until she let out a cry of pain. He breathed heavily into her face. "Don't lie to me," he snarled.

He let go and Constanza walked toward the stove, rubbing her wrist. Agnes and Alfonsa rose to help her, but she waved them away and the girls quickly left the room before Filastro turned his aggression toward them. Gandolfo made to rise as well, but Filastro placed his hand on his son's shoulder and violently pushed him back into his seat. "You're not going anywhere, you hear?"

"Let him be," Constanza pleaded.

"Shut up! I don't want to hear a thing from you!"

Gandolfo remained seated, staring at his hands on the table with fixed concentration.

"Look at me," Filastro demanded.

Gandolfo's gaze remained on his hands.

Filastro leaned over and flicked Gandolfo's ear. "You'll look at me when I'm talking or else I'll beat you until your jaw can't open even if you wanted to use it, you deaf mute!"

Gandolfo looked up at his father, but his eyes were distant; he appeared to be staring at his father's nose.

"Nothing but worthless sons," Filastro said to Mendigo. "Don't you think I have the most worthless sons you've ever come across?"

Mendigo laughed nervously, unsure how to respond. Filastro turned to Edmund, who'd been sitting quietly. "What are you doing, you sneaky little shit?"

"Nothing."

"What were they all talking about?"

"Nothing."

"You piece of—I can't even trust you anymore. Now go get your guitar and show my compadre how good you play."

Edmund sprang from the table, excited to play another new song he had learned. He found the guitar and began tuning the strings as he entered the kitchen. He stopped short when he saw his father with his hand wrapped around Gandolfo's neck, pressing his brother's head to the wall. Mendigo was watching the scene, shifting from side to side, saying, "Now compadre, now compadre, tranquility, tranquility!"

"Shut up, Mendigo!" Filastro shrieked. "Gandolfo, I'm going to speak slowly and clearly so there's no chance you'll misunderstand me. I want you to tell me exactly what you were talking about when I came in just now. I want you to tell me all information about your brothers—who helped pay for them to go, which coyote arranged their passage. I want you to tell me if you're planning on joining them. I want to know if Abel has been in contact with you, with your mother, with any of your aunts. Now I'm going to let go and I want you to answer my questions or else, you understand?"

Filastro slowly loosened his grip. Gandolfo's face had turned purple and he immediately began to choke, placing his hands on his knees, struggling to regain his breath. Constanza quickly brought him a glass of water, which he gulped down, spilling half on himself. He started to sit, but suddenly he lifted the glass above his head and brought the butt crashing onto Filastro's head. There was a dull thud and Filastro cried out in pain. Gandolfo lifted the glass again and brought it back down, blood beginning to gush from his father's forehead. Filastro fell back, mouth open, head tossed limply backward.

Constanza screamed and ran toward her son, afraid he would continue raising and lowering the glass until her husband was dead.

Mendigo remained frozen in his chair, his eyes wide with fright, as if expecting to be the boy's next victim. He held up his hands and cried out, "I told him to go easy on you, I told him!"

Gandolfo let the glass fall. Edmund watched it drop to the floor, waiting for the sound of breaking glass, but Filastro's boot stood in the way, preventing it from shattering. Gandolfo's eyes scanned the room, shocked and horrified. He was panting, his arms and legs trembling violently. Then, without saying anything, he walked out the door.

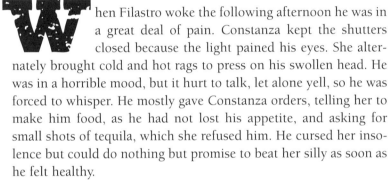

hen Filastro woke the following afternoon he was in a great deal of pain. Constanza kept the shutters closed because the light pained his eyes. She alternately brought cold and hot rags to press on his swollen head. He was in a horrible mood, but it hurt to talk, let alone yell, so he was forced to whisper. He mostly gave Constanza orders, telling her to make him food, as he had not lost his appetite, and asking for small shots of tequila, which she refused him. He cursed her insolence but could do nothing but promise to beat her silly as soon as he felt healthy.

Edmund felt it wise to stay outside of the house as much as possible. He was now the only son left, and, with his father laid up in bed, he felt the burden of being the man of the house. He didn't quite feel up to the challenge. The only challenge with which he cared to be preoccupied was how to get Ingrid Genera to fall in love with him. Jorge el Gato had recently given him an excellent idea as to how to do this.

"Women love a vulnerable man," Jorge had explained, limping on his clubfoot as he pushed his cart. "They love when men show feelings, but they love it even better when they can care for the man, nurture him, bring him relief. Tell a woman a sob story and she'll want to wipe your tears."

"But what kind of sob story do I got?" Edmund asked.

"It seems to me like you got plenty now. Don't you miss your brothers?"

"Um . . . I guess."

"What about how Filastro beats you?"

"He doesn't want to beat me on account I'm so small."

"Oh, yeah. What about how he beats your mother and goes out on her? Tell Ingrid something like it hurts to see your mother treated so badly, and that you wish you could do something about it."

"That's true. I could probably cry about that."

So Edmund walked the streets looking for Ingrid in order to tell her his sob story, but along the way he happened upon a cross-eyed mangy dog, the same cross-eyed mangy dog that had peed on his shirt when he had removed it to play soccer the day before. He decided to show the pitiful looking mutt that it couldn't just go around peeing on people's shirts. He chased the dog and quickly cornered it, the little mutt yapping away. Upon realizing it was trapped, the dog cowered, its crossed eyes opened wide, staring at its muzzle.

Edmund picked up a sizeable stick and began trying to hit the dog's backside, saying, "Don't be peeing on my shirt, you little dog! What? You think I got like twenty shirts or something?" The dog began yelping in pain. Edmund swung the stick a few more times before noticing the dog was no longer nimbly jumping back and forth to avoid his blows.

Edmund stopped and the mutt whined. He bent forward and the dog tried to drag itself away using its front paws, but couldn't get far. Its hind legs were broken. Realizing what he had done, Edmund felt awful. He picked up the mangy dog, its hair sticky and tangled. He petted its head and repeatedly gave his apologies. "I didn't mean it, I didn't mean it, I was just trying to teach you a lesson."

He walked frantically in no particular direction, unsure of what to do. Finally he decided he'd ask Jorge el Gato to make a splint. He looked around, somewhat disoriented. He shushed the dog, promising him first aid as soon as possible, and listened for Jorge el Gato's distinctive call. It was then, however, that he realized his feet had taken him in his previously intended direction: he was standing in front of Ingrid Genera's house.

"What are you doing?" a voice, sharp and irritated asked. He looked up and saw Ingrid through the wire-screen door.

"Nothing."

"Why are you standing in front of my house with that ugly dog?"

He stuttered momentarily, "Uh—uh—well—uh—" But suddenly Edmund was struck with an idea. "What, this dog?" he feigned mild indignation. "Don't call him ugly, can't you see he's hurt?" "How'd he get hurt?" she asked, staring at the dog curiously. "What's wrong with him?"

"His legs are broken, and if you must know, I came across some little kids beating this poor little dog for no other reason than he's just a poor little cross-eyed dog with no family to take care of him. So I chased the kids away and told them to never be beating on little dogs again. And then I come and pick up the dog and see that he's hurt badly. So I'm going to bring him to my brother-cousin and get him a splint so his legs heal properly. Then I'm going to make sure he's well taken care of, 'cause dogs—you know—it just isn't right how people treat those who are weaker and smaller."

He stopped and breathed deeply, having used a single breath for the entire delivery. He could tell Ingrid was impressed. But instead of coming up and giving him a kiss for his valor and compassion, all she said was, "That's nice."

He waited for more. When none came, he pushed further. "So you see, I'm a nice guy and I just wanted to come by and show you that I'm good at caring for things—and well, maybe we could get an ice cream sometime or something?"

Ingrid shook her head disapprovingly. "You should do good things because it's God's work, not just so you can show off!"

"What are you talking about?" he asked, suddenly finding himself on the defensive.

"Don't pretend you care for that poor dog if you're just doing it to get me to go out with you. You're full of tricks, you know that, Edmund?"

"Tricks?"

"Yes, tricks! Why don't you just be honest for once, and *then* maybe we can have a friendly conversation."

"I am honest!"

"All right, then tell me where you found that dog because I know for a fact you didn't chase off any kids with a stick. No one would be afraid of you!"

"See, you're always being mean to me! I told you the truth. I beat the dog with a stick and then I chased off them kids and—" he stopped, realizing his blunder.

Ingrid's eyes bugged out. "You did what?"

Edmund tried to explain, but his voice began to tremble, "Look, see, I just wanted to . . . show this dog that it can't be peeing on my shirts, and—"

"So that's why you broke its legs?"

"No—I didn't mean to, but I—I did, so then I was really trying to help it by bringing it to Jorge, and then I was going to try and adopt it or something, and then I was in front of your house and you asked me what I was doing and I—I—wanted to tell you— something that would make you see that I was—um—just . . ."

Edmund realized the futility of his plea. He lowered his head and turned around, muttering, "Forget it," as he walked away. He cradled the dog with one arm and petted the top of its head, desperately hoping she would call him back.

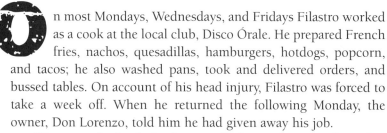

CHAPTER 9

O n most Mondays, Wednesdays, and Fridays Filastro worked as a cook at the local club, Disco Órale. He prepared French fries, nachos, quesadillas, hamburgers, hotdogs, popcorn, and tacos; he also washed pans, took and delivered orders, and bussed tables. On account of his head injury, Filastro was forced to take a week off. When he returned the following Monday, the owner, Don Lorenzo, told him he had given away his job.

"You son of a bitch!" Filastro yelled. "I've been working five years and you just give away my job like that!"

"Look, Filastro, you are slow, you drink while you work, you have no respect for the customers, and you give away too much free food to your friends, who are too old to hang out in a disco anyway."

"But I have a family to feed, Don Lorenzo. Don't leave me like this."

"Ay, Filastro, don't take me for a fool. We all know what you do with your money, and now that your sons have left, you'll be getting plenty from them, no? Plus, I've hired someone who—"

"Tell me his name and I'll kill him!"

"Never mind, Filastro. You'll find out soon enough, and if you think harming him will do any good, it won't. There are plenty of others I'd take before hiring you back."

Filastro kicked a few chairs as he left the disco, garnering curious stares from the young clientele drinking at the tables, playing billiards, and dancing to banda music. He went to the nearest cantina, had a drink on the bartender, promising he'd pay his bill next paycheck, then headed for the only other club in town, Disco Chido. This disco attracted a different clientele than Disco Órale, for in addition to billiards, darts, dancing, and alcohol, one could find a whore. Older men and drunkards frequented the club; the only women were of ill repute.

Filastro saw Hortensia in the corner, holding a tray and talking to a man he didn't know. He bought a drink at the bar with his remaining money and waited impatiently. He showed his impatience by pacing back and forth, occasionally stopping to stare at Hortensia until she noticed him. Finally, she picked up an empty glass from the table and said something to the man that made him laugh; then she walked away.

Hortensia was the only whore Filastro went to now, except she wasn't technically a whore. She did work in a place of ill repute, but merely as a waitress. No one, including Filastro, drew the distinction, though she didn't necessarily stress the point, either. He used to sleep with anyone he could convince or pay, and although he paid far more often than he convinced, his conquests were not infrequent. But that was when he was younger. His desire had waned in recent years almost to the point of disappearing completely. So Filastro's relationship with Hortensia was not as sordid as one would assume. In fact, there was a touch of innocence to it: she liked him, and he came to her when he was in the worst of his moods and found the dank room in which she lived oddly calming.

"I don't like to beat my wife and kids," he once told her.

"Why do you do it, then?" she asked as she changed the television channel.

"Because I always have and because I'm expected to."

"Who expects you to? Surely they'd rather you not hit them."

But he hadn't answered her and instead stared blankly at one of the many soap operas she enjoyed watching. Hortensia was twenty-seven and reminded him of his wife when she was younger, before she had put on weight and her skin had become wrinkled, before she began looking sad all the time. He told Hortensia this once and she told him that she already knew.

"How did you know?"

"Because of the way you look at me."

He considered this for a moment, and then said, "I was never faithful to her and I never cared to be, but now . . . now, I don't know, it's too late. Why is it that you all have to get old, and so quickly at that?"

Hortensia stared at Filastro's naked torso, his breasts as large as hers, his mountainous hairy stomach rising from his stocky frame. She looked at the lines around his eyes, his sagging cheeks and double chin. She reached over and tousled his thinning hair, which he parted over his head. She began to laugh. She laughed long and hard and he couldn't get her to tell him why.

When Filastro arrived that night she saw his distraught face and knew that he needed her. She took her break, then led him down a dark corridor and into her cramped room that she rented behind the club. She pulled him over to the bed, removed his shirt and pants and said, "Lay down, mi amor." Then she went to the television and found her favorite soap opera. She pulled her dress over her head, leaving her underwear on, and crawled next to Filastro, placing her leg over his and resting her hand on his chest. They watched the television in silence, Filastro sighing deeply every couple of minutes.

When the show finished he abruptly stood up and began putting on his clothes.

"You can stay longer," she said.

He grunted.

"What's wrong?" she asked, rising from the bed and touching his arms, gently rubbing them.

"Nothing," he said.

"Tell me."

Filastro fastened his belt and told her to shut up.

"Is it about your sons' leaving?" she asked without thinking.

He slapped her suddenly with the back of his hand. "I said shut up!"

It surprised him just as much as it did her and he immediately apologized, "I'm sorry, I'm sorry, please, damn it, come here." She backed away, waving away his embrace. She put on her dress hastily, cursing to herself as she did so, wanting to cry.

Filastro took out his wallet and remembered he had no money. "I'll pay you when I get some money, OK?"

Hortensia gave him an incredulous glare. "How many times do I have to tell you?" she scoffed. "You're a real son of a bitch, you know that?"

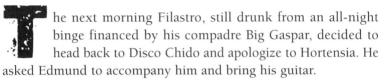

CHAPTER 10

The next morning Filastro, still drunk from an all-night binge financed by his compadre Big Gaspar, decided to head back to Disco Chido and apologize to Hortensia. He asked Edmund to accompany him and bring his guitar.

"Why, Papá?"

"Don't ask why, just put down that dumb dog, bring your damn guitar, and shut up!"

Edmund set Cross-Eyes down, grabbed his guitar, and began tuning the strings as he struggled to keep pace with Filastro, who was almost running. When they arrived at the plaza heading in the direction of Disco Chido, Ingrid Genera was shopping at the flea market with her mother. She noticed Edmund carrying a beat-up guitar that looked much too big for him and his father yelling at him to hurry up.

"Ay, this should be funny," she thought to herself. She told her mother that she was going to buy a soda and slipped away. She followed Edmund and Filastro down a side alley that ran along the side of the club leading to a dilapidated apartment building. She lost them for a moment, but then she heard Edmund's voice arguing with his father. Ingrid peeked her head around the corner of a discarded mattress and saw the two of them standing below a balcony, its shutters closed.

"I don't wanna sing, please don't make me," Edmund was saying.

"What do you mean you don't want to sing? You always are singing for no good reason and now I'm telling you to and you refuse? Damn you, now sing!"

"No, I can't."

Filastro leaned forward and swatted Edmund on the top of his head. "Now, I said play that song you're always playing!" "What song you talking about?" "The song you play a hundred times a day!" "I can't sing that song yet, it's not ready," Edmund said, shaking his head adamantly. "What do you mean? Ready for what?" "For the person I'm going to sing it for! I still gotta practice!" "Think of this as practice, then. Sing it right now!" Filastro raised his hand as if to hit Edmund again, but then stopped, drawing his hand behind his ear and scratching it. "Look, mijo, I need for you to sing this song for someone who is very special to me. I did something wrong and I need to make up for it."

Edmund looked confused. "Like one of your compadres? Who, Big Gaspar? He doesn't live here."

"No, not one of my compadres. A woman who always gives me a—uh—um—a good discount at the store and she—she—I insulted her the other day for no good reason."

"So why don't you just say you're sorry? I'm sure she'll continue giving you discounts. Why do you want me to sing?"

"Because I just do, now do what I say, no more arguing!"

Edmund looked around himself and realized where he was: everyone knew only lowlifes and prostitutes lived in this place. Suddenly it clicked and his brow furrowed. "Jorge el Gato told me that men sing songs to make women love them."

"Well, Jorge doesn't know what he's talking about," Filastro said angrily. He didn't like to be reminded of his clubfooted son. He grabbed the back of Edmund's neck and brought their faces close. "Now you play the damn song, you little shit, or I'll take this guitar and smash it on the road. You get away with too much, you hear?"

Once Filastro let go, Edmund shrank back, shielding his guitar with his body. The thought of losing his guitar filled him with desperation. He slowly positioned the instrument in front of his body and began to strum.

"Now that's more like it," his father grumbled.

Edmund found angry tears falling from his eyes and he tried to wipe them away with the shoulder of his sleeve, but he couldn't do so and continue playing. He sniffed but felt the snot drip from his nostril anyway.

Ingrid Genera felt bad for having spied on Edmund; she had been hoping for something to tease him about later. She turned away and began walking back down the alley, but curiosity compelled her to stop when she heard the shutters open and a woman's voice.

"What do you want, Filastro?" Hortensia asked, her voice impatient.

"I've come to apologize!"

"For what?"

"For what? What do you mean for what?"

"You have no need to apologize to me."

Filastro was taken aback. "Look, I've brought my son to play for you—my little guitarrista!"

Hortensia shook her head. "You should have come by yourself, Filastro. A little boy shouldn't have to see his father here." She gestured around her.

"Oh, he's not *that* little—he's just scrawny, but he's almost a man, has pubic hair the color of his red head, I'll tell you that much!" Filastro laughed. "Play another song for her, mijo!"

Hortensia was not amused. "Filastro, come back when you're ready to come to my room, and not with your son—"

"I'm trying to win you back with romance, can't you see?"

"Don't you know I don't need romance?" With that she closed the shutters. Filastro called her name over and over, made Edmund begin playing again, this time the two of them belting out the lyrics, but she wouldn't come to the window.

Finally Filastro gave up and said to Edmund, "Let's go, mijo, maybe she needs more time." He started to walk away but Edmund remained.

"Come on, let's go, I said."

Edmund didn't budge.

"Damn it, you want me to break your damn guitar after all?"

Edmund held the neck of the guitar with both hands and raised it above his head. He stared at his father, his jaw clenched.

"What are you going to do?"

"I'm going to break my guitar."

"And what good would that do?"

"So I never have to play for you or your women again."

"Put the guitar down, mijo, or I'll break it myself, and then what would you do, leave like the rest of your brothers? You want to leave, is that it?"

"No, that's not it! I don't want to leave at all! But I don't see why you gotta have me sing songs when I don't want to!"

Filastro began to laugh. "Seems to me like you're a little softy. I should have beaten you more, then maybe you'd be a man. When you get older, you'll understand. You'll be just like me, watch."

"I won't ever be like you!" Edmund cried. With that he took off running, guitar in hand. He ran past his father, past the broken videogame shell, the dismantled furniture and old bedsprings, around the corner, down the alley, right past an old armoire and discarded mattress, where he thought he saw Ingrid Genera in the corner of his eye. He couldn't be sure, so he turned around, and just as he did so, tripped over an old boot left in the middle of the narrow path.

He crashed to the ground; his fall broken by the guitar beneath him.

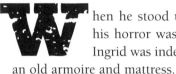hen he stood up and found his guitar in splinters, his horror was somewhat assuaged by the fact that Ingrid was indeed there, somewhat concealed behind an old armoire and mattress.

"Oh Edmund, your guitar!" she exclaimed, emerging from her cover.

Edmund was too surprised to speak. He still held the guitar neck in his hand, the strings hanging askew.

"Look at your guitar!" she cried again.

Edmund looked at his guitar.

"It's broken!" she said, her voice quivering.

Edmund continued looking at his guitar in a daze, wondering why Ingrid was there in the back alley with him. What was she doing in a place reserved for whores and lowlifes? Had she seen him cry? Did she see him sing for his father's mistress?

After what felt like minutes he turned to her: "What are you doing here?"

She stuttered, "Uh, I was just in the market shopping with my mother—and—uh—I—uh—I heard you singing . . . it was good."

"It was good?"

"Yeah."

Edmund had never heard such kind words. He felt like crying with joy. His mouth was forming a broad smile when he heard his father's voice. "What happened, damn it! Sounds like something broke—"

Filastro came around the corner and stopped in his tracks. "What did you do to your guitar?"

"I have to go!" Ingrid said. She hurriedly walked off down the alley toward the plaza, shrieking when a dog barked at her through a screen door. Edmund watched her as she disappeared into the busy square.

He turned to his father. "What?"

"What the hell did you do?"

Edmund once again looked at his splintered instrument. "She said I was good, Papá."

"Well, little good that does you now! I'm not buying you another one!"

His guitar destroyed, Edmund now had two challenges occupying his time. Although Ingrid was the ultimate goal, buying a new guitar was just as important. He was sure the way to her heart was perfecting the serenade he had already so laboriously practiced.

Never having worked in his life, Edmund wasn't too sure how to go about earning money. So he found Jorge el Gato and asked him, "How do you get a job?"

"You must apply for a position."

"Did you apply for your position?"

"No, I just found the cart, fixed it up, borrowed money for a freezer, and then borrowed more money to buy popsicles wholesale."

"Well, should I look for a cart?"

"Depends, are you interested in a long-term investment?"

"Not particularly, I just want to make money for a guitar."

"Then go around town and see if there are any jobs."

Edmund headed to the town square and asked at every shop off the plaza if they needed extra help. One glance at Edmund and each shopkeeper laughed. "You're just a little kid; you should be in school!"

"I'm not so little, I'm thirteen, almost fourteen."

But they merely waved him on. When he asked at the market, however, he received somewhat favorable news. "We hire kids to help people carry their bags home," the manager said.

"I could do that. How much does it pay?"

"It doesn't pay anything. If you get a tip, you get a tip."

"Do I get a uniform?"

Edmund got a green vest to wear over his shirt. His first customer was his neighbor, Doña María, who didn't recognize him in his green vest and new position as bag carrier. He picked up her bags and said, "I'll take these for you, ma'am."

"Oh thank you, little boy, I live on 45 Carranza Street."

"I know where you live! We live right next to each other, Doña María."

The woman lifted her glasses and inspected Edmund more carefully. "Oh, Edmund! I didn't recognize you. How nice of you to offer to carry my bags."

"It's my job."

She nodded and smiled. When they arrived at her door, Doña María fished in her change purse and brought out two pesos, hardly the tip he was expecting, especially from his own neighbor, who should want to help out a local kid trying to make something of himself. He took the two pesos anyway, but then he heard his mother's voice, "Oh, no, no, no!" She emerged from the house. "Edmund, give her back the money. Sorry, Doña María, my son has obviously lost his manners."

"But, Amá, it's my job now!"

"Your job is certainly not to charge your neighbors for little more than carrying their groceries."

"But look at my green vest. They hired me. I work for tips!"

"Not for Doña María's tips or any one of our neighbors, you hear?"

Edmund looked at Doña María for support. She clearly wanted her two pesos back. He gave them to her and she said, "Thank you so much for your help, Ed-mun-di-to." He wanted to throw her bags into the street. He walked back to the plaza in a huff. "I'll never make enough for my guitar," he lamented.

When he arrived at the store he waited along with the other kids for customers in need of help. There were four other bag carriers. He introduced himself.

"My name's Edmund, what's yours?"

"Francisco, I'm six."

"Pedro, and I'm seven and a half."

"Mariana, I'm gonna be nine."

"Kelly, I'm almost—"

"What are you guys saving your money for?"

"Help my mamá."

"Help my mamá, too."

"Food for my brothers and sisters. I'm the oldest!"

"Help my grandma."

"Well, that's nice. I'm saving for a guitar. I used to have one but I fell on it and it broke, so here I am, saving for another one. Do you think it'll take long?"

His colleagues' eyes grew wide. "A guitar?" they exclaimed in unison. "It's going to take you like three years."

"I can't wait that long! What makes you think it'll take such a long time?"

"We don't make much money here."

"Shit, what am I going to do then?"

"You can take this woman," Pedro, the first in line, offered.

"Are you sure?"

He nodded.

"Thank you so much, I appreciate it." Edmund stepped forward and picked up the woman's bags on the counter. "Where are we heading?" he asked cheerfully, truly appreciative of Pedro's kind gesture. The woman turned around and said, "48 Carranza Street, Edmund!"

Of course, it had to be another neighbor. Suddenly he pretended that he had sprained his ankle. "Oh, oh, I can't go, look at my damned ankle. I should get better shoes."

His neighbor shook her head and wished him well. Pedro took her bags instead and as soon as they were out the door Edmund began walking straight again. "Why'd you do that for?" Mariana, the next in line, asked.

"My mom says that I can't take any tips from neighbors."

"Oh."

That would have settled it if the store manager hadn't seen his stunt. "You, the new boy, come over here! Go to my office." Edmund cautiously walked to the back of the store, wondering what his boss was so worked up about.

hat kind of games are you pulling on the customers?" the manager asked, his face scrunched in a frown.

"I don't know what you're talking about. Where is your office? I thought you said go to your office."

"*This* is my office!"

Edmund thought it looked more like a storage closet and told the man so.

"That's beside the point. Now tell me, how old are you? You act too smart for a child."

"I'm thirteen, almost fourteen."

The manager threw up his hands. "This job is reserved exclusively for children ten and under, otherwise I'd have to pay wages! And although you may look like one, I cannot have you disrupting my store."

"But I didn't do nothing. I just didn't—" Edmund stopped. "I don't look like a child! Why's everyone always saying that? Look, I gotta mustache and hair under my armpits, what kind of kid has that?"

"The only reason I hired you is because we needed another bag carrier. All other positions are filled."

"Ay, I need the job," Edmund pleaded. "I have to save a lot of money!"

"I'm sorry, son, I can't help you."

*   *   *

Now that he was unemployed, Edmund felt that he should go sit on the plaza benches next to the taxi stand, for that's where all the other unemployed men sat. He walked over dejectedly, wanting someone to ask him what was wrong. But no one paid him any mind. He sat down on the end of a bench and sighed loudly. "It's tough out here!" he said, grunting to no one in particular. The unemployed men ignored him.

"What's a man have to do to earn money these days?" he said a little louder.

He was ignored.

"It's almost like you have to rob a bank or something!"

No response.

"I'm almost ready to move out of town, see what's up the road—" He directed a question to the man closest to him. "How are job prospects up in Crucero?"

The man shrugged and turned to the conversation next to him. Two taxi drivers were playing a game of checkers. Edmund rose from the bench and approached the board. He inspected the game momentarily before offering one player some advice. "I'd move that one, give it up, and then you got your guy safe there in the corner."

"Get lost, you little twerp," one of the checker players told him.

"I'd like to," Edmund responded, finally having someone's attention. "But you see, I need to earn some money so that I can buy a guitar. I was just fired from my job for unjustified reasons, if you know what I mean."

The checker player, without turning to him, said, "Well, maybe you should go visit Tres Pasos."

The whole crowd of men started laughing, including the checker player who had actually acted upon Edmund's suggestion and was now kinged as a result.

"Who's Tres Pasos?" Edmund asked, remembering the name from Abel's postcard.

"No, I'm just joking, little boy," the man said, still laughing. "Don't go see Tres Pasos. It was a joke, nothing more. Now get out of here before I lose this game."

Edmund decided to ask Jorge el Gato about Tres Pasos. He listened for his best friend's distinctive call but to no avail, so he walked toward his tía Lupe's house. He found his aunt mopping the floor, the music blasting. He had to scream her name before she recognized his presence. "Where's Jorge?" he asked when she turned down the radio.

"Oh, he's in the back yard," she said. "How's my sister?" she asked as Edmund passed through the house. The two sisters hadn't spoken in twenty years ever since Lupe became pregnant with Filastro's son. They still inquired about one another through Edmund.

"She fine, a little tired," he responded. "She's going to the bakery later on this afternoon because it's Agnes and Alfonsa's birthday."

He found Jorge el Gato in the backyard fixing his cart.

"What happened to your cart?" Edmund asked.

"The usual, the wheels loosen and then the freezing unit gets thrown off."

Edmund watched as Jorge tinkered with the bolts and screws. He admired his half brother's handiness. He waited until Jorge lost the fixed, concentrated look he wore when working. "Who's Tres Pasos?" Edmund asked finally.

"Why?"

"Just wondering. The men in the plaza told me today that I should go ask Tres Pasos for money. They were just joking though, I think. And the other day we got a letter from Abel and he mentioned something about paying back Tres Pasos."

"He loans people money, that's all I know."

"Do you think he'd lend me money for my guitar?"

"I don't think that's a good idea."

"Why not?"

"Because he charges interest and if you can't pay him back then he hurts you until you do."

"Hurts you? Like how?"

"I don't know, but I've heard that he's killed people in other towns."

"Killed people? But all I want is a guitar."

"Yeah, well who knows? I'd stay away from him."

"Do you think my brothers borrowed money from him?"

Jorge el Gato shrugged and recommended working on the cart. Edmund answered his own question. "I bet they did because they didn't have any money but they made it all the way up to Nebraska and Wyoming. I wonder if Gandolfo is already there. And I bet Tomy and Paty are already married, too. It would be too bad if they couldn't pay back Tres Pasos and he tried to do something to them, huh?"

Jorge el Gato shook his head. "He couldn't do anything to them; they're too far away. He'd hurt someone close by."

Edmund scrunched his brow. "Like who?"

"Like other members of their family."

"What do you mean? Like *me*? But I didn't do nothing."

"Tres Pasos doesn't care, he just wants his money back—" Jorge stopped, noticing the concerned look on Edmund's face. "But don't worry, I'm sure it's fine. That's why he usually just loans money to guys going north because they earn money quickly up there."

Edmund relaxed somewhat. "How long do you think he'd let me take to pay back 1,000 pesos?"

"I said don't think about it," Jorge el Gato said sternly. "It's not worth it."

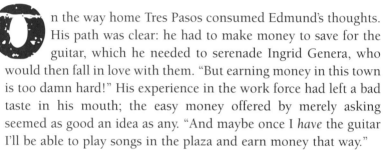

n the way home Tres Pasos consumed Edmund's thoughts. His path was clear: he had to make money to save for the guitar, which he needed to serenade Ingrid Genera, who would then fall in love with them. "But earning money in this town is too damn hard!" His experience in the work force had left a bad taste in his mouth; the easy money offered by merely asking seemed as good an idea as any. "And maybe once I *have* the guitar I'll be able to play songs in the plaza and earn money that way."

He was rounding the corner, his excitement growing as he pondered the idea, when he ran into six girls walking home from the high school. They were wearing uniforms: white blouses, plaid skirts, and socks hiked up to their knees. For this reason, Edmund didn't recognize Ingrid amongst them and he kept his head lowered as he passed, thinking only of Tres Pasos's impending loan.

"Hi, Edmund," Ingrid said.

He looked up, somewhat startled. In front of him stood a wall of white blouses. "Oh," he said, scanning the faces. His jaw dropped when he noticed Ingrid. "Hi," he managed.

Silence ensued.

"Look how dirty he is," one of the girls said, pointing.

Edmund frowned. He knew for a fact his shirt had a pink stain on it because he'd spilled Kool-Aid on it at his tía Lupe's.

"I know, and his red hair is so funny—he looks like a squirrel!" screeched another.

Edmund started to tell her what she looked like when a fat girl with glitter on her cheeks chimed in, "I knooooow, and you want to know why he's sooooo small?"

"Why?" two of the girls responded.

"Because he—"

Edmund answered Glitter-Cheeks's question. "I'm small because that's how God made me. Just like he made you fat—" he addressed the others, knowing from his sisters the last thing a girl wanted to hear—"and he made you with black skin, and you with thick ankles, and you with a flat chest, and you with a big nose!"

He stopped when he came to Ingrid. "And, and—you—you . . ." his heart sank when he saw her disapproving look. He made to count his losses and turn away, when two boys sauntered around the corner, also wearing their uniforms—navy blue dress pants with green cardigan sweaters—kicking a soccer ball.

The big-nosed girl called out, "Rafa, Chico, he said you guys were sissies!"

"No, I didn't!" Edmund said, trying to walk past the two boys. He knew them because they never let him play soccer. They cut off his escape, cornering him against a wall. Rafa said, "You calling us sissies, Edmund, huh? Big words for such a runt!"

"I swear, Rafa, I didn't," Edmund pleaded.

Chico pushed Edmund with both hands, causing him to trip backward and fall.

"Come on, man," Edmund said, picking himself up from the sidewalk. "I didn't say anything. They started it," pointing to the girls.

The girl who had first called him dirty said, "Nuh uh! Rafa, he said I had thick ankles!"

Rafa turned to Edmund, his eyes wide. "Did you say that? You think it's funny telling girls they got thick ankles?"

"No, no, I don't, my sisters have them, I didn't say that, I just—"

Rafa punched Edmund in the nose and Edmund fell to the ground once again, blood spurting from his nostrils. He sat there, defeated, this time making no effort to get up. Chico slapped Rafa on the back and said, "Ah, you got him good!" The crowd of starched uniforms continued on their way, laughing and joking, quickly turning to other topics of interest.

Edmund tilted his head back, his fingers pinching his nostrils, trying to stop the bleeding. He saw Ingrid looking back at him, a sad look on her face. Then he saw Rafa place his arm around her waist.

"Son of a bitch, he's not even that good-looking," Edmund said to himself. Then he stood up and walked home, trying not to cry.

When he arrived home, his mother shrieked when she saw him covered in blood. Agnes and Alfonsa stood up from the kitchen table, clamoring around him, "What happened, what happened?"

Edmund noticed the birthday cake on the table and remembered it was their birthday. "Happy birthday," he said, his voice nasal as he was still holding his nose. Constanza went to the washbasin, wet a towel, and wrung it. She brought it to Edmund and began wiping his face, cleaning off the blood. "Take off your shirt," she ordered. He removed his shirt and sat down at the kitchen table.

"Do you really want to know what happened?" he asked, having already worked out a story.

"Yes! Tell us! Who hurt you?" Agnes and Alfonsa exclaimed.

"Well, the truth is, one of our brothers has fallen behind on his payment to a man you might know by the name Tres Pasos. A few of his thugs cornered me this afternoon and took me for a little ride. This is the result."

His sisters gasped. Constanza continued wiping his face and then stepped back, eyeing her son.

"What did these men look like?" Alfonsa asked.

"Oh, they were big guys. They had big mustaches and boots with steel toes. They also had cowboy hats. They drove a blue truck."

"Who could they be?" Agnes asked.

"Yeah, who but us would care to hurt our little monkey?" Alfonsa followed.

"Hey, I held my own. They threatened me with much worse, I'll tell you that."

Constanza told the twins to run to Doña Flabia's for ice to put on Edmund's nose. It had begun to swell and already there was discoloration around his eyes.

"I kind of feel tired," Edmund admitted when they left.

"Go lie down," his mother said. "Take a nap before we celebrate tonight. A few of your aunts and uncles and cousins are coming over for your sisters' birthday."

She sighed when he left the kitchen, wondering what had really happened. She had heard from all of her children, Abel, Ezekiel, Tomy, Gandolfo; they had arrived safely and were working. Abel and Ezekiel were in Nebraska, Tomy and Paty were already married in Wyoming, and Gandolfo had found work in Texas. So far they had all sent or wired money, indicating what was for her and what was for Tres Pasos. She herself had gone to Tres Pasos and paid him the agreed installment. She found the loan shark agreeable, if not a little eccentric. Certainly he wouldn't have sent men to beat up Edmund.

It wasn't long before she found out her son's true assailants. She heard a knock on the front screen and found a pretty girl standing outside.

i, is Edmund home?"

"Yes, but he's not feeling well right now. What's your name? I'll tell him you came by."

"I'm Ingrid. Can you tell him I'm sorry? I was there when Rafa and Chico beat him up. I should've stopped them, but it happened too quickly. They're just bullies. I should've said something, I—I really should have. So tell him I'm sorry."

"OK," Constanza said. "Did they beat him up for any reason?"

Ingrid shook her head. "No, not really. My friends were just being mean to him and he said some things back. But it wasn't his fault, really. I hope he feels better."

She turned and walked away quickly. Constanza walked to the kitchen and began preparing the pans, feeling sorry for her youngest son. She went to the backyard and gave Cross-Eyes a bone and some water. The mutt limped over and rubbed against her leg. She petted the top of its head and said, "Poor little thing." When she came back into the house, Edmund stood before her, still shirtless. He was smiling radiantly.

"She loves me!" he exclaimed.

Edmund didn't mention the part about trying to touch Ingrid's breasts, breaking Cross-Eyes's hind legs, and singing for Filastro's mistress, but on the whole, his mother received a thorough report concerning his attempts to win over Ingrid Genera's heart. Constanza looked at her prepubescent-looking son and then thought of the pretty girl at the door who could have passed for eighteen. His enthusiastic and positive outlook made her feel sorrier than when Ingrid had told her about the boys beating him up. But Edmund wasn't fazed; he felt the more important thing was that she came to *his* house explicitly to *see* him.

"So, Mamá, I have to buy a new guitar. Then I'll be able to sing that song I was singing—you remember how good it sounded, huh? And I'm sure she'll be mine."

"But, mijo, it's not as simple as that. A song is just a song, and even though you sing it so very good, it still—it—how do I explain—there needs to be more there than just a simple song."

"I know, but—"

Just then Agnes and Alfonsa rushed back into the house. "Guess what?" they exclaimed. "Guess who's coming to play at Disco Órale this Friday! Oh my God, I can't wait!"

"Who?" Edmund asked.

"Benni Terraza is coming!" Agnes shrieked. "Oh, I love his voice! He sings like an angel!"

"I would marry him, I swear I would!" followed Alfonsa.

"No, I would marry him. He's amazing! His voice makes me melt!"

Edmund looked at his mother and raised his eyebrows in triumph. She laughed and told him to go put on his shirt because his aunts and uncles and cousins would be arriving soon.

The family members arrived and the twins' birthday was celebrated with food and cake. They waited for Filastro, but he never showed up. Those in attendance were somewhat relieved, including the birthday girls; Filastro had ruined many a celebration with his drunken antics. Since being fired from his job at Disco Órale, he had been working for Don Gabriel Ponce, a position his compadre Big Gaspar had secured for him at a ranch on the outskirts of Retorno, a town about thirty miles away from La Prudencia. Sometimes they worked until late at night and the workers stayed in the barn, sleeping on grain sacks.

Don Gabriel was generous with his workers, and when they worked past dark he gave them food and plenty of homemade ponche. On the evening of his twin daughters' sixteenth birthday, Filastro, Big Gaspar, and three other workers from town sat around a fire and cooked a pig, drinking merrily.

"I think my daughters' birthday is coming up!" Filastro announced to the group.

"Well, I congratulate you, compadre," Big Gaspar said. "Do you have a gift in mind?"

"No, not really, but maybe I'll have an extra sip of ponche for myself!" Filastro laughed.

The men raised their glasses. "A toast, Filastro!"

"To my daughters' birthday whenever it might be—hopefully not tonight, eh?—may they marry rich men and . . ." Filastro paused to think. "And have sons with big peckers!"

Everyone drank.

A half hour later, Filastro's two other compadres, Mendigo and Jerry, arrived, honking the horn as they drove up, letting the gathering know it was a friendly approach.

"Is that Jerry's truck?" Big Gaspar asked. "Who told them we were here?"

"I did!" Filastro exclaimed. "As long as Don Gabriel supplies the ponche we might as well invite some friends!"

Big Gaspar looked nervously at the other workers, knowing one of them was bound to mention something to the boss. "But, Filastro, we might lose our jobs, Don Gabriel said—"

"Oh, compadre, you are always worrying. Don Gabriel, that rich bastard, has plenty of food and drink for Mendigo and Jerry. Mendigo hardly drinks a sip before he's drunk!"

"That is beside the point," Big Gaspar muttered as Mendigo and Jerry stepped out of the truck, hollering, "We have arrived! Let the party begin!"

The compadres began passing the bottle and cracking open the beers. The other workers soon grew tired and left the fire to sleep in the barn. Big Gaspar tried to leave several times, but his three friends demanded that he stay. Periodically the workers, unable to sleep, stuck their head out the door and asked for quiet. "We have to work early tomorrow!" they cried.

"And we'll be dead the next day!" Filastro yelled back. "So drink up while you can!"

When they were sufficiently drunk, Mendigo and Filastro decided to piss into the fire. Midstream, Mendigo asked Filastro why he hadn't gone to his daughters' birthday party. "I was there for a little bit to have some cake. Your wife mentioned it to my sister at the market. I thought you'd be there."

"It was today?" Filastro asked. "Well, damn, I guess I missed it! A working man can't dance at all the parties."

Jerry, who had been lying on the ground and staring at the sky, interjected, "Hey, Filastro, speaking of your daughters, I saw one of them the other day with her boyfriend and man, compadre, he had his hands all over her! I thought to myself, if Filastro saw them he'd kill them!"

Filastro zipped up his pants. "What the hell did you say?"

Jerry continued, "Yeah, compadre, girls these days, I wouldn't wish a daughter on my worst enemy. They're no different than the boys, nothing on their minds but—"

Filastro violently kicked the ground, showering Jerry with dirt. "What boyfriend? Who was it?" he demanded.

Jerry tried rising from the ground, but settled for resting on his elbows. "No need to kick dust on me. I don't know who her boyfriend is, I couldn't see his face because—well, just because."

Filastro glowered at his compadre. "Damn whores," he muttered to himself. "Come on, let's go. I'm going to teach them a lesson."

he family was asleep when Filastro, Jerry, and Mendigo showed up at four in the morning. How Filastro made the thirty-mile windy drive back to La Prudencia was the first thing that entered Constanza's mind when she opened the curtain and noticed the three compadres stumbling out of the truck. Mendigo could hardly stand up.

"Stay out here," Filastro ordered them as he fumbled in his pocket for the key. Constanza opened the door, but Filastro continued digging in his pocket, unaware of her presence.

"What are you doing?" she asked finally.

He looked up, his face full of rage. "You mother of sluts," he snarled.

"Husband, be quiet. Just come in and I'll make you something to eat and—"

"No!" he entered the house, pushing her aside. "I want Agnes and Alfonsa to come out here right now!"

"But, Filastro, they're asleep. It was their birthday. Let them be."

Agnes and Alfonsa were already awake, having heard the truck stop with a squeal of brakes and their father's unmistakably drunken voice. They looked at each other, wondering why he would want them at this hour.

Filastro screamed their names, but they remained huddled in the bed they shared with their mother. For his part, Edmund kicked off the covers and walked into the front room. He was wearing his pajama bottoms with the spaceships on them. "Hey, Papá," he said. "You missed Agnes and Alfonsa's birthday. It was a lot of fun cause what's-his-name brought over a—"

"Shut up, you shit, before I slap you silly!" Filastro screamed at him.

Edmund stopped in his tracks. "But, Papá, I was going to tell you about—"

"Agnes and Alfonsa, get out here before I drag you out like the trash you are!"

After several moments of quiet, the twins emerged from the bedroom in their nightgowns, their faces full of fright.

Constanza stood next to her daughters, ready to shield them from her husband. "Filastro, please, let's just go to bed—"

"Shut up, woman! Now, look at me. I want you to tell me right now who your boyfriends are!"

"Boyfriends?" they squeaked. "We don't have boyfriends."

"I know you do. One of my compadres told me that he saw you the other day and some boy had his hands all over you. Now which one was it, you or you?"

"I don't know," they trembled in unison. "I don't know what you're talking about."

"Jerry! Come in here!"

Jerry entered the house, removing his hat as he did so, and looked down at the ground. "Yes, compadre?"

"Which one did you see with the boy?"

Jerry looked up at the two girls, then his eyes shifted to Constanza, who glared at him. "Uh, compadre, I can't be sure . . . they're twins, after all. Maybe it wasn't even them. Maybe we should just call it a night, eh?"

"Damn it, Jerry, you tell me now! I know when you're lying."

Jerry lifted his hand and pointed between the two girls. "It was her."

"Who?"

"Her."

"Who? You're pointing at both of them, compadre!"

"Filastro, they look the same to me! How can I tell?"

Filastro turned to Constanza. "Did you know they have boy-friends? Did you know they're out on the street necking like prostitutes? If I get my hands on whoever these guys are, I'll kill them!"

"But, Filastro—"

Filastro slapped her and she fell backward onto the couch. Then he took his daughters by the wrists and dragged them to the kitchen. They were crying hysterically. "No, Papá, no, Papá, please, please don't!" Constanza followed them.

Edmund scowled at Jerry, who stood abashedly, head bowed, his hat in his hands behind his back. They could hear screaming in between slaps and chairs being knocked over in the kitchen. "Why'd you have to tell him for?" Edmund asked.

"I—I—didn't know—he—"

"You're a donkey's ass, you know that? Get out of my house!"

"Don't get fresh with me, I'll tell your father—"

"Tell him, then! See if I care! Now, get out!" Edmund screamed. He rushed at Jerry, trying to push the man over. He was swinging his arms wildly. Jerry held him at a distance, his hands outstretched, restraining the boy.

Finally, exhausted, Edmund backed away. "It was their birth-day! You didn't have to say nothing."

Jerry left the house and Edmund heard the truck drive away. He sat down on the couch and gently rubbed his tender nose, which had been banged in the exchange. Agnes and Alfonsa passed him crying. He walked into the kitchen and found his mother at the stove heating up food, wiping her face periodically with her apron.

Filastro sat at the table, his eyes bloodshot, his face drained. He didn't even notice when Edmund sat across from him. They remained silent for several moments before Filastro told Edmund to get his guitar and play for him.

"Can't."

"Why not?"

"Remember? It broke."

They were silent once again.

"Go to bed, then," Filastro said.

Edmund rose and walked to the bedroom. When he was gone, Filastro asked his wife, "What happened to his face?"

"He got beat up."

"By who?" Filastro said, his voice rising.

"Does it matter?" she said quietly, scooping the beans onto the plate.

"What'd you say?"

"I don't know who did it. He wouldn't say." Constanza set the food on the table, then walked to the stove to heat more tortillas.

n hour later, close to 6:00, Big Gaspar showed up in his truck. He banged on the front door, and Constanza, unable to sleep, rushed to open it. "Is my compadre here?" he asked gruffly.

"Yes, he's asleep."

"Wake him, then. He has to come to work or else we'll both be fired. I vouched for him, told Don Gabriel that he'd work through the harvest."

Constanza went to the bedroom and gently shook Filastro's shoulder. He didn't stir. "Filastro!" she whispered loudly. She was afraid of waking Edmund and the twins, who slept in adjoining beds. "Filastro!"

He grumbled, but did not turn. She went to the front door and told Big Gaspar that his compadre wouldn't wake up. Big Gaspar swore and spit on the sidewalk. "Let me wake him."

He brushed past Constanza and walked into the bedroom. "Filastro! Get up! I'm not getting fired on your account. We have half an hour to get there and start working!"

Everyone woke except Filastro.

"What happened?" Edmund asked, through sleepy eyes. "Oh, Big Gaspar! What are you doing here?"

Big Gaspar ignored him. Agnes and Alfonsa moaned and pulled the covers over their aching heads.

"You want to know how to wake him up?" Edmund asked, jumping up from bed. "You gotta tickle his feet, watch!"

Edmund moved his father's blanket and found that he still had his shoes on. He removed the dirt-caked boots, then the hole-ridden socks, and began to lightly move his fingers across the soles of Filastro's feet.

Filastro squirmed and grunted. Edmund continued. "Watch, you have to do it real fast." He picked up speed, moving up and down the sole. "Stop it, stop, stop," Filastro grumbled, finally jerking his feet away. He rose, holding his head. "Ah, damn you, Edmund, what do you want?"

Big Gaspar spoke. "Compadre, get up. We have to go to work."

"I'm in no condition. We didn't get in until late—"

"I'm not getting fired because of you. I need Don Gabriel's work, and I told him that I'd make sure you were there every day."

Constanza handed Big Gaspar a clean shirt and socks. "Here, take him with you," she said quietly.

Filastro rose from the bed, grabbed the shirt from Big Gaspar, and walked outside, barefoot, holding the socks and boots in his hands. His compadre opened the passenger door and Filastro stepped inside, leaning his head against the seat rest. He grimaced in pain. Big Gaspar walked around to the driver's side, said goodbye to Constanza and Edmund standing at the door, and drove off.

Edmund looked at the clock. "Papá wasn't even home two hours, huh?"

*   *   *

When Agnes and Alfonsa woke up four hours later, they were both black and blue with welts on their faces. They were silent as they sat at the kitchen table drinking atole. Constanza prepared breakfast in a daze, her right cheek red and swollen. Edmund had two black eyes, but his mood was considerably more chipper.

"Agnes, I'm thinking of a number between one and ten, guess which one?"

Agnes ignored him.

"Alfonsa, I'm thinking of a number between one and ten, guess which one?"

"Shut up, Edmund."

Constanza brought a plate of eggs to the table. "Edmund, eat your breakfast and let your sisters be."

He scarfed his food down and rushed outside, his mouth still full. "Bye!" he called out.

"Don't get into any more fights," his mother called after him wearily. She brought her daughters bags of ice.

Edmund headed to his tía Lupe's house to visit Jorge el Gato. On the way he passed the high school. He could see the students inside the classrooms; they sat facing forward watching the teacher in front of the chalkboard. He scanned the faces for Ingrid's but didn't find her. His eyes rested on a poster, a cartoon of an orange cat playing the piano with one hand and holding a book with the other. "That's stupid," he thought to himself. He continued walking. "I'm glad I'm not in school anymore. It looks boring." He kicked a rock and watched it bounce across the cobblestones.

He found Jorge el Gato in front of the house wiping down his cart with a handkerchief.

Edmund approached, hoping his half brother would ask about his black eyes, but Jorge was too engrossed in the cart to look up.

"Going to work?" Edmund finally asked.

"Yup. Want to come along?"

"Can I push the cart?"

They walked along the side of the street, Edmund pushing the cart while Jorge el Gato called out, "Popsicles! Treats for the kiddies!" In between cries, Edmund found an opportunity to ask Jorge questions.

"Have you ever been beat up?"

"No."

"If you could be anything in the world what would you be?"

"I don't know, maybe a doctor."

"I'm glad I quit after primary school. Don't you think school is boring?"

"I don't think so. You get to learn about a lot of different things."

"Yeah, but who cares most of the time? If they taught guitar in school I'd go back."

"They do have music class."

"They do?"

"Yeah, I'm pretty sure."

"Why didn't you go to high school?"

"Couldn't afford it."

"Yeah. My mom said that I could continue if I wanted because all my brothers and sisters were working, but my dad said no."

"Why?"

"Because it cost too much. After the uniform, the books, the pencils, the binders and papers . . . the stapler and paper clips, the backpack . . . the entrance to the school dances. It'd all be a lot of money."

"Yeah."

After an hour of pushing the cart, Edmund decided he'd had enough. They sat together in the central plaza and Edmund enjoyed a lime-green popsicle (his payment). In between bites, Edmund described what had happened when Filastro had arrived home early that morning.

"Is that how come you got black eyes?" Jorge asked.

"No, I got these from two kids in the high school . . . had to fight them off."

Jorge el Gato was quiet, his face pensive.

"They're just bullies," Edmund said. "Picking on some little kids, so I felt like I had to say something."

Jorge el Gato unwrapped a popsicle for himself and began eating it.

"I don't even care, really," Edmund persisted.

A long pause ensued.

"Yeah?" Jorge finally responded.

"Yeah, it don't even hurt."

"That's good."

Edmund was quiet for a minute. He looked down at Jorge's club-foot, the boot misshapen. "Can I ask you something? Why do people always have to focus on the funny looking or the bad parts, almost like they don't notice the parts that are good or not funny looking?"

"How do you mean?"

"I mean—" he grew silent. "Never mind, forget it."

"No, I know what you're saying."

"You do?"

Jorge nodded. "That's just how people are, I guess."

"Yeah." Edmund got up to leave. "I have to go. I'll see you later."

He decided to go home by the back route, which meant he had to cross through Don Pascual's yard. The old man wasn't around, but his donkey was, so Edmund petted it and then continued on his way. He climbed a fence and dropped down into his own backyard. The chickens scattered. The house was quiet as he approached, but he could hear subdued voices talking in the kitchen.

He crept closer, careful not to wake Cross-Eyes curled up at the base of the washbasin.

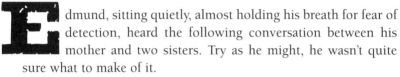

Edmund, sitting quietly, almost holding his breath for fear of detection, heard the following conversation between his mother and two sisters. Try as he might, he wasn't quite sure what to make of it.

"Are you sure, Agnes?" his mother asked.

"Yes, I'm sure. I was sick for an entire week so I went to Doña Ignacia and she confirmed it. I thought maybe she had told Papá, and that was why he came home so mad."

"What are we going to do, Mamá?" Alfonsa asked. "Papá will kill her!"

"So tell me, what exactly did Doña Ignacia do?"

"She cracked an egg on my back and massaged it into my skin . . . and she . . ." Agnes paused.

"Yes, go on."

"She told me to crow like a rooster."

"Like a rooster?" Alfonsa gasped. "Oh my God, sister, did she really make you do that?"

"Yes, and when I had done that she took some ashes and smeared them over my belly and made chanting noises."

"And then she said that you had conceived?" Constanza asked.

"Yes."

"Well, Doña Ignacia has confirmed the results of more than one missed period in this town. She must be right."

There was a knock at the door and the women quieted. Edmund saw his mother walk out the kitchen toward the front door. She opened the screen and looked to her left and right.

"Who is it?" Agnes asked.

Constanza returned to the kitchen table. "Just the tortilla vendor knocking on everyone's door."

Edmund decided to enter the house. He walked back a few yards and then stomped his feet as he approached the door, waking up Cross-Eyes, who started whimpering. "Stop whining, little dog, you're always whining," he said loudly. He opened the back screen so that it slammed against the wall. He wanted to be sure they were aware of his arrival.

"Hello!" he said. "I'm back."

He took a seat at the table and asked his mother for some horchata.

"We don't have any," Constanza responded.

Edmund took note of each one's swollen face. "What were you guys talking about?"

"What do you mean?" Agnes asked warily.

"The weather, the concert this weekend, neighborhood gossip? I don't know, that's why I asked."

"Oh. Well, we weren't talking about anything, really."

Constanza brought Edmund a glass of water and he drank it thirstily. "Why do you have a green stain all over your lips?" she asked him.

"Huh?" He took his shirt and wiped his mouth, noticing the green dye now on his sleeve. "Because I worked for Jorge el Gato and in payment he gave me a popsicle."

"You're such a little kid," Agnes said, ruffling his hair. Her eyes were sad. "Don't ever grow up, OK?"

Edmund eyed his sister. "I don't know about you, but I'm already grown up."

Later that evening, Edmund went for a stroll around the town plaza. "Why had Agnes gone to Doña Ignacia?" he wondered. "And why does Alfonsa think Papá is going to kill her?" The beating last night was harsh but surely not out of the ordinary. At least Filastro had a reason for his rancor: Agnes and Alfonsa were forbidden to date. Edmund was ruminating upon possible scenarios when he heard a voice ask, "How did the love letter work out?"

Edmund turned and noticed Ricardo the Notary sitting by himself on one of the plaza benches. He was wearing a beret, round wire-rimmed glasses, and had a pencil in his ear. His eyes were glassy. In his right hand he held a black book.

"Why you got a Bible?" Edmund asked.

"What? Oh this. This isn't a Bible, just a journal of sorts."

"What's that for?"

"Just musings, thoughts, little sketches. Throughout the day I'm struck with certain revelations, if you will, ideas that require fleshing out. I write them down so as not to forget, and later I return to them when my mind is not so preoccupied, and I try to expand upon them."

"Did you go to high school?"

"Yes, I did."

"Too bad. It was boring, I bet."

"Yes, it was, in fact. Boring and deplorable, I'll tell you that much. I hated my days in high school with such intensity, I couldn't wait for its end; already I had my sights set on the advanced learning to be had in a university. Only there, away from the provincial nature of this town, can one find true thinkers, true cultivation."

Edmund had no idea what Ricardo was talking about, so he changed the subject. "What's a period?"

"You mean a historical epoch?"

Edmund shrugged. Now he was even more confused as to the meaning of his mother and sisters' conversation. "Well, tell me this. Why if my sister missed a historical epoch would she have to go to Doña Ignacia's, the healer?"

Ricardo the Notary thought for a moment and then said, "You must mean a period, as in menstruation." He laughed. "Your sister is probably pregnant!"

Edmund doubted this interpretation. He must have heard wrong.

"Makes sense," Ricardo continued. "Why else would she go to a healer? But more importantly, tell me, how did things go with that girlfriend of yours? Did she enjoy the love letter?"

Edmund shook his head. "No, she knew I didn't write it."

"Not to worry. I'm sure she appreciated your effort. In retrospect, I shouldn't have been so heavy-handed; not everyone can appreciate a poet's touch. My father, for instance: he couldn't recognize an artist if his life depended on it. It seems your father is much the same way, am I right? They have no appreciation for subtlety, for delicateness, for sensitive natures. Culture eludes them; words beyond labels they can't understand, images beyond television and rag magazines they have no time for, music other than the backwoods type like Benni Terraza they—"

"I like Benni Terraza!" Edmund exclaimed. "He's the best. And my dad likes him, too. He's good, huh?"

Ricardo the Notary sighed and removed a flask from his pocket. "To Benni Terraza, may this town jump back and forth like ignorant monkeys." He took a swig.

"You drink mescal?" Edmund asked.

"This, no, this is anisette, secured from a friend of mine with connections in Guadalajara. Of course no one drinks it in these parts. Would you like a drink?"

Edmund declined. "I have to go."

"Goodbye, little Edmund," he said, taking another drink. "May you not be as miserable as yours truly."

"OK, bye."

dmund woke before sunrise and found himself alone in the room where they all slept. His father hadn't come home from Don Gabriel's since leaving with Big Gaspar several mornings before. He heard the front door slam and his mother say, "Shh, you'll wake Edmund." He moved the curtain aside and peeked out the window. By the dim light of a streetlamp, he saw that Agnes and Alfonsa were both carrying suitcases. His mother put her finger to her mouth and beckoned the girls to follow.

Edmund jumped up from bed and put on a sweatshirt. He looked for his pants but couldn't find them in the dark. He frantically moved aside articles of clothing, only coming across his sisters' pants. Finally he decided he'd have to go in his pajama bottoms, the spaceship ones. Then he looked for his shoes, also without success. "Ah, man, they're going to be gone—where's all my stuff?" He gave up the search, deciding to wear one of the pairs his brothers had left behind. The sneakers were much too big for him, and he almost fell over just getting out the door.

He left the house and walked as quickly as he was able in the large shoes that became untied the second he tied them. He looked down each street for the silhouettes of his mother and sisters. An occasional dog emerged from the shadows and greeted him, but for the most part the town was still asleep. An old woman sat outside her door, holding a basketful of pan dulce. At her side stood a large silver canister from which billows of steam rose in the crisp air. He stopped and asked her if she had seen Doña Constanza and her two daughters.

"Would you like a taco?" she asked.

"No, I'm looking for my mamá, you know her, right? Doña
Constanza. Did she pass by?"

"Would you like a taco? Two for ten pesos."

"No, I don't want a taco, I'm looking for my mamá and sisters.
Did you see them?"

"How about some pan dulce for your little tummy?"

"No, I don't want pan dulce, either! Listen, I'm looking for my
mamá. She's about this tall and she's wearing a scarf. My sisters are
about this tall and they had suitcases. Did you happen to see what
direction they went?"

Someone from inside the house called out, "She can't hear,
damn it! Do you want a taco or not?"

"Ah, forget it!" Edmund said, exasperated. "It's like you can't
ever get a simple 'this way' or 'that way'!" He tried to run, but the
big shoes made it difficult. Finally, just when he was about to turn
back, he spotted three dark forms in the distance, two of them
holding suitcases.

Tres Pasos's assistant was nicknamed Tomato on account of his bulbous nose. He was sitting on a recliner watching an early-morning
talk show. He laughed at everything the host had to say, everything
the guests had to say; he laughed at the commercials, too. He stood
up and dropped the remote and the batteries fell out; that got a
cheerful rise as well. He laughed because he loved the early morning. He was at his best from three in the morning until eight. Come
nine, Tomato's mood would begin to sour so that by ten he was
ready to bite your head off. The afternoon was when he went to
collect Tres Pasos's debts. Fortunately for Constanza and her twin
daughters, they had arrived at the crack of dawn.

Constanza knocked on the front door and heard, "Come in!"
followed by a chuckle. She pushed the door open and beckoned
her hesitant daughters to follow. She had been there before and
knew Tomato, whom she mistakenly believed was Tres Pasos.
Tomato was in such a good mood the last few times Constanza had
visited that he hadn't bothered to correct her.

Tomato greeted the three of them with warm hugs, arms spread wide. They returned the kind gesture awkwardly. "Look, look," Tomato said, "let's watch this great show. It's so damn funny!" He pulled up plastic lawn chairs for them to sit on. They all sat down and watched a few minutes of the program, and Tomato chuckled and giggled, turning to them and pointing to the screen with delight. Constanza, Agnes, and Alfonsa all looked at each other hesitantly, wondering if the man were insane, not finding the show on traditional Oaxacan window decorations the least bit funny. When the program went to commercials, they expected Tomato to turn to them, but the subsequent advertisements kept his attention. Finally Constanza said, "Excuse me, Tres Pasos, I need to ask a favor once more. This time for my daughters."

Tomato straightened up. "Oh, yes! Forgive me, sometimes the television just makes me lose track of time. Forgive my manners. So, Constanza, did you change your hair? What beautiful daughters you have! Would you like some coffee? What would you like?"

Constanza wasn't sure to which question or comment she should respond, so she merely stated what she'd intended to say initially. "My daughters need money to go to the United States. Their brothers are already in Nebraska, Wyoming, and Texas. They will go to them and be taken care of."

"Sounds just fine!" Tomato said. "How can I assist them?"

"Well, they need money."

"Sure thing. You already know our policy, so I won't go into detail, but remember Tres Pasos is a hard man when he needs to be. This isn't a bank, this is a 'you pay us back or else' institution. Understand?" He said this so cheerfully it almost seemed in jest. Agnes and Alfonsa had lost their nervousness and were now smiling.

"We need something else," Constanza continued. "One of my daughters . . . Agnes, this one here—she's pregnant. Her brothers were able to go on their own; they found coyotes closer to the border, but my daughters, they are just young girls; they need more assistance, someone to protect them—"

"No need to explain, Doña Constanza. I know exactly what you're requesting and I'm granting your request on the spot. Good thing your daughters—Agnes and Alfonsa, beautiful names, such angelic faces—brought their suitcases. A bus is leaving this morning at nine on the dot. How does that sound?"

"Thank you, Don Tres Pasos, thank you. We appreciate it so much and we will pay you as soon as possible, of course."

"No need, no need to assure me. You and your family are trusted customers, Doña Constanza. But just a reminder, a little reminder to place in the back of your head." Tomato looked so kind as he spoke. "We will get our payment, in *whatever* form. There is no doubt about it." With that he laughed and proceeded to give each of them affectionate taps on the hand.

"What a beautiful sunrise, no?" he exclaimed, as he moved aside the curtain. "I just love the early morning!"

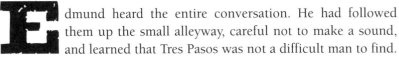

Edmund heard the entire conversation. He had followed them up the small alleyway, careful not to make a sound, and learned that Tres Pasos was not a difficult man to find. In fact, he lived and operated in proximity to his tía Fredy's house and Güero's Pizza. "I should have just asked around some more," he thought to himself. "I could already have my guitar and be practicing Ingrid's song."

He had crept as close as possible, just outside the door. He hid behind a large plant and listened while his mother asked Tres Pasos for a loan. The man sounded so friendly and good-natured that Edmund couldn't understand how the loan shark had developed such a harsh reputation. "Just goes to show you," Edmund thought. "Here's a guy who just wants to help people out, give them money so that they can make something of themselves, and the entire town has to assume he's a bad person. Even Jorge el Gato!"

Edmund heard that his sisters were going to leave at nine; they still had a few hours of waiting. Inside, Tomato decided to make breakfast. He asked them how they liked their eggs, how many tortillas they wanted, if they took two or three spoonfuls of sugar in their Nescafé. He donned an apron and rushed to and from the kitchen, laughing at whatever the television commentators had to say. Constanza left after breakfast, kissing her daughters with little ceremony. They had already exchanged tearful good-byes the night before, not knowing their dealings with Tres Pasos would be so easy and convenient. She walked past Edmund without noticing him huddled behind a plant.

Edmund decided to return to Tres Pasos's after Agnes and Alfonsa had departed. He was still wearing his spaceship pajama bottoms and big tennis shoes, but he didn't want to go home and risk his mother questioning his whereabouts. So he decided to stick to the back streets and stay out of people's way. When he grew tired of the back streets, not knowing what else to do to kill time, he headed to the main streets, then to the plaza. His excitement about the impending loan allowed him to ignore the glances and smirks at his attire.

When he returned to Tres Pasos's place it was almost 10:00 and Tomato's good mood, as always, had soured considerably. The morning talk shows full of chipper people had given way to more serious news programs and soap operas—not his favorites by far; they were depressing, but more depressing was turning off the television. The transport van had shown up late, and if that wasn't enough, his mother had called and asked him where he'd hidden the saltshaker. "I never even looked at the saltshaker," he yelled at her, "how am I gonna know where it is then, huh? Answer me that!" When Edmund knocked on the door, Tomato was gnashing his teeth, moaning aloud, "People always coming by asking for money like it grows on trees and then I gotta go beat up their great uncle, the only poor sucker I can get my hands on, in order to get Tres Pasos's money back, and usually they want the—"

"Hello! Anybody home?" Edmund asked, stepping inside. He expected a warm hug like the one his sisters had received. Instead he found Tomato with his head against the chair, staring at the ceiling.

"Hey, Tres Pasos! I'm just coming by to—"

"Get out of my life!" Tomato yelled.

"What?"

"I said to get the hell out of here, you scum of scum. I can't tell you how much you make me sick coming in here without being asked to. You knock, you stay outside until I come and answer the door!"

"But—but—"

"What do you think this is? Your goddamn aunt's house? This is Tres Pasos's place of business, where deals of life and death are made, and you walk in here like it's your own living room. What did you come in here for?"

"Uh—uh—I—" Edmund didn't know what to make of Tres Pasos's change in demeanor. "Sir, I—uh—came to ask—if—"

"Did I ask you what you came for—no! I told you to get the hell out of my face. You little shit with your red hair like a goddamn rooster—"

"But—I—"

"Like a goddamn sneaky red fox—"

"It's just that I—"

"Like a little red jackrabbit—"

Edmund was overwhelmed. He knitted his brow and allowed Tomato to list all the reddish animals that came to mind. As soon as Tomato finished, Edmund volleyed off, "Oh, yeah, you think I got funny red hair, well look at your nose, your big ugly red nose—I'd rather look like a rooster than have a big tomato on my nose. Look at your big tomato nose! People should call you 'Big Tomato'!"

Tomato snarled at Edmund, "Get out of here before I snap your toothpick neck. If you weren't a little boy I'd beat the living shit out of you."

Edmund suddenly realized his hopes for a loan were disappearing. He changed his tone. "Wait, please, wait! Just hear me out. I'm sorry for calling you a big tomato; it's just I get real mad when people make fun of my hair. But please listen—" He tried to say it as quickly as possible before the man could tell him to get lost. "I need money to buy a guitar so that I can practice a song so I can serenade Ingrid, who will fall in love with me and there's nothing more in life that I want but I need that, I need her to love me because I love her!"

"I don't care what you want or what little slut you want to sing for, what do you think this is? A charity for lovebirds? My God, I should—"

They heard a voice from the back room. "Tomato!"

They were silent.

"I said, Tomato! Tomato!"

"Yes?" Tomato said meekly.

"Get over here now!" the scratchy voice called.

"Who's that?" Edmund asked.

Tomato hung his head and mumbled, "Tres Pasos." He walked dejectedly to the back room. "Coming!" he called out.

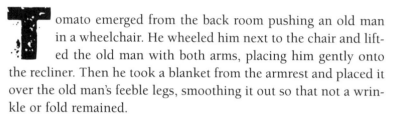

omato emerged from the back room pushing an old man in a wheelchair. He wheeled him next to the chair and lifted the old man with both arms, placing him gently onto the recliner. Then he took a blanket from the armrest and placed it over the old man's feeble legs, smoothing it out so that not a wrinkle or fold remained.

"What happened to your legs?" Edmund asked.

"Age, son, age. What the hell are you wearing?"

Edmund looked at his pajama bottoms and big shoes—he had gotten used to them. "I was in a rush. Are you Tres Pasos?"

"Yes, that is my name. This here is my assistant, Tomato."

Edmund thought Tres Pasos must have heard the exchange of insults. "I'm sorry, I was just upset, so I called him the first thing that I thought of because his—"

"His nose. Don't think you're the first to make that connection. His name *is* Tomato and it's been Tomato as long as I've known him. Forgive his bad humor, he's better in the morning."

Edmund looked at the clock.

"Early morning, I should say. Now look, son, you appear much too young for any monetary request, but in my extensive studies of our great revolution I've read of small boys as young as eight or nine becoming commanders of entire regiments. So I'm always willing to be proven wrong. How old are you, nine, ten?"

"I'm almost fourteen."

"Oh, well, then, you're just small."

"I'm not that—"

"Never mind. What did I hear about a guitar and a serenade?"

Edmund told him about his plan to win Ingrid over.

Tres Pasos chuckled. "Ah, what I wouldn't give for my youth, for my first love. Tell me, son, what is it about this Ingrid that makes you love her?"

Edmund thought for a moment. "I don't know. I just do."

"Is she beautiful?"

"Yes."

"Well, sometimes that's reason enough. Is she sweet to you?"

"Sweet? Like how do you mean?"

"Does she smile with a twinkle in her eye? Does she say kind words to you, does she tremble in your presence and giggle?"

Edmund shook his head. "No, for the most part she's kind of mean to me. She calls me a troll sometimes. The other day she was with her friends and they all made fun of me and then her boyfriend came and beat me up."

Tres Pasos frowned. "So this is a tough case then. Tell me, how did you first meet?"

"I was walking down the street one day and I saw her drop a wrapper so I went and picked it up and brought it to her. 'Excuse me,' I said, 'you dropped this over there.' She laughed and told me it was trash and she meant to drop it. So I just said OK and I dropped it, too, and we both laughed. But then this woman saw me and she started screaming at me that I was littering in front of her property that she had spent so much time sweeping and that she would beat me with her broom if I ever so much as stepped on her sidewalk again. So that was when I told the woman that it wasn't me who was littering but Ingrid—"

Tres Pasos scoffed, "What are you, some kind of idiot?"

"No, but I didn't see why I had to get in trouble when it was her who was throwing trash around in the first place. Anyway, Ingrid got mad at me and I apologized, even though I didn't know for what—she was the one who got me in trouble—and then we didn't talk again until Jorge el Gato told me that all I needed to do was tell her I had to speak to her about a 'matter of great importance'."

"Did that work?"

"Yes, it did, but then I ruined it when I tried to—ah, never mind, it's just stupid stuff. What I know is that she once heard me playing the guitar and she said that it was good. And Jorge el Gato told me that the way to a woman's heart is through serenading."

"This Gato fellow seems to know what he's talking about. Now, listen, I have a proposition to make. Are you listening?"

Tres Pasos's proposition went as follows: first, he would give Edmund his son's guitar.

"Won't your son need it?"

"He's dead."

"Oh. How did—"

"I'll get to that."

Second, Edmund would come to him every other day for lessons because in addition to loan sharking, Tres Pasos was an accomplished guitarist.

"Why didn't you become a professional?"

"I was."

"What happened?"

"I'm getting to that."

Third, in exchange for the guitar and the lessons, he would have to kill Tomato.

"I can't do that!"

Tres Pasos laughed. "Hear that, Tomato?"

Tomato was not amused (he was cracking his knuckles).

"No, just joking, Edmund. In exchange for the lessons you must listen to the stories of my life."

"What do you mean?"

"I mean this: Tomato here is just a big brute, all fat and muscle. All my sons, same thing. They couldn't sit still one minute and if they ever did they just wanted to hear stories about drunken brawls. Which I told them, and is probably the reason they're all dead. None of them in drunken brawls, but close to it. So anyway, this is the thing. A man gets to a certain age and he feels the need to pass on his wisdom, the experiences he's collected over the years, you understand?"

"No."

"That's all right. All I'm asking is for you to listen. Can you do that?"

"I think so."

"You little devil, I'm offering you the deal of a lifetime—a guitar, lessons from a master. All you have to do is listen to some good stories—and your response is 'I think so.' What's your problem?"

"Well, about how long are these stories?"

Tres Pasos laughed. "What else could you possibly have to occupy your time?"

Edmund was offended. "I gotta lot of stuff to do, just things."

Tres Pasos laughed again. "OK, now are you ready for the first story and lesson?"

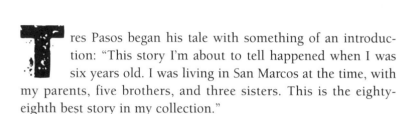
Tres Pasos began his tale with something of an introduction: "This story I'm about to tell happened when I was six years old. I was living in San Marcos at the time, with my parents, five brothers, and three sisters. This is the eighty-eighth best story in my collection."

"There are eighty-eight stories!" Edmund exclaimed.

"No, of course not. There are 500. This is just the eighty-eighth best one. And by best, I mean there are certain criteria. You got action, you got passion, you got sexual overtones, you got sex itself, you got heartache, you got death, so on and so on, and they all get consideration. If a story has action, sex, and heartache, it's most likely ranked pretty high, you understand?"

Edmund was dumbfounded. What had he gotten himself into?

Tres Pasos began. "OK, so when I was six years old . . . "

* * *

The first story wasn't too long and it was actually pretty good. Turns out Tres Pasos, a long time ago in a place called San Marcos, decided he wanted to be a matador, so he climbed into a corral, red blanket and skewering rod in hand, and fought one of the neighbor's defenseless cows.

"Damn cow wouldn't fight back, so I kept hitting it over the head to get it angry, but it wouldn't charge me."

"Of course it didn't. One time—"

"Wait, I was only six years old; I didn't know better. Just let me tell the story without interruption."

So Tres Pasos the six-year-old took the skewering rod and plunged it right into the cow's udder. The neighbor had been watching him, enjoying the child's play, but upon witnessing the violent act, he went berserk, hopped over the fence, and proceeded to beat Tres Pasos just as the boy had been beating the cow.

"I learned a lot that day," Tres Pasos said in conclusion. "I learned that there are certain forces acting upon the will of man, playing both with his ignorance, his naïve nature, his aggressive disposition . . . latent and yet lurking. I was a fool, yes, but a child's folly is nothing to nod your head about (Edmund was nodding his head as Tres Pasos spoke); it is a chapter in the longer book of life, no less important than the middle and end. Do you understand what I'm saying?"

Edmund continued nodding.

"Are you sure?"

"Yes." And then after a moment's pause: "One time I tried to ride a cow, so I got a step stool and climbed on top but the cow wouldn't move. So then I began to yell at it and my brother Ezekiel heard, so he went and told my dad."

"Did he find you and beat you?"

"No, he beat my brother for being a tattletale."

"Did he then beat you?"

"No, on account I'm so small—anyway, that was a good story. Can we start our lesson?"

Tres Pasos and Edmund began their lesson. When Tomato brought the son's guitar from the other room and placed it in Edmund's hands, Edmund almost felt weak. How he had wished for that moment! He ran his fingers over the smooth wood. He held it up to his nose and breathed in deeply. He lightly touched the strings as if afraid to make a sound.

"Good, son," Tres Pasos said, "someone already taught you how to handle the guitar—like a woman, yes?"

Edmund shrugged, somewhat embarrassed. "I just like it, that's all."

They commenced the lesson, Edmund showing Tres Pasos all the chords and songs in his repertoire.

"Not bad," Tres Pasos commented.

The old man instructed Edmund on the proper way to position the guitar. "Don't watch those amateurs in the plaza; they'll show you nothing but bad habits. Look, this'll be awkward at first, but don't put your thumb over the neck . . . "

After the first day's instruction, Edmund couldn't have been more satisfied with the deal he'd struck with Tres Pasos. There was one drawback, however: he wasn't able to bring the guitar with him. It wouldn't be his until they were through with the lessons and the stories.

"But how long will 500 stories take?" Edmund asked.

"Do you want to be a maestro or not?"

"I just want to play my song for Ingrid."

Tres Pasos laughed. "Here—you'll thank me later—help me adjust my position in this damned lumpy chair."

*　　*　　*

On the way home Edmund ran into Ricardo the Notary sitting by himself eating a piece of barbecued corn with chili pepper sprinkled on top.

"What are you eating?" Edmund asked, smiling.

Ricardo looked at him, his eyes hollow. "Why do people ask questions the answers to which they already know? What do you *think* I'm eating?"

"Barbecued corn with chili pepper sprinkled on top."

"Very good," Ricardo sneered. "Now what can I do for you?"

"Forget you, man. You're a downer. Here I just come from a guitar lesson with Tres Pasos himself, who, if you didn't know, is a great guitarist, and I'm excited because I learned how to hold the guitar properly, and even though it's awkward, I can already see—"

"Wait," Ricardo sat up straight, suddenly animated. "Did you just say you're taking lessons with Tres Pasos?"

"Hah! Why do *you* ask a question you already *know* the answer to? I just told you—"

"OK, you got me, but are you really taking lessons with Tres Pasos? That's incredible! How'd you get him to do that?"

"Easy. All I have to do is listen to the 500 stories of his life and in exchange he gives me a guitar and lessons. Today the story was pretty good and it wasn't even that long."

Ricardo the Notary was reeling. "You get to listen to the stories of Tres Pasos's life! Oh my God, that's amazing! What I would give for those stories!"

"Why? Do you want guitar lessons, too?"

"No, no, not at all. I just need stories. That's it. I'm writing a book, you see, or I'd like to, at least." As he spoke he stared curiously at Edmund's attire. "But my stories are humdrum, my life is boring; it's the curse of the intellectual, I'll tell you that—possessed with reason and language but lacking in the nuts and bolts of life, do you understand?"

Edmund shook his head. "No, but I could tell you the story if you want."

"Could you? That would be perfect! My God, this is going to put me on the map. I'll be chumming around with Fuentes in no time."

"With Don Roberto? Why do you want hang out with—"

"No, not Roberto Fuentes. Anyhow, tell me the first story." Ricardo brought out his black book and a pen, his hand trembling with excitement.

hat's it! That's the story?" Ricardo exclaimed after Edmund finished.

"Yeah, what did you expect? I thought it was a good story. It happened to me once, something similar. I was on top of the cow trying to ride it—"

"I don't care about your story! I want Tres Pasos's. And all you give me is 'He wanted to be a matador, but the cow wouldn't chase him, so he skewered its udder and was beaten by the neighbor.' Where are the details?"

"What details? I told you exactly how he told it to me. Or almost."

"I need more to work with," Ricardo said, shaking his head. He placed his black book and pen back in his coat pocket and sighed.

Edmund couldn't understand why Ricardo the Notary was so upset. "Hey, man, don't you hear people's stories all the time when they come to you for letters?"

"Ah, just boring, meaningless lives. I've heard enough about quinceañeras, weddings, baptisms, and ailments for five lifetimes. That's why I quit."

"You quit? But that seems like a good job. You get to sit in the shade and talk to people and you get paid for it."

"Ah, Edmund, you wouldn't understand. I have big dreams— big dreams! And as long as my dad keeps me under his reins, I'm kept from reaching my true potential."

"You should leave, then, like my brothers. Go to Nebraska or something."

Ricardo moaned. "I'm a Man of Letters, can't you see? I'd have to start from scratch there, working as a dishwasher. I imagine you'd be fine with that, but me, no, my mind requires creative stimuli—"

Edmund's face colored. "I'm not going be a dishwasher! I'm going to be a guitarist."

Ricardo chuckled. "Ah yes, Edmund, then maybe you do understand what I'm going through. Is that why you don't join your brothers?"

Edmund shrugged. "I don't know. I never even thought of going. I got all my friends here, Jorge el Gato . . . you . . . my mom, my tía Lupe, and plus, Ingrid lives here, not there."

"So if she left, you'd follow her?"

Edmund thought for a moment. "When I play her my song, she won't think about going."

Ricardo stared hard at Edmund as if recognizing him for the first time. "I admire your tenacity."

"What does that mean?"

"Nothing, forget it."

While Edmund spent the afternoon striking deals, listening to stories, and practicing the guitar, his mother was at home doing the unprecedented: she sat on the couch watching television. She watched a game show, a soap opera, music videos, another soap opera, and the news, until finally she fell asleep. When she woke from her nap she decided to iron clothes. She put on the radio and turned up the volume. After three shirts, starched and wrinkle-free, she found herself smiling. She couldn't stop. Her sons were gone, her daughters not yet safely across the border, but she couldn't shake the feeling of peace that had enveloped her. "They are free from their father," Constanza repeated to herself.

There was always Edmund, she thought, and she worried that with all the other children gone maybe Filastro would finally turn his aggression toward him. She wondered where her youngest had disappeared. "Always up to something," she chuckled to herself. After ironing she decided to prepare dinner. She pulled a large metal pot down from the nail on the wall and stopped. It was then that she began to cry. All her children were gone save one. Yes, free from their father, but gone from her as well. "What's left to do?" she asked herself.

She looked again at the large pot. "What do I need with this?" Constanza wiped her eyes and placed the pot back on the nail. She looked at the clock and wondered when Filastro would be coming home. A moment later the screen door opened and slammed shut, startling her.

"Who's there?" she asked.

There was silence.

"Hello?" she said again, walking slowly toward the front room. The sun had set and the house was dark. She reached for the light, but stopped, seeing something next to the sofa.

Edmund jumped out from the shadows. "Hey!" he yelled.

His mother shrieked. "Ay, Edmund!" In one motion she took him by the arm and swatted his backside. He looked at her in disbelief. "What'd you do that for?"

"You should know better!"

"But you don't have to hit me like a little kid!"

"Well, if you keep acting like one, jumping at your mother like that! And where have you been all day? It's enough that your father is gone without me knowing when to expect him, but you do just as he does, about your business as you please! And just what are you wearing—your pajamas, at this time of day! And whose shoes are those—"

Edmund's face stopped her.

"What's wrong?" she asked, calming.

He looked around the room. He had been too occupied by his own dealings with Tres Pasos to absorb the fact that his sisters were gone. "It's just us now, huh?" he said quietly.

Constanza nodded and stepped toward her son, drawing him close. "Yes," she sighed. "But it is for the best."

"Are you going to make me go, too?"

"No, no, mijo, what makes you ask that?"

He shrugged. "I don't want to go."

She laughed gently. "Oh, my little one, you will be the one to stay with me, you will take care of your mother."

Edmund stepped back, his brow furrowed. "Why do I gotta take care of you?"

"I was just saying, my Edmundito—"

"No, see, you don't understand me." The conversation with Ricardo the Former Notary had resonated. "I have big dreams—big dreams! I'm a Man of Guitar Music and I need to stay here to focus on that, not working as some dishwasher in Wyoming! My mind needs creative sti—stimu—— can't you realize that?"

His mother eyed him suspiciously. "What are you talking about? Who have you been talking to?"

Having mentioned a Man of Guitar Music, Edmund was suddenly reminded of the concert. "Agnes and Alfonsa are going to miss Benni Terraza tonight! Why couldn't they leave tomorrow?"

"They had more important things to worry about than Benni Terraza."

"But—but who's going to take me?"

"Here," Constanza said, struck with an idea. She went to the cabinet and removed a tin from the shelf, opened it, and took out several bills. She knew this would make her son happy. "I'll go with you."

"You! But—"

While Edmund and his mother headed to the Benni Terraza concert, Filastro and his three compadres, Big Gaspar, Mendigo, and Jerry, were planning a concert of their own. Drunkenness was the score. Filastro and Big Gaspar had worked all week and made more than enough money for a three-day revelry. Which is why Filastro invited Mendigo and Jerry to join them. No need to have more than enough money when thirsty friends are waiting at home!

Big Gaspar was hesitant. "Why do you always have to call Mendigo and Jerry? It'd be nice to just get drunk for a night and then go home with a little money saved. My woman keeps asking me—"

"That's your problem right there, you listen well enough to your woman that you can tell me later what she said. I don't remember a single word Constanza has told me since she said 'I do.' And that wasn't even to me—that was to the judge. Your woman must respect your hard work; you deserve a good time with your compadres."

"Yes, but why three days?"

"Why? You ask me why? You weren't here for the Best Compadres' Time Ever, so I'll tell you why—"

Just then Mendigo and Jerry drove up, honking the horn repeatedly. When they stepped out of the vehicle, Filastro said to them, "Compadres, our compadre Big Gaspar here has just asked me why we must go on a three-day spree. Shall we inform him?"

Mendigo hopped forward. "Rule number one for the Best Compadres' Time Ever: Never shall you drink for less than three days!"

Jerry raised his hand, index finger extended. "Rule number two for Compadres' Time: at every given moment the compadres must be on the brink of disaster, not possible unless following rule number one—"

"Never shall you drink for less than three days!" Filastro and Mendigo chorused. Filastro followed, "And you're forgetting rule eight, Jerry. You must always say, 'Best Compadres' Time Ever,' no shortening!"

Jerry slapped his forehead. "Oh, you're right, compadre. What a good memory!"

Big Gaspar shook his head. "Ah, we'll see. I'd rather rest tomorrow, save some of this money I've earned, you know?" He looked to them for some semblance of understanding. His compadres *did* understand and they were not amused.

Filastro took a sip of beer. "What's happening to you, compadre, or should I call you 'comadre'? Hey woman-friend, maybe your wife would like it if you cooked the food, too!"

Jerry screwed off the top of the bottle. "Yeah, Big Gaspar, for the last year or so you haven't been the same. That's why you missed the first Best Compadres' Time Ever. You said you were off working somewhere, but maybe that was a lie, maybe you were at home with your woman and mother-in-law watching soap operas."

Mendigo giggled. "Yeah, comadre. I never thought I'd call Big Gaspar my comadre, but times change, I guess."

They soon moved onto other topics. "OK, compadres," Filastro said, "Let's lay out the plan for tonight. First I'd like to play a few games of pool. Anyone against that? All right, next I'd like to play a few games of cards, and if not cards, then let's look for a rooster fight, and if not roosters, then dogs, and if not dogs, I say—what the hell!—we wrestle one another and place bets. How does that sound?"

"Sounds good to me," Mendigo said. "And I'd like to visit a you-know-what afterward, if you know what I mean."

"No, I don't know what you mean by 'you-know-what.' Remember rule number five of Best Compadres' Time Ever—honesty without shame, compadres."

"He wants to go to a whorehouse!" Jerry said, laughing. "Why are you ashamed to say it, Mendigo?"

"It's because he's always the one suggesting we go!" Big Gaspar added in, beginning to enjoy himself after a few shots.

After an hour drinking on Don Gabriel's ranch they headed into the town of Retorno. They played several games of pool, inventing new rules for Best Compadres' Time Ever as they went along. "Rule sixteen," Filastro suggested, "you can only talk to women if it's in your compadres' interests."

"How do you mean?" asked Mendigo.

"Watch." Filastro tapped a woman on the shoulder. She turned around and looked Filastro over, having no qualms about displaying her annoyance. "Oh, don't worry," he reassured her, "I don't speak for myself, but on behalf of my compadre Mendigo." The woman turned her eyes in the direction Filastro pointed. He seemed to indicate Jerry, who some considered handsome.

"Oh, yeah?" she said. "Well, why can't he speak for himself?"

"You see, he'd like to, but there was an unfortunate accident in his childhood, making him incapable of even the slightest utterance."

Jerry laughed and called out, "Yeah, he can't even say his own name."

The woman was confused. "But he just spoke!"

"Who? Oh, no, that's my compadre Jerry. I'm talking about my compadre Mendigo." Filastro and the woman turned to the elfish man standing next to Jerry.

"Oh, well, I'm here with someone," the woman said. "Plus, I'm not one for circus helpers."

Filastro laughed. "Hear that, Mendigo? She called you a circus helper!"

Mendigo glowered at Filastro as he drank his entire beer in one gulp. "Oh, yeah, well, guess what I heard today about your—" he stopped mid-sentence, not drunk enough to make such a stupid mistake. Instead, he said to Jerry, "If only he knew what we know."

"Let him find out from someone else," Jerry said. "That'd end our fun real quick."

"What are you guys talking about?" Big Gaspar asked.

"Word's around that Filastro's daughter Agnes is—" he stopped as Filastro approached them carrying four more shots.

"Drink up, compadres!"

They continued well into the night, following Filastro's itinerary almost exactly as planned. Several games of pool, a few rounds of cards, then they found a rooster fight, but it was just some back-woods amateurs. So they sought out a dogfight but to no avail. They decided to wrestle one another—in jest, however. Still, Jerry managed to sprain his ankle trying to trip Mendigo. After carrying Jerry to a whorehouse along the highway, the compadres were exhausted. They passed out waiting for a room to open up. When the owner of the establishment emerged from his office and found the four of them leaning on one another, he kicked their boots. "This isn't a hotel, damn it! Get out of here!"

Filastro and Big Gaspar helped Jerry, whose ankle had swollen considerably, rise to his feet. They walked out of the building, the sky beginning to brighten over the distant mountains. "Where's the truck?" Mendigo asked, struggling to keep up. They stumbled around town until they found it. Filastro, Big Gaspar, and Jerry slept in the cab, while Mendigo was forced to crawl onto the truck bed, where he fell asleep shivering.

A t first Edmund was hesitant about attending the concert with his mother. But he quickly changed his mind when he found he enjoyed acting the part of tour guide. Constanza rarely left the house, and then, only during the day for errands. It had been years since she had taken her little ones for an evening outing to the carnival, the dwarf bullfights, or ice cream in the plaza. Edmund saw his mother's eyes widen or narrow, her brow wrinkle, her face brighten, and he pointed out the sights accordingly.

"That's the pool hall where we-know-who likes to go. And that's the video game place where I like to play shoot-'em-up. That's the corner where Jorge el Gato gets the best business. That's where Doña Claudia has her taco cart, and it's probably my favorite of all the carts. We should go there after the concert, OK?"

When they arrived at Disco Órale it was clear that no other mothers had accompanied their teenage children. Most of the girls and young women were decked out in skimpy tops, tight pants, and boots or high heels. Constanza wore a long, thick skirt, house-slippers, and a black knitted shawl. She was self-conscious, but Edmund was unfazed as he pointed out the sights of interest. "And that's where everyone goes to get their popcorn. Do you want some popcorn, Mamá?"

She nodded her head and they walked toward the concession cart. He ordered two popcorns with plenty of hot sauce. They stood outside the club along with the other young people, all of them anxious for the ticket office to open. Edmund ate his popcorn fast, becoming nervous as he considered the possibility of running into Ingrid. What would he say? Would his mother mind if he talked to her? He then thought it'd be nice for his mother and Ingrid to meet under circumstances other than the occasion of his getting beaten up.

The ticket office opened and the crowd formed a haphazard line. Young people kept slipping in front of them, either out of rudeness or not realizing Constanza and Edmund were in line. "Hey, no cuts!" Edmund said after two cowboys knocked his popcorn, but they just turned around and shrugged. Edmund decided to assert himself. Grabbing hold of his mother's hand, they stepped forward together so that no one could get through. The line moved quickly and soon they were at the ticket counter.

"Two tickets!" Edmund said, smiling.

The bouncer looked at Edmund, then at his mother, and said, "Sorry, no children."

"But I'm almost fourteen."

The bouncer laughed. "Yeah, sure you are. Well, no one is allowed under sixteen."

Meanwhile people continued filing past, the tickets bought, the hands stamped, and several kids Edmund knew to be younger than him passed by without even a second glance.

"Hey, those kids aren't even thirteen!"

The bouncer looked at Edmund and then at Constanza. "Are you his mother?" the man asked.

Constanza nodded.

The man smiled.

"Well then you can enter, but you can't let go of his hand. Under no circumstances, you hear? If anyone gets hurt we'll be in big trouble with Benni's managers."

Constanza said OK, squeezing Edmund's hand. They paid for the tickets and entered through the doors, deciding to throw away the popcorn because it was too hard to hold hands, maneuver through the crowd, and eat at the same time. Edmund happened to look behind himself and noticed the bouncer and the ticket-taker looking in their direction and laughing. Edmund was ready to give the bouncer what-for when he heard a guitar chord struck. He turned and saw Benni Terraza and his band warming up onstage.

"Look, Mamá, look! It's him!"

They pushed forward, skipping past the bar, moving as close to the stage as possible. Edmund admired Benni's guitar and paid close attention to the chords played. "I think that's a combination I know," he told his mother. Constanza watched her son's attentiveness and laughed inside. She was happy to see him so excited. "What chords are those?" she asked.

"Oh, just the C and then G and G7, I think. He moves his hands too quick to be sure."

She continued asking questions and Edmund answered in great detail even though she couldn't hear a word he was saying over the crowd. The club was now completely packed. The band left the stage and the dance floor darkened. The crowd grew quiet, some people whistled, and girls' voices called out, "I love you, Benni!" Pink smoke emerged from behind the stage and an announcer boomed, "Here we have our hometown favorites on tour through the country but they always come back to the place that started it all, I present, Benneeeeee Terrrrrazaaaa and his Banda del Fuego!"

The crowd went crazy, roaring and clapping. A chord was played and the stage lights flipped on, the spotlight on Benni Terraza. He sang into the microphone and the crowd cheered wildly. Soon everyone was dancing, taking partners, and swinging one another around. Edmund looked up at his mother and smiled. They were still holding hands, and though they didn't dance, they couldn't help but swing their arms in beat to the music. Edmund hopped from one foot to the other. "Isn't he good?" he screamed to his mother.

After several songs, Constanza turned and observed the crowd. Everyone's attention was either on the stage or on his or her dancing partner, which was why she easily spotted a group of young people staring in their direction and laughing. She turned around, thinking they must be looking past her, but nothing but the far wall stood behind them. One of the boys pointed in Edmund's direction and screamed something unintelligible. Then she recognized the girl who had come to apologize the other day. She was trying to make the boy stop.

Constanza looked at her son to see if he noticed, but he was staring at the stage, his eyes transfixed on Benni Terraza.

The next day Edmund woke with a heavy feeling in his chest. He had seen Ingrid and Rafa dance together during the first song, and then again when Rafa noticed Edmund and decided to call everyone's attention to the boy holding his mother's hand. Edmund tried ignoring them, not for his sake, but for his mother's.

For the first time he felt as if playing a song for Ingrid wouldn't be enough. "Clearly, she likes assholes like Rafa," he grumbled. Then he wished he hadn't taken his mother to the concert. "Now everyone thinks I'm a mama's boy." He could hear her in the kitchen. He peeked his head out the bedroom, wanting to just slip away and go for a walk. But then he smelled something good. He couldn't quite put his finger—or nose—on it. He inched toward the kitchen, his nostrils wide. Then he knew.

"Ah, you made pancakes!"

"Of course, my love. I had such fun last night that I thought I'd treat you. Do you want jam?"

They ate and the heavy feeling in Edmund's chest was assuaged somewhat. His outlook was no longer so bleak. "I should run this all by Jorge el Gato before rushing to any sort of conclusion," he thought.

After breakfast, he walked around town listening for his best friend's distinctive cry. When he didn't hear it, he went to the plaza and found Jorge sitting on one of the benches reading a comic book, his cart beside him.

"What are you reading, brother-cousin?" Edmund asked.

"Ah, just a dumb comic book to pass the time."

Edmund skipped any further small talk and told Jorge el Gato exactly what had happened the night before. He also told him about his sisters' leaving, but not about Tres Pasos. Instead, he told him that he had met an old man who was willing to give him guitar lessons in exchange for stories.

"Where did you meet this old man?"

"Oh, you know, around the way."

Jorge el Gato nodded and asked. "This old man wouldn't happen to be Tres Pasos?"

"How do you know?" Edmund exclaimed.

"I sold his assistant several popsicles yesterday evening and he told me that his boss had finally found some idiot to tell his stories to—in exchange for guitar lessons. I went to Tres Pasos for money once—to buy my cart—and he had tried to give me the cart in exchange for listening to his stories."

"But you should have; it's easy, and they aren't even that long. Why didn't you?"

"Edmund, I told you before. He's a not a man to get close to. He's dangerous—"

"No, you're wrong! You just have to get to know him better. He has a lot to share and he—he—well, I haven't known him long, but he's promised to give me his son's guitar."

"His dead son's, right?"

"Yeah."

"Did he tell you how his son died?"

Edmund thought for a second. "No, but he did say that it *didn't* happen in a drunken brawl."

Jorge el Gato placed the comic book on the bench. "Just be careful, Edmund."

"OK."

They were quiet for a moment before Edmund asked what he should do about Ingrid.

"Maybe . . ." Jorge el Gato hesitated. He had thought about saying this for some time. "Maybe you should just forget her. It sounds like she's kind of stuck up, and if she is dating this guy, then what can you do except wait? There are other girls out there—" He stopped when he saw the pained look on his half brother's face.

"But you said that if I sang for her and she heard me once and said that I was good, and she also said hi to me one time even though I wasn't looking at her, and . . ." his voice trailed off.

Jorge put his hand on top of Edmund's head, ruffling his frizzy red hair. "The thing is, you can't place too much stock in any one girl. There are many out there, and Ingrid, she might be special to you, but there are others who might be less special, but still real nice to be with. If you want my advice, I'd go for someone else. You don't have to forget about Ingrid, but it might make things easier if there's not so much at stake."

Edmund considered this for a moment, not at all happy with the idea. But he knew Jorge gave good advice regarding women, so before leaving his side he promised that he'd at least consider other girls if only as a healthy distraction.

Edmund's foray into womanizing didn't go half badly. He asked Laura, who lived a few doors over, if she wanted to accompany him for a cup of ice cream. She said yes without a moment's hesitation. They walked together for a half a block and Edmund decided to hold her hand. She eyed him warily and asked, "What do you think you're doing, Edmund?" He smiled and said the first thing that came to mind, "Just you know, just distracting myself." She laughed and didn't let go. "OK, whatever, Edmund."

When they got to the plaza, however, she dropped his hand, which discouraged him somewhat. "I don't care, her hand was sweaty anyway," Edmund reassured himself. They arrived at the ice cream shop and ordered their favorite flavors—Edmund, vanilla, Laura, strawberry. When it came time to pay, Edmund pulled out some change his mother had given him. He paid for his, but Laura didn't reach for her money. She looked at him in surprise. "Aren't you going to treat me?" she asked.

"What do you mean?"

She huffed and took some money out of her pockets. "Whatever, Edmund." She walked home at a fast pace, Edmund struggling to keep up while eating his vanilla ice cream. When they were back on Carranza Street, Edmund tried holding her hand again. She pulled away and said, "You're just a little kid, you know that?"

He was about to say, "Oh yeah, sweaty-hand-girl," but right away the thought hit him: "It doesn't feel even close to as bad as when Ingrid says it."

After Laura, he received three rejections and was ready to give up when he came across Juana, the daughter of Lety la Flor, a woman of ill repute. Apparently, the daughter was following in the mother's footsteps because Juana told Edmund that she didn't want ice cream but that she'd fuck him for twenty pesos.

"But don't you like ice cream?" Edmund asked.

"Are you paying?" she said.

"Yes, of course." He had asked his mother for a few more pesos.

"Well, how about you just give me the money?"

"But then we wouldn't have a date."

"Why do you want to go on a date for?"

"Because . . ." he couldn't think of one reason why he wanted to walk to the plaza with Juana. She wasn't even a good distraction, and he had already had his fill of vanilla. "You know, forget it," he said.

"I'll fuck you for ten pesos."

"No, that's OK, thank you. I have to go."

"You can touch my chi-chi for a peso," she called after him.

Edmund stopped. He had only grazed Ingrid's breast before she pulled away and called him a troll, but his brief contact had piqued his curiosity. So he turned around, fumbled in his pocket for a peso, and said, "Only one peso?"

"Two," she said when she saw his eyes.

"OK, fine." He stepped forward, his hand leading the way. He felt as if he shouldn't watch. She took his hand and started to put it underneath her shirt. Edmund touched her skin and jerked his hand away. "What are you doing?" he exclaimed.

"So you can touch my chi-chi, stupid."

"I didn't know that you meant underneath!"

"What difference does that make?"

"It makes a big difference."

"How?"

Edmund didn't know how, except that he really never expected to touch her *actual* breast. In truth, Juana's soft skin had scared him, but he wasn't about to tell her that. So he racked his brain for excuses. "Well, to tell you the truth, I'm saving myself for someone."

"Touching chi-chis don't count, stupid."

"Yeah, huh, when you care about her as much as I do."

"You're a fag, that's what I think."

"No, I'm not. I don't expect you to understand."

She rolled her eyes. "OK, then give me three more pesos."

"For what?"

"I'll tell everyone that you were afraid to touch my chi-chi because you're a fag."

Edmund considered three pesos a fair price to pay for her silence. He walked away cursing whores of all ages. Suddenly he felt guilty for what he had done. In just a few hours he had held a girl's hand, picked up on three others though they denied his advances, and touched Juana's breast, or at least part of it. What if word got back to Ingrid? He didn't know about the three girls he had passed on the street, but he knew that Laura and Ingrid were classmates. And Juana, the insolent slut, may have read Ingrid's name all over his face and was now on her way to tell Ingrid what Edmund had just paid three pesos to suppress.

"Shit! What have I done?" Edmund said aloud.

An old man with a large white mustache heard him and growled, "Shut up, kid, can't you see I'm trying to listen to the game?"

Edmund lashed out. "Forget the game! Can't you see I've betrayed her! Why did I do it?"

The old man was silent, one wrinkled finger in his left ear, the transistor radio pressed to his right.

Edmund could hear the announcer, "*and Vásquez passes to Galván, who crosses it to Blanco, who heads it in . . .*"

Suddenly the old man jumped up and cried, "Yesssss, a goal! We've won! We've won!"

"Who scored?" Edmund asked, jumping too, the spry man's excitement contagious. The old man was waving the transistor above his head calling out, "We've won! He did it! He's redeemed himself! We've won!"

"Which team?" Edmund asked again, unable to hear the announcer over the old man.

"The Chivas beat Necaxa!"

Edmund stopped jumping. He hated the Chivas. He walked down the street, now dejected for two more reasons. The Chivas had won, his team had lost (at that moment he decided Necaxa was his hands-down favorite), and he was sure that Ingrid was bound to discover that he was nothing but a lowlife chasing whatever tail came his way.

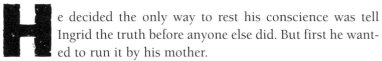

He decided the only way to rest his conscience was tell Ingrid the truth before anyone else did. But first he wanted to run it by his mother.

"Isn't it best to tell the truth," he asked her, "even when the thing you're going to say is bad?"

Constanza surprised him. "No, not always. Sometimes it is necessary to lie."

"Like when?"

"Like how your brothers left. I couldn't have told your father. He would've hurt them, prevented their leaving."

"Oh." He tried to rephrase the question. "But in all other cases, like when you're not dealing with someone who beats people up?"

"What are you talking about, Edmund?"

"The thing is, I've done a few bad things. Not bad-bad, but sins in most people's eyes. Not bad sins, but just sins. And, well, I think I should confess them."

Her son's piety surprised Constanza. "Of course, mijo. And I'm sure you'll feel much lighter afterward."

So Edmund headed to Ingrid's house to confess his sins and halfway there he thought to himself, "My mamá must think I mean a priest." So he turned back and rephrased the question.

"OK, Mamá, say someone did something bad that affects you in some way, would you rather hear it from them or not at all?"

Constanza had a headache, but she tried her best. "I guess not at all. If I knew all the things your father did I don't think I could stand it . . ." Then she thought for a moment. "Actually, maybe I would want to know. Sometimes I think the doubts are worse than what actually happens. Your father's having Jorge with my sister was the most horrible betrayal, but at least I know my nephew is also your brother. What's worse is looking at half the children that come by and wondering if they're your siblings too!" She laughed despite herself.

Edmund wasn't sure what to make of her response. "Sooo . . . you're saying it's better to know or not to know?"

"Ay, my son, look at me right now. I don't know where your father has been for a week. A part of me is glad that he's not here and there's peace; another part of me wishes he were home causing me trouble just so I'd stop imagining all the trouble he's causing elsewhere. Honestly, God knows, I'd rather *nothing* bad have happened in the first place!"

"It's too late, what's done is done," he said solemnly.

"Why don't you just tell me what happened?"

He shook his head and sighed. "No, I should just go tell her."

He walked out the door, slowly, waiting for his mother to call him back and tell him definitively that it was better *not* to know. But she didn't and he continued on his way to Ingrid's house.

Ingrid was sitting on the couch watching television with her mother, Doña Celeste. Their favorite soap opera was on. At that moment they were both particularly riveted because Don Eladio, a real Don Juan, was begging his love's forgiveness, on the verge of tears. Ingrid and Doña Celeste were also on the verge of tears. Just when they thought everything was going to be all right, the couple to live happily ever after, Don Eladio's love, a very pretty young girl who resembled Ingrid (so Ingrid thought), decided to confess her own infidelities. Suddenly, all was not right. Don Eladio went crazy with anger and all but tore the brim off his cowboy hat.

When the show had ended, Ingrid turned to her mother and exclaimed, "Oh, why did she tell him? She was unfaithful because she was hurting, for no other reason!"

And Doña Celeste, wiping her eyes, said, "Yes, but what kind of future can they have if she's not absolutely honest with him and he with her? Now only if he can forgive her. It's a real man who can swallow his pride, confess his sins, and accept the same from his woman."

This is what Edmund heard as he walked by the window and prepared to knock on the door. He didn't know the context of the statement, but it stuck in his head all the same. Which is why when Ingrid came to the door and said, "Hey?" he remained mute, Doña Celeste's comment having jumbled his thoughts.

Finally, he said slowly, "I . . . forgive . . . you?"

"What?"

"Uh—I meant to say—"

"Edmund," she said, an impatient tone in her voice, "I'm sorry that they teased you the other day and that Rafa punched you, but it—it wasn't *my* fault."

"Ingrid!" her mother interrupted. "Is that true? Rafa beat up this little boy!"

"Yes, but—"

Edmund took courage, knowing the mother was on his side. He collected his thoughts, reorganizing them, and said, "Ingrid, I understand that sometimes girls are attracted to rougher bigger guys, so I forgive you for dancing with Rafa at the Benni Terraza concert. And also for letting him put his arm around you after he punched me. I also forgive you for calling me a troll. Now I want to ask you something." He paused.

Ingrid waited for him to continue. She looked at her mother, whose eyebrows were raised in astonishment.

Ingrid clenched her jaw. "Yes?"

"Forgive me," he said, still standing on the sidewalk.

"For what? Look, Edmund, I'm sorry I don't want to be your girlfriend. You're funny, and I thought you were—"

"Forgive me for betraying you. I went on a few dates and I did something I regret with one girl. I felt so guilty. I just needed to tell you. Now please forgive me, and whatever you hear, from Laura or anyone, please don't think for a moment that I love you any less."

Doña Celeste almost laughed out loud, but she stopped herself when she saw her daughter's face redden. Ingrid asked him, "Which girls did you say you went out with?"

"Well, let's see. Laura was one of them. Juanita was another. The other girls meant nothing, I promise you. I went with them trying to distract myself, to keep me from thinking so much about you. It hurt to see you dancing with Rafa and so I did something I thought would make me feel better. It didn't. And I'm sorry." Ingrid was silent before asking, her voice hesitant, "Do you like Laura?"

"No, I swear it. And you can ask her; I didn't even pay for her ice cream even though I know that's what guys usually do on dates, but I just couldn't bring myself to do it."

Ingrid sighed and an awkward silence followed. Finally, she opened the screen door. "Do you want to come in?"

Edmund stepped backward. "No, I just ask you to understand. I'm going now to let you think things over." And with that he hurried down the street, afraid he'd trip on the cobblestones because his legs felt so weak.

Ingrid turned to her mother.

"Mija, what's going on?"

Ingrid shrugged. "He has a crush on me, that's it. I feel bad for him."

Doña Celeste chuckled. "Seems like it bothered you that he went out with Laura."

"No, it's just that—forget it."

"You know, Ingrid," her mother said, thinking of the boy's ardent face. "Sometimes it just takes boys longer to develop."

"So?"

"So, that's something to consider."

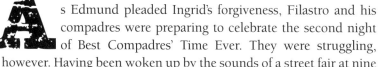

s Edmund pleaded Ingrid's forgiveness, Filastro and his compadres were preparing to celebrate the second night of Best Compadres' Time Ever. They were struggling, however. Having been woken up by the sounds of a street fair at nine in the morning, they stumbled around town looking for a good cheap meal. They found a stand selling menudo and birria and ate several bowlfuls each. Afterward they felt a little better, except for Jerry, whose ankle had swollen to the size of his knee. The compadres decided to head to the plaza. They found an empty bench in the shade and for the next five hours watched people pass to and fro.

They considered an afternoon beer but decided against it as it meant rising from their comfortable plaza bench.

"Maybe we're too old for this, compadres," Big Gaspar said at one point.

Filastro lifted his head. "There you go again, always trying to dampen our spirits!" He looked to Jerry and Mendigo for support. Mendigo was doubled over, his head on his knees. Jerry was staring at his enormous ankle. "Maybe it's broken," he said.

"It's not broken," Filastro responded, annoyed. "It just needs some ice. Here, damn it, I'll go get some ice, and then maybe we'll be able to focus on more important things, like Best Compadres' Time—"

"Give it a rest!" Big Gaspar moaned. "Can't you see we're all dead? I have a headache like I've been hit by a truck, Jerry is in pain, and look at Mendigo, is he even alive?"

As if prompted, Mendigo raised his head from his knees and threw up all over the pavement.

"Good God, Mendigo!" Filastro roared, slapping Mendigo on the back. "That was a throw-up to end them all! I think I can see the entire goat in there!"

Big Gaspar and Jerry couldn't help but laugh. A passing police squad, however, didn't find it funny at all. A truckload of uniformed men hopped out the truck bed and cab in unison. They ran over, all wearing helmets and sunglasses, shotguns in hand.

"What's going on here?" a policeman said.

Filastro answered, "Ah, nothing, we're just sitting in the shade. Our friend here has a stomachache, it seems."

"Where are you from?"

"We're visiting from La Prudencia. We all were working at Don Gabriel's, and now we're resting after the harvest."

This seemed a good enough response for the squadron spokesman. "All right, then, take your friend to Doña Clea over there. Tell her I sent you. She'll make him a good tea."

The officers filed away and the compadres watched them, relieved. Filastro said, laughing, "Hear that, compadres, the police in this town send you to their mothers for tea!"

The compadres chuckled, appreciative of Filastro's jibe after a slightly tense moment. The policemen, though, were still within earshot. They came rushing back, and once again, were not amused.

"You think you're real funny, no?" sneered the spokesman, holding his shotgun as if a bayonet were attached. He didn't wait for the reply Filastro was about to give him. "Get in the truck. We're taking you in!" he ordered.

"But—"

"Get in! Damn it, off your asses! All of you!" The plaza full of people turned and stared at the spectacle. Filastro held his hands behind his head even though they hadn't told him to do so. "All right, all right, you got us for the big crime we committed. People, be glad your police force is on top of things. Four men were just prevented from—"

"Shut up, Filastro!" Big Gaspar said through his teeth.

"Ay, compadre, what can they do to us—"

This time, Jerry, the pain in his ankle excruciating as he hopped along, told Filastro to shut his mouth. The four of them climbed into the back of the truck, the squadron surrounding them. They were driven to the jail in silence. Upon arrival they had to fill out documents before placement in a holding cell. Filastro felt bad for putting his compadres through so much trouble. He had only intended a bit of fun and didn't expect the police force to be so quick-tempered. Worse, he saw the second night of Best Compadres' Time Ever quickly slipping away. He knew that after a night in jail they'd all be ready to forget the third night, too. "I didn't work that entire damn harvest for one lousy night of drinking!" he said to himself. He looked for a way out.

Providence smiled upon him, or so he thought. In walked the squadron commander, a man with the face of a shovel, a face Filastro knew well. He recognized his old friend and drinking buddy Don Esteban. Filastro called out to him, "Esteban, compadre, how are things? How long has it been?"

Captain Esteban squinted his eyes and looked none too friendly at the four vagabonds who had just been brought in.

Big Gaspar, assuming Filastro was up to his tricks, told him, "Please, for the sake of God keep your mouth shut." Filastro waved him off. "Don Esteban, don't tell me you don't recognize me. Remember that night in Crucero? My God, we drank through three horse troughs of tequila!"

Captain Esteban walked closer, and suddenly his wide, flat face broke into a smile. "Filastro Agustín! What a miracle, I can't believe it. After all these years!"

"Yes, and look at you. You were only thinking about joining the force then. I see it has worked out well!"

Captain Esteban looked at his name tag and badge and shrugged, raising his hands in a dismissive gesture. "Still the same old me! Now I get to have fun without the fear of being thrown in jail!" He pointed at the four compadres and winked—"And all my drinks are paid for!"

"That sounds ideal, compadre! I should have joined with you. Look at me now, not a day different than myself at twenty!"

"Oh, let me tell you, I envy your carefree lifestyle, old friend. Now let's see"—he addressed the police clerk who was helping the four men fill out their forms—"these men were arrested for . . .

insulting officers, disorderly conduct, vagrancy—sounds like a reasonable rap sheet." The captain looked up and smiled.

Filastro returned the smile, not in the least abashed.

"I'll tell you what. I can't let you guys go; it wouldn't be good for the men's morale, but your compadres seem decent enough. How about you guys tramp around with me tonight? We'll do some police business, add in some fun along the way, how about it?"

Filastro, Mendigo, and Jerry were willing participants. Only Big Gaspar nodded hesitantly, wishing they could just spend the night in jail and return home the next day. He didn't trust the look of the police captain.

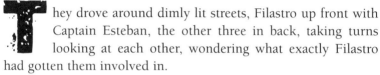
They drove around dimly lit streets, Filastro up front with Captain Esteban, the other three in back, taking turns looking at each other, wondering what exactly Filastro had gotten them involved in.

They passed around a bottle of tequila, the police captain turning from the wheel to make sure they drank healthy amounts. "Drink up, no, more, do it again, take another swallow! That sip my mother could handle! Don't be a bitch! Ah, you're a bitch if I ever saw one!"

The first stop was at a bar on the edge of Retorno. The whorehouse the men had visited the preceding night was next door. The five of them walked through the barroom full of people—mostly truck drivers, passers-through, and loose women. They exited out the back. The alcohol had deadened the pain in Jerry's ankle and he only limped slightly. They entered a large shed and knocked on the door. A small window opened, a man's eyes visible.

"Captain! Come in, come in!" the man said, opening the door.

"These guys are with me," Captain Esteban said. The man nodded his head nervously.

The dark entrance opened up into a larger room; there in the center was a desk and a stool. In the back of the room a man was on his knees riffling through papers in a file cabinet. He turned around when he heard the men enter and said, "Be right with you!"

The captain and four compadres remained standing, watching the man throw papers left and right. Finally, he found what he was looking for and said, "Got it! Thank God above!"

He rose from the floor and shook each of their hands, clasping theirs in both of his. He was bald except for a few strands around the ears, which he ran his fingers through over and over. "Good, good, good, glad you could come, very nice of you!" He paced back and forth, unable to look any of them in the eye. The four compadres watched him, sneaking glances at the police captain, curious to know the purpose of their visit. Captain Esteban remained silent, his shovel face unflinching as he stared at the nervous man.

"Paco, I suspect you know why I've come," he said finally.

"Yes, of course. And I really would like to make you happy, but the truth is, I'm just not ready, I don't have it yet, as hard as I've tried—here, take this paper as proof that I'm good for—"

"Clearly you have not tried hard enough. Look, Paco, I'm going to be real clear on this matter, are you listening? By tomorrow, noon."

With that he turned around and beckoned the four compadres to follow him. When they reentered the bar, the police captain signaled the bartender to bring his friends some drinks. Filastro, Mendigo, Big Gaspar, and Jerry raised the shot glasses to their lips, eyeing one another warily. They swallowed and grimaced, as the tequila was little better than rubbing alcohol. Captain Esteban slapped Filastro on the back. "'Atta boy, compadre! Take it like a man. You don't mind a little business with our pleasure, do you? Your friends look a little white in the face. We policemen keep municipalities together, prevent them from falling apart at the seams. That son of a bitch in there would put every bar in town out of business if I didn't keep tabs on him, you understand?"

Filastro nodded, coughing, "Yes, I can see, that makes sense." He didn't remember his compadre Esteban being such a hard-ass. Then again, they had merely been drinking buddies, twenty years ago at that.

"Good. Then let's go. This place is a shit hole!"

The four compadres and Captain Esteban visited five more establishments; in each one they found a nervous man pacing back and forth, asking for more time. Over the course of a few hours, they drank four shots of tequila and five beers, insulted three women, eyed a few others, and played a round of cards. Only on the sixth visit did they meet any resistance.

"This'll be the last one, friends," promised Captain Esteban. "Then we'll really let loose!"

It was a ranch several miles off the main road. They drove along a bumpy path and pulled up to a dark, humble house, barely more than a barn. When the captain knocked on the corrugated tin door, the man inside refused them entry. "No! Please! Come back later, I beg you!" he shouted through the door. The captain told Filastro and his compadres to step back. He shot through the lock and kicked open the door. In mere seconds, he had rushed into the back room, grabbed hold of the man's hair, and slammed the man's face into the closest hard surface—in this case, a table. The man screamed in pain, blood pouring from his nose as steadily as from a faucet. Captain Esteban threatened to do it again.

"Please, no, please, no! Tomorrow, tomorrow! I'll have it by then."

But the captain had been insulted; his wide face beet-red from anger and exertion. "I want it now! You hear me? Now!"

The man limply pointed to a drawer and the captain called to Filastro, who had remained standing outside the door with Big Gaspar, Mendigo, and Jerry, each of them listening to the sounds of torture, quite ready to go home and sleep away this nightmare. "Get in here, Filastro!" the captain yelled again.

Filastro entered the room cautiously, peeking around the partition that separated the entranceway from the main room. "Yes?" he asked.

"Get over here! Grab the key that's in the cupboard and open up that bottom drawer!"

He hesitated, looking around as if expecting someone to step forward and offer his services. But there was only the bloodthirsty captain and a bloodied man Filastro wished he'd never laid eyes on. He realized he had no other option but to obey. He found the key and walked to the drawer. His hand shook as he tried to open the lock but couldn't for the life of him match the key to the hole.

"Hurry up, you worthless ass!" the captain yelled at him.

"OK, OK!" Finally he managed to fit the key and open the drawer. In what unsavory business was he now entangled, he wondered, expecting stacks of money or drugs. It was empty save for a small bag of seeds. He breathed a sigh of relief and turned around. "There's nothing but a pack of seeds."

"A pack of what!"

"Seeds."

"Seeds? What the hell! Are you sure?"

"Uh . . . yeah," Filastro examined them closer. "They're pumpkin, I think."

Captain Esteban raised the man's bloody face again and smashed it against the floor. The man screamed, several of his teeth now on the concrete, "It's in the next one, I swear it, the next one. It must be!"

Filastro tried the next drawer. He saw only a few nudie magazines. He hesitated, wondering what to do. He turned around and asked, "What am I looking for exactly?"

Once again the police captain raised the man's head to smash it against the floor, when two gunshots rang out, one after the other. Bang! Bang! The windows shook and the floor vibrated. Filastro heard a grunt, then another gunshot. Bang! Filastro dropped the key.

He heard Mendigo scream, "Let's get outta here!"

Then Big Gaspar said, "No, please! Please! Please!"

"What the fuck is going on?" Captain Esteban let go of the man's limp body and reached for his gun. He walked toward the door and another shot rang out. Bang! The windows shook and the police captain slumped to the floor, first to his knees, and then face forward, his head hitting the concrete floor with a dull thud.

Filastro called out, "Compadres! Compadres? Are you there?" He received no response. His hands were shaking uncontrollably. He saw the deep red pool grow slowly larger underneath the captain's body.

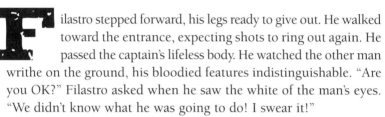

Filastro stepped forward, his legs ready to give out. He walked toward the entrance, expecting shots to ring out again. He passed the captain's lifeless body. He watched the other man writhe on the ground, his bloodied features indistinguishable. "Are you OK?" Filastro asked when he saw the white of the man's eyes. "We didn't know what he was going to do! I swear it!"

The man looked at Filastro as if to say something and then passed out cold. Filastro called again for his compadres. "Jerry? Mendigo? Gaspar? Where did you guys go?"

He stepped toward the entrance and peeked around the partition. The door was open and he saw Mendigo crawling, clutching his side, his hands covered in blood. He was trying to raise himself from the ground.

"Compadre, what happened?" he asked Mendigo.

Mendigo looked up, his eyes bleary, "Filastro, she shot me! Why did she shoot me?"

Filastro crept closer to the door. "Calm down, we'll get out of here," he said. He looked around for Big Gaspar and Jerry but didn't see them. Then just a few feet away he saw his compadre, Jerry, face forward in the dirt, moaning. Filastro whispered loudly, "Jerry, you alive?"

Jerry moaned in response.

"Where's Big Gaspar?"

Jerry moaned again.

"What was that?"

This time Jerry's moan was cut off by a scream followed by a gunshot.

Filastro tried to cry out, but he couldn't breathe.

Suddenly, as if realizing for the first time that his own life was in danger, he turned around frantically, unsure which direction to run. He was about to turn back and get the keys and the gun from the police captain when a woman stepped out of the darkness carrying a shotgun. He stopped. She was dark-skinned, chubby; she had long black hair pulled back in a braid. She raised the weapon. He held up his hands.

"Get down on the ground," she said.

Filastro was too scared to move. "Please," he said, his voice barely audible. "I didn't know, I swear. We were his prisoners."

"Get down on the ground," she repeated.

He still couldn't move. Then she shot him in the knee. He fell to the ground and screamed until he lost consciousness.

* * *

When he woke, he saw a child's face staring at him. "Hello!" the child said. Filastro guessed it to be a boy, but he wasn't sure; the child possessed a perfectly smooth face, large eyes surrounded by impossibly long lashes, and a head covered in delicate black ringlets. Filastro attempted to speak but couldn't.

"What happened to you?" the child asked in a squeaky voice.

He could only stare at the child, wondering if he was awake, dead, or dreaming.

"Did you hurt my papá? Is that why my nana shot you?"

Another child entered the room. "Hello!" that child said (Child One returned the hello). This child also appeared androgynous, possessing green eyes and long lashes, a head covered in curly brown hair. "What happened to you?" the child asked, its voice even more shrill than the first.

Before Filastro could attempt to speak, another child entered the room, this one more angelic than the first two. "Hello!" it squeaked (Children One and Two responded hello). Before the newest could ask what happened, yet another child entered the room and said, "Hello!" And then another one, this child with milky white skin, was followed directly afterward by another child repeating the same shrill "Hello!" Each time the entering child said hello, the other children responded so that there was a general chorus of "hello!", then "what happened?", then "hello" again. Two more children entered.

Filastro lost consciousness when the seventh child entered the room playing an accordion.

When he woke again, a woman stood over him. He immediately recognized her as the woman who had shot him. He stiffened.

"Calm down," she said. "If I was going to kill you I'd have done it already."

He relaxed. "Where am I?" he asked, his mouth dry.

"You should know. You came here several days ago and roughed up my son."

"I didn't do any—"

The woman slapped him. "No excuses, you hear?" Her voice was calm, but her hand was still raised.

"But—"

She slapped him again with the back of her hand. "Learn to shut your mouth."

He remained silent. The woman had a bowl of hot water. She took a washcloth, wrung the excess water, and then placed it on his knee. Filastro cried out in pain.

"I need to clean your wound," the woman said. "The spray just missed your knee cap. You're lucky."

Filastro felt his eyes water. He wanted to cry out again, but he had no strength. "Your son?" he whispered.

"He is alive . . . barely. If he lives, you can go."

"And if—"

"Then I'll kill you with my bare hands." She continued cleaning his knee, placing the washcloth in the bowl of water, wringing it out, then wiping the wound.

"There were children here . . . earlier?"

The woman called out seven names in rapid succession. Filastro heard the tromping of feet and children's laughter. They entered the room all at once, practically climbing over one another to get through the door. Their squeals caused shooting pains in Filastro's head.

"Yes, Nana?" the oldest of them said. Filastro examined the children. They were dark and chubby, their hair tangled and standing on end. Their faces were dirty.

"Children, this is the man that came to kill your papá."

The children crowded around him, their eyes wide and curious.

"Why didth you hurth our papá?" a child no older than three asked.

Filastro shook his head. "I didn't. The man who did made me and my friends come along."

"Nana shot them and I helped," an older child said. "I pretended to be a little dog going 'ruff, ruff.' "

Filastro turned his head to the woman. "Did you kill my compadres? They didn't do anything wrong, they were just there, like me."

She chuckled. "Are you an innocent man, señor?"

He nodded.

She raised her brow. "Ay yay yay. I'll ask again. Señor, are you an innocent man?"

"Yes, I am. And so are my compadres."

She repeated her question.

He repeated his answer.

The woman took the bowl and slowly poured the hot water over his head. He tried to raise himself; that was when he realized his arms had been tied down. "Goddamn woman!" he screamed.

"For the last time," she said, her voice never losing its calm, "are you an innocent man?"

Filastro writhed in agony. "I've done nothing wrong!"

The woman spit in his face. Then she said to the children, "Spit on him until he drowns in your saliva." She walked out of the room laughing.

The children began spitting. They crawled on top of the bed, jumping on top of him. They squealed and giggled, pushing one another aside to get the chance to spit. One child, knees on Filastro's chest, dribbled his saliva slowly toward Filastro's mouth. Filastro moved his face and groaned in pain and disgust. Then the children began to hit him. All he could hear was the repetitive slaps of their little fists against his face. Finally they stopped and crawled down from the bed. They stared at him, once again their eyes wide, curious. One child asked, "Do you want to hear a song?"

He shook his head. They began to sing anyway. He felt as if his head was going to explode. Then he recognized the lyrics. It was the song he had forced Edmund to play for Hortensia. When they stopped singing, he lost consciousness.

week passed and Constanza and Edmund heard no word from Filastro. Agnes and Alfonsa had arrived safely and were living in Nebraska with Abel and Ezekiel. On the phone the girls asked if their father had gone mad when he discovered they were gone. Constanza answered that he had, mentioning nothing of his disappearance.

He had left for days at a time before, a week once, but always left word with a friend or a compadre whose wife would invariably tell another wife, who'd tell another, until the juicy news reached Constanza. "Oh, yes, I heard—and this is between you and me, although I promised I wouldn't tell, but it's because I care for you— you should know that Filastro and Mendigo really caused some trouble the other night, and . . ." But this time the gossiping neighbors weren't knocking on her door. She decided to visit Big Gaspar's wife and ask if she knew anything regarding Filastro's whereabouts.

"How should I know where your husband is?" Big Gaspar's wife said, keeping the screen door closed. "All I know is he forces my husband to accompany him on all his drunken escapades."

"So you haven't seen Gaspar, either?"

"No, I have not! I hope he knows to stay away this time."

Constanza visited Jerry's wife next. They had become friends over the years, having commiserated so often about their husbands. She hoped to at least get some information from her, but all she found was a note on the door reading: "Jerry, I'm with my mother. I took the children." Underneath, someone else had written, "Jerry, she's with me now." And someone else, barely a child's scrawl, had written, "Chivas suck!" An attentive neighbor noticing Constanza's concerned face as she read the note said, "She left it there about three days ago. Jerry hasn't been around and neither has she."

"If she returns, tell her I'm looking for my husband."

"I don't think she's going to. I think she's at her mother's for good, poor thing. Got tired of her husband's ways, I imagine. How she put up with him that long, I'll never know."

Constanza nodded her head in thanks and walked to Mendigo's house. Mendigo had never married, nor left home, so she spoke to his parents, who were both too senile to be of any help. Their house was dark; it smelled of rotting fruit. Mendigo's father kept asking, "Hah? What was that you said?" He'd turn to his wife and ask, "Who is she talking about?" and Mendigo's mother would say, more softly than Constanza, "She's asking about José María, I believe." Constanza left with nothing save for the knowledge of Mendigo's given name.

So Constanza waited, too worried to appreciate her first week of peace in thirty years. And Edmund continued his lessons with Tres Pasos, never thinking for a second that his father was in trouble. Even when Tomato interrupted the fifty-seventh best story to tell his boss, "Tres Pasos, guess what? They got Captain Esteban! Found that son of a bitch's body by the side of the road with a sign that said, 'Have you accepted Jesus Christ as your Lord and Savior?' What do you think about that? I guess he disappeared a few days ago with four prisoners."

Tres Pasos looked up, his mouth still forming whatever word he'd been about to say. "Tomato, next time you interrupt my story time with Edmund here I'll shove a piece of paper down your throat with that same message." He turned back to Edmund. "Now to continue, where were we?"

"You were at the part where the woman is giving you a you-know-what and you have two pistols, one pointed at the window, one at the door, in case your enemies decided to catch you off guard."

"Oh, yes, that's right. So I wasn't about to do without any sort of fornication, even though I had those growths I mentioned, but . . ."

Tres Pasos had lived the most violent, revolting, promiscuous, immoral life Edmund could ever have imagined. He was horrified, yet enthralled. They upped the stories to five a day because most of them were short, and Edmund's appetite was insatiable. He couldn't get enough. After Tres Pasos imparted, in one sitting, the 22nd, 300th, and 465th-best stories, Edmund asked for the last story of the 500.

"These have all been so good, I want to know what's a bad story."

"Bad stories wouldn't be ranked! I have more, many more than 500 stories in my long life, but not a small number of them are worthless. Meaning most of them I didn't learn a thing from, or it was merely a repetition of something I learned in a better story. So I'm just serving you the stories—and by stories, I mean lessons—that have made the cut."

Tres Pasos took great time and effort to convey each story's moral. Sometimes the story was only a few minutes long but the effect on Tres Pasos's life required an additional hour to explain. Surprisingly, Edmund enjoyed these elucidations, and added to their length by asking question after question.

In one story, the 318th best, Tres Pasos told Edmund how he had once bought some sour milk, but he was too far away from the roadside store to go back and demand a refund, so he went into the nearest store and asked the clerk to either give him some new milk or his money back. The clerk didn't recognize the brand and told Tres Pasos that it must be from a different locale. So Tres Pasos wrestled the clerk to the ground, pinned him, and forced the innocent man to drink the sour milk, chunks and all. When he left the store he felt no better for what he had done.

"So you see, Edmund, I learned that day that one must always be careful, as meticulous in his dealings—every dealing, no matter how small!—as an accountant reviewing digits—one misplaced zero, one decimal in the wrong location and it means bankruptcy, death, shame. I should have checked the date on that milk, I should have smelled it before I took it to my lips, I should have done this in proximity to the place of purchase, but no! I was lazy, I left my fate up to God's will, and I suffered the price, and so did that store clerk! Is that clear?"

"I think so, but didn't you also realize afterward that the store clerk had nothing to do with it?"

"I'm not sure I understand your question, Edmund."

"Didn't you think that maybe you were taking your frustration out on someone you shouldn't have, for all the wrong reasons? Isn't that the moral of this story—to control your anger rather than take it out on the wrong people?"

"No, you're wrong there. Maybe you're partially right, but the moral of which you speak is better encapsulated in my seventy-second best story."

"Well, can I hear that one?"

"Sure you can."

And so in no time Edmund was making a dent in Tres Pasos's considerable oeuvre. The guitar lessons continued as well, and every day he made progress; he himself could hear the difference. He grew embarrassed when he thought about how he used to play and sing, remembering that Ingrid Genera had heard him play such puerile clunks and clanks.

"She's going to fall in love when she hears this," Edmund told Tres Pasos.

"Fall in love? Hell, she'll tear her clothes off!"

PART

II

Three weeks passed before a grain farmer discovered Filastro by the side of the road. The farmer thought the man was dead, so he wrapped him in a grain sack, and with the help of his father and son, lugged the body onto the back of his truck. The son, a boy of five, asked, "Do you know who this is?"

The grandfather, a man who had shrunken smaller than the boy, said, "I know who it is, but I'm not telling."

"And why not?"

"Because I love a good secret," he said, winking.

The grain farmer told his father and son to sit in the back and make sure the body didn't fall out.

As the truck drove along the dusty path toward town, the son kept trying to get his grandfather to confess the man's identity. "Please, Grandpa, I want to know."

"You must think I'm a softy if I'm going to give it up that easy," the old man said laughing. They both sat cross-legged on top of the grain sacks, each of them with a hand on the bag containing the body.

Finally the old man relented. "OK, let's play a game."

"All right."

"You ask a question about who this man is and I'll say yes or no."

The boy had few options to choose from as he'd rarely been off his father's grain farm, but they played anyway and after thirty minutes the boy had determined that the body was not that of his Uncle Carlos, nor his Uncle Valentín, nor his Uncle Juan, nor was it their neighbor Don Sapo.

"This is hard," the boy said.

"Yes, but that's what makes a game fun, no?"

"Yes, it is."

They arrived at the police station in town and the grain farmer stepped out of the truck and spoke to the guard at the door. The guard approached the back of the vehicle and asked, "Do you know who it is?"

The grain farmer shrugged. "My father says he knows."

"No, I don't," the old man said, winking again at the boy. When the guard left, the boy asked his grandfather, "Why did you say that?"

"Better to play dumb with the police, otherwise they try and put you in jail."

Several police officers came outside and began lifting the body off the truck when they heard a grunt. They almost dropped the body. "Set it down, set it down!" one of them said. They unwrapped the sack, and Filastro, his eyes still closed, groaned again.

"Didn't you check to see if he was alive?" a policeman asked the grain farmer.

The grain farmer shrugged and looked at his father and son. They both shrugged, too.

They pulled Filastro out of the sack and laid him on the sidewalk. "Get him a doctor, call the doctor!" a policeman said. He examined the man's swollen face, his bruised body, the bandage around his knee. He bent down and lightly slapped Filastro's cheek. "Wake up, wake up, a doctor is coming soon. You've been on quite a ride, it seems." Suddenly his superior officer came behind him and said, "Holy shit, that's what's-his-name!"

"Who?"

"Ah, God, I can't think of his name—what's his—he's been in lockup before."

"Don Gregorio?"

"No."

"Is it that guy that lives on Calle Juárez?"

"No."

"Don Macario's friend?"

"No."

"The guy who used to work at the hardware store?"

"No."

The grain farmer's son turned to his grandfather, his eyes wide. "They know the game, too," he whispered. The grandfather winked and placed his finger to his lips.

It was the doctor who finally identified Filastro. "Oh, my God, I feel horrible—I warned him of his ways, but I never thought he'd actually meet such an end!"

That was when the police captain clarified that the man was still alive; he had merely passed out again.

"Oh," the doctor said, placing two fingers on Filastro's wrist, then placing his ear to Filastro's chest. "Yes, of course. Well, that's a relief. Can we get this man delivered to my office?"

The grain farmer and his family departed and Filastro was transported to the clinic, where a nurse stripped and bathed him as the doctor administered shots to prevent infection. Meanwhile, a messenger ran to Doña Constanza's house and notified her that her husband had been found. Constanza and Edmund had just sat down for the midday meal. They left the house hurriedly, Edmund taking a tortilla to nibble on. When they arrived at the clinic, the doctor himself greeted them.

"The good news is that he's alive," he said.

"What's the bad news?" Constanza asked.

The doctor peered down at Edmund, suddenly recognizing him. "Oh, my, it has been a while, no? You haven't grown much at all since you came in to see me. How long ago was that? A few years? But didn't I save you some beatings? I use that speech with many an aggressive father—'You don't want your sons to hate you; otherwise there's no telling what might happen'" he nudged Constanza, then stopped, remembering that Filastro was comatose in the other room. "Well, sometimes mishaps happen regardless. Now where was I?"

"You were going to tell us the bad news?"

"Yes, the bad news. You see the thing is . . ." he sighed. "The fact of the matter . . ." he sighed again and pursed his lips. "As far as I see it . . ." He crossed his arms as if in deep contemplation. "In my estimation . . . what's going on here is that, how shall I put it, let's see . . ."

Edmund and his mother exchanged worried glances.

"Well, how about this? We should visit your husband, Doña Constanza . . ."

The doctor placed his hand on Edmund's head and ruffled his hair affectionately. "It's all right, son." Edmund shrugged off his hand.

They walked to the examining room where Filastro was laid out on the table. The lower half of his body was covered with a white sheet. Constanza gasped when she saw the body. "Oh, my God! What could have happened?" Edmund stared curiously, hardly able to believe it was his father. "Look how skinny he got," he commented.

"He looks dead," Constanza murmured, afraid to get closer.

"No, no, he's not dead," the doctor assured her, "He's merely in some form of coma. It's not a deep one by any means; he should emerge from it in a matter of days, no more than a week—well, maybe several weeks at the most. His vital signs are fine—this coma almost seems self-induced, which is common, or I shouldn't say common because I've never seen a case like this, but it appears to be so, as I've read . . . heard . . ." He stopped, having lost his train of thought. "Anyway, where was I? Ah, yes, he's certainly not dead. In fact, it may be good to have you close, help him if he heard a familiar voice. Say something to your husband."

Constanza couldn't move, let alone speak. She could only stare horrified at her husband's bruised and swollen face. Edmund, on the other hand, had loads to share. "So I've been taking guitar lessons, Papá, and I think you're going to be real impressed with how good I'm getting. I mean, you used to like me to play for you before, but now, oh now it's almost like I'm a professional. I mean not exactly like one, but I'm getting there. And guess what? A few weeks ago I went to the Benni Terraza concert with Mamá. I had to go with her because Agnes and Alfonsa—"

This roused Constanza from her momentary shock. She rushed forward and placed her hand over Edmund's mouth. "That's enough, mijo, no need to tell him everything." She turned to the doctor. "Does he need to stay here?"

"For the night. We should monitor him some more, but tomorrow you can come and pick him up bright and early."

Constanza and Edmund turned to leave.

"Just one more thing, Doña Constanza. The police, I believe, need to talk to him when he emerges from his coma. They need to ask him questions about his—his ordeal."

She nodded and they left.

On the way home, Constanza began to cry. She tried to hide it from her son, but he heard a sniffle and asked, "Why are you crying?"

She gently scoffed. "Ay, Edmund, isn't it obvious?"

"Yeah, but he's back. And the doctor said he'll be all right again. Maybe now he won't be so up to beating you on account he got beaten up himself."

The thought of her husband ceasing his abusive ways hadn't entered her mind; it was a given, but then again, Filastro had never been beaten up before. Fights, yes, but so drastically on the losing end? She looked at Edmund and said, "Yes, maybe you are right."

"I think it's good that he's home because with all my brothers and Agnes and Alfonsa gone it gets kind of boring around the house. I'm busy with my lessons and stuff, but when I come home it's too quiet."

His mother looked down at her feet as they walked. "Yes, I know. I wish you didn't have to feel alone, but these last couple of weeks I have been so worried. I didn't know what could possibly have happened. Now that he's back, I realize just how little energy I have left. I'm exhausted. As soon as we're home I'm going to sleep."

The next morning Edmund woke and went into the kitchen looking for his mother. She wasn't there. He walked out to the backyard and she wasn't there, either. Cross-Eyes looked at him and whined. His limp was no longer so bad, but it seemed the dog would always hobble. "Where's my amá, little dog?" Edmund asked, petting Cross-Eyes's head and ears. Edmund returned inside the house and entered the bedroom to change out of his pajamas. He turned on the light and found his mother still asleep on her bed. He merely thought she had left the blankets undone.

"Mamá!" he said. "Wake up! It's late and we have to go get Papá."

Constanza moaned and turned over. "Mijo, you go by yourself. Get someone there at the doctor's to help you."

"But—but you have to help, too."

Constanza turned over and pulled the covers over her head. "I will, I just need more rest right now."

So Edmund went alone to the clinic. The doctor beckoned him inside. "Where's your mother?"

"Asleep; she doesn't even want to get up!"

"Yes, sometimes trauma can have an adverse effect on our behavior. Our psychological states sure are fragile. Remember that."

"Yes, I still remember," Edmund said, pausing. "OK, then, can I bring my papá home by myself?"

"No, you need help transferring him, plus, we only release patients to adults. Tell your mother that when she's ready to pick him up we'll have two men drive Filastro home in one of the clinic trucks. Until then I'll transfer him to the infirmary where he can be watched over by the nursing staff. He'll be fine there, I'm sure."

So Edmund went home and relayed the message to Constanza.

"They won't bring him home until I go get him?" she asked.

"Yes, so let's go right now."

Constanza looked out the window, lost in thought.

"OK, Mamá? Let's go, yeah?"

She turned her head slowly toward Edmund. "No, mijo, let him rest there for a while. I'm still too tired."

"From what?" Edmund asked, exasperated. "You had more to do when all my brothers and sisters were here, and they're gone, and Papá has been gone, too, so what can you be tired from? You slept late this morning, anyway."

His mother didn't answer him. She returned to looking out the window. Edmund sighed loudly and walked outside.

Edmund found Jorge el Gato on Cuatrero Street surrounded by a group of children, each one clamoring for a look
inside the popsicle cart. One boy tried sticking his hand
inside the freezer and grabbing a few popsicles before his turn. Jorge
el Gato had to swat him away. When the children dispersed, Jorge
counted the money and placed the bills and change in his fanny pack.

Edmund told him about their father.

"He had it coming," Jorge el Gato mumbled.

Edmund's face scrunched into a frown. "What's that supposed
to mean?"

"There's talk around town. A police captain's body and several
others were found in a ditch. The day before the captain was last
seen, the police had arrested Filastro and his compadres. Later, they
were all seen together going on the captain's rounds, collecting
money, some say drugs and contraband, too."

"Well, so what about it?" Edmund asked after a long pause,
not sure what to make of this new development.

"Maybe your dad was involved in things he shouldn't have
been, and now he's paid the price."

"You know what, brother-cousin, he's your papá too, and
instead of listening to what 'some people' are saying, you should
stick to selling popsicles!"

"Edmund, don't get upset; I'm just repeating what people are
saying. They're pretty sure Big Gaspar, Mendigo, and Jerry are the
other bodies. How did Filastro escape?"

"He *didn't* escape. Let's go to the clinic. I'll show you. He's practically dead himself."

They headed to the infirmary. The head nurse told Jorge el Gato to leave his cart outside, but Jorge refused, arguing that in less than a minute his popsicles would all be gone. "I'm sorry," the head nurse said. "But we can't have you pushing the cart with that bell on it. We have sick patients who need their sleep."

So they compromised: Jorge left the bell with the nurse, who, as soon as the two visitors had left, set it down on the front counter. Edmund and Jorge walked to Filastro's bed. He remained comatose, but some color had returned to his face.

"See, look how bad he is," Edmund said.

Jorge el Gato stared at his father's sunken face. Never before had he been in such close proximity. He always diverted his eyes in Filastro's presence, and Filastro had never recognized him. Even the time he tried buying a popsicle from Jorge's cart. He had merely said, "Give me the green kind! I love the green kind!" And Jorge responded, "I'm all out of green." Filastro turned to his friends, "Hear that, compadres? This popsicle seller doesn't even have the green flavor! What kind of popsicle seller is this? Hah! Well, give me the purple!" and Jorge had said, "I'm all out of purple." And Filastro turned to his friends and repeated his previous comment. Then he asked for red, to which Jorge responded, "No red, either." And this continued until they had gone down the list of colors and Filastro finally asked, "What kind *do* you have left, damn it?" and Jorge, pushing his cart away as fast as possible, called out, "The kind for sons of a bitch!" He had wanted Filastro to come after him, to start beating him as he'd heard Filastro did to his other children. He wanted someone to tell Filastro afterward, "Did you know that the popsicle seller you beat up is your own son?" But Filastro didn't chase after Jorge el Gato; he merely called out, "Go on, you gimpy bastard! Hah, hah!"

Now Jorge el Gato stared at Filastro's withered, lifeless body and felt nothing whatsoever. He didn't care if he was alive, dead, or in a coma for the rest of his life. He looked at Edmund, who couldn't turn away from his father. After observing him for a minute, Jorge asked, "Brother-cousin, why do you care if he's dead or not? He's caused everybody nothing but trouble, including a lifetime's worth for your mamá."

"Shh!" Edmund said, putting his finger to his mouth. "The doctor said that he can hear us!"

"So what? I want him to hear me. He's better off dead."

Edmund looked at Jorge in disbelief. "How would you feel if you were in a coma and a whole bunch of people came in and started talking like you weren't there, saying things like 'Oh, I'm glad he's this way, and how much better things will be when he's gone for good?' Do you think you'd want to wake up after that?"

Jorge el Gato shrugged, continuing despite himself; the sight of his comatose father had stirred his rancor rather than sympathy. "I don't care, Edmund, and people wouldn't say that about me, they wouldn't say it about you, they wouldn't say it about most people, but your father deserves whatever hateful remarks come his way. And you know what else? Your mother doesn't come to pick him up because she feels the same way."

Edmund shook his head. "No, you don't know. She's just tired, that's all."

Jorge el Gato held up his hands. "I'm sorry, Edmund, but I have to get back to work." He walked away, pushing his bell-less cart, not knowing why he wanted to hurt his half brother's feelings, except that Edmund's ignorant adoration had frustrated him. When he was at the front desk he asked the nurse for his bell. She looked around and raised her brow. "I don't see any bell." She summoned the head nurse, who also looked around her and shrugged. "I don't know where it could have gone, I'm sorry." She pointed to a sign that read, "WE ARE NOT RESPONSIBLE FOR LOST OBJECTS."

Jorge el Gato sighed and spent the rest of the day looking for his bell. He found it tied around a dog's neck. Luckily, the owner was not around and he reclaimed his property without confrontation.

For the next week Edmund spent most of his time shuttling between two bedridden people: his comatose father at the infirmary, and his mother at home still complaining of exhaustion. Constanza stayed in bed until ten, then she'd move to the couch and either watch television or sleep some more. In the afternoon, she'd move back to the bedroom, which remained dark throughout the day, the curtains never opened. She told Edmund, "Don't mind me, I'm just not feeling well, just a little tired. I'll get over it soon, I'm sure."

"But what about dinner?" he asked. The first few days she heated up beans and tortillas for him, but nothing for herself, then returned to bed. Then she sent him to his aunts' and uncles' homes for meals, but he didn't go because he knew they would make him play with the little kids. Too many times he had been caught for hours playing racecars, house, jump rope, goalie-wars, tag-you're-it—all perfectly respectable games, but it had become a matter of principle: he wasn't a child anymore.

So Edmund decided to fend for himself and try his hand at cooking. He opened the refrigerator, finding it mostly empty. There was a pot of beans, some cold meat, three eggs, and pico de gallo salsa. He lit the stove and poured all the contents into a pan. He realized pretty quickly the food was burning, but didn't know how to remedy the problem. So he turned the stove to low and went to ask his mother.

"How do you keep food from burning in the pan?"

She was asleep, so he roused her, shaking her shoulder gently. She woke, smelled the burning food, and asked, "Is that our kitchen?"

Edmund shook his head, "No, I don't think so."

Constanza rose anyway, sniffing. "Edmund! I thought I told you to go to your aunt's house!" She rushed into the kitchen and turned off the stove. She saw what he had been trying to do and started to cry. "Why didn't you just go to your aunt's like I said?"

"Because I don't want to play with the little kids."

"But just do it for a few more days until I get better, OK?"

She ended up cooking the meal for him and serving it on the table. Then she returned to the bedroom.

"Mamá, you have to eat, too, or else you're going to keep being tired!" Edmund called after her, his mouth full. But she didn't respond.

The situation at the infirmary wasn't much better. He'd sit by his father's side, but Filastro just lay there, looking dead. Once Filastro opened his eyes and Edmund jumped up and down, calling for the doctor, "He's awake, he's awake!" but apparently all he did was wake the neighboring patients. The doctor rushed over and told Edmund that opening and closing the eyes was a mere matter of reflexes.

Still, Edmund considered this positive news, and while Filastro's reflexes kept his eyes open, Edmund spoke to him about the events of his day, namely his mother's condition. "It's like she just wants to lay in bed all the time, but I tell her, 'Amá, you got to come get Papá at the hospital so we can take care of him.' But she just goes, 'Ahhhhh, I'm tired, mijito,' so what can I do, huh?"

In addition, Edmund told his father about things he saw on the way to and from the infirmary. He also caught him up to date on all that happened during his absence. Edmund even told him some of Tres Pasos's stories, the tamer ones, passing them off as things he'd heard on television. He talked so much that after one visit the head nurse stopped him and said, "Little boy, could you be a little quieter when you're visiting your father? Some of the other patients have started to complain."

Edmund wanted to know which patients, but she merely said, "Just keep your voice down and all should be fine."

* * *

If it weren't for Tres Pasos's lessons and stories, which were now daily, Edmund's life would have been lonely indeed. He and Jorge el Gato had yet to make up after their heated exchange, and every time he visited Ingrid's house, her mother came to the door and said coldly, "Ingrid is not feeling well." Edmund always responded, "Tell her to feel better. My mother is also not feeling good. Maybe something is going around."

Following his confession and plea for forgiveness, Ingrid had invited him over for hot chocolate. The mother and daughter sat on the couch, Edmund on a chair, his feet dangling, of which he wasn't the least self-conscious because he kept swinging them back and forth. They watched television and talked during commercials. But after a mere two dates the invitations ended.

Doña Celeste asked her daughter when Edmund left, "Such a nice boy. Tell me again, who's his mother?"

"Constanza," Ingrid muttered.

"Constanza . . . hmm?" she racked her brain. Then it hit her. "Not Don Filastro's wife?"

Ingrid shrugged. "I think."

Doña Celeste's face colored. "Oh, well that will not do!"

She decided the boy's overtures were no longer so romantic. All of Filastro's sons had dealt with this at one time or another, and now it was Edmund's turn. In a way, though, Doña Celeste helped his case. Ingrid was at the age where she wanted what she couldn't have, especially when forbidden by her mother. So her desire to see Edmund went from feeling sorry for him to genuinely desiring his presence. When word spread that Filastro was found close to dead, her wish to see him increased, owing in part to curiosity, in part because she wanted to see how Edmund was faring.

s Ingrid headed toward the infirmary, she thought she recognized the woman whom Filastro and Edmund had serenaded at the window. She was walking on the other side of the street. The woman was dressed in her Sunday best and wore a dark shawl over her shoulders. After several blocks, corresponding lefts and rights, it became clear that they were headed in the same direction. The woman, her head focused on the cobblestones to avoid falling in her heels, didn't notice Ingrid until they were both at the clinic entrance.

Ingrid opened the door for the woman, the woman muttered a thank you, and they walked inside together. The woman allowed Ingrid to go ahead of her and the girl obliged. The nurse at the front counter asked Ingrid whom she wished to see. "Uh—Filastro Agustín."

"You're here to see him, too," the woman said, gently touching Ingrid's shoulder.

Ingrid turned but avoided looking the woman in the face. The smell of the woman's perfume was strong.

"I'm a friend of Filastro's. My name is Hortensia. How do you know him?"

"I'm a friend of his son," Ingrid mumbled, her face turning red.

The nurse interrupted, "Do either of you know that little red-headed boy over there?"

Hortensia and Ingrid turned their heads and looked down the long row of beds. Ingrid recognized the back of Edmund's head. She suddenly felt nervous. "Yes, I know him."

"Well, we feel so sorry for him. His father is in a coma and all, but he comes in every day and talks and talks and talks. He talks so much that he disturbs the other patients and their families have begun to complain. We've told him numerous times, but maybe if you said something, he'd listen."

Ingrid and Hortensia both nodded. They walked past each bed, coming closer to Filastro's. They could hear Edmund telling his father about some guy who beat up a store clerk over sour milk. They turned to one another and raised their eyebrows simultaneously. They both broke out in smiles, and each felt a little relieved.

"So isn't that crazy, Papá? Here this guy beats up a completely different store clerk for a mistake that he made and he doesn't even realize that he's taking out his aggression on the wrong guy! When I heard that I was like, 'No way! Who's going to believe that?' But that's what I saw on television—" Edmund stopped. He'd felt someone approach while he was talking, but he assumed it was the head nurse coming to instruct him to be quiet. He turned around and to his surprise found Ingrid Genera and his father's mistress staring down at him.

"Hi, Edmund," Ingrid said.

"Hi," he responded dumbly.

"I'm so sorry about your papá," Hortensia said, her voice breaking. She bent down toward Edmund and embraced him.

Edmund felt a lump in his throat for two separate reasons. First, because this woman—never mind that it was his father's mistress— was hugging him and was the first person who seemed to care that Filastro was in a coma, and second, because Ingrid was there in the infirmary to see him. But he wasn't sure of the latter fact, so he asked her, "Who are you here to see, a sick relative or something?"

"I came to see you, Edmund. I wanted to know if you were all right."

Edmund now felt tears of joy coming to his eyes. Relief and joy, and he wanted to hug Hortensia again and then hug Ingrid and then call over the nursing staff, even though they were rude to him, and introduce everyone to one another. He clasped his hands. "So!" he said, trying to compose himself. "This is where I've been spending most of my days. It's not too bad. And my papá seems to be improving. Watch this!"

Edmund took the cross pendant from his neck and approached Filastro, whose eyes were fixed open. Edmund moved the pendant back and forth and his father's eyes followed it. Edmund turned to Ingrid and Hortensia. "See? I know he's getting better because he didn't do that before."

Hortensia began to sob. She walked closer to the bed and Edmund moved out of the way. She knelt down and took Filastro's hand in hers and brought it to her face, tears streaming down her cheeks. Edmund watched, unsure of what to do. He turned to Ingrid, who now looked scared, and said, "Do you want to go outside?"

They left Hortensia at Filastro's side and sat on the benches in front of the clinic, but the benches were about to fall apart, so they moved to a sparse patch of grass. Edmund sat cross-legged, Ingrid with her long, skinny legs stretched out in front of her. They were silent for a long time; something about Hortensia's tears had left Edmund at a loss for words. Finally he spoke, "My mamá won't pick him up. She won't get up, she won't eat. I don't know what to do."

Ingrid looked at the cars passing along the main road out of town.

"It's all right," Edmund continued. "I'm sure she'll feel better soon."

Ingrid nodded and said, "Yeah."

"Ingrid, can I ask you something?"

She nodded again.

"Well, it's just that I thought we were having a nice time when I came over for hot chocolate and we watched television with your mamá. But then your mamá kept saying that you were sick. Were you really sick?"

Ingrid shook her head. "No. My mom doesn't want me to see you because she found out your dad was Filastro."

Edmund perked up. "Really?" He didn't mind this idea. He thought of Tomi and Paty both forbidden to date because of Filastro, and look at them now, married and living in the United States. "So it wasn't because you didn't want to see me?"

She shook her head and smiled.

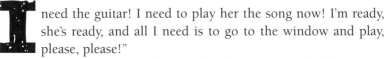

need the guitar! I need to play her the song now! I'm ready, she's ready, and all I need is to go to the window and play, please, please!"

Tres Pasos was stooped over in his chair, his wrinkled face stern. "Look, Edmund, Tomato has brought something to my attention that's a little more disconcerting than your not being able to serenade your girlfriend."

"She's not my—wait, what happened?" Edmund turned to Tomato, who was in his usual bad-and-getting-worse afternoon mood. Tomato scowled, making his bulbous nose protrude even more. "Shall I go get him, boss?"

Tres Pasos nodded, not moving his eyes off Edmund.

They waited in awkward silence, Edmund wondering what could be going on, Tres Pasos glaring at him, and the sounds of Tomato busy in the other room, obviously struggling with someone or something. He emerged from the back leading a man whose mouth was taped, his hands tied behind him. Edmund recognized Ricardo the Former Notary immediately.

"What'd he do?" Edmund asked, surprised.

"Are you saying you don't know what he was doing lurking in my patio area?"

Edmund shook his head.

"Are you saying you don't know what he was doing scribbling word for word all my stories into his little black book?"

Edmund shook his head, this time less convincingly.

"Are you saying you don't know that he had plans for writing a book and you told him that I was telling you the stories of my life?"

Edmund hung his head.

"Did you betray my exact order that you should not speak to anyone about our agreement? Did you renege on your vow of secrecy?"

Edmund looked up, scrunching his brow. "I never vowed secrecy, and you never told me I couldn't tell nobody!" His ears began to burn when he thought of all the stories he'd told his father at the infirmary.

Tres Pasos turned to Tomato. "Do you remember the vow of secrecy?"

Tomato shrugged. He wanted to say yes, but despite his surly temperament he tried to be a man of his word. "I don't know," he grumbled.

The old man sighed. "All right, so maybe you did vow and maybe you didn't, but the real issue here is this worthless piece of crap listening in on my stories, writing them down, and trying to pass them off as his own. Are you saying you haven't been planning this together?"

"I swear," Edmund exclaimed. "The other day I was walking home all excited because I was getting better at the guitar and I ran into him and I explained our deal. I didn't know he was going to try and copy the stories."

Tres Pasos nodded to his assistant and Tomato removed the tape from Ricardo's mouth.

Ricardo gasped, "Edmund, convince him to let me write down his stories!"

"Why did you tell them I planned this with you?"

"I didn't! He tied me up and taped my mouth before I could say anything—they read my book!"

Tres Pasos shifted in his recliner and said, "A whole lot of complaining, whining, 'My papá this, my papá that.' What you ought to do if you got problems with your father is—"

Edmund had heard this story. "Yeah, that's a good one!"

Tres Pasos turned to him. "Don't you see, son, this isn't some sensationalized rag magazine I'm imparting to you. I'm giving you life's wisdom as I know it, and if I may say so, mine is a fortunate perspective to be had. For the rest of your days you can reflect back on what I'm saying, you can learn from my mistakes, make judgments based on my sound or unsound decisions, you understand? And here this little sneak is out there just copying down the juicy details. I've read through his black book and he doesn't have one word of the sound wisdom I've shared with you. All he has is the fights, the whores, the deals, the abuse given and received, the loves lost, the family members dead, all the surface details, none of the morals or the lessons learned!"

"Those are my favorite parts," Edmund said.

"Exactly! And he has not one word! Now what kind of book can he be writing without lessons and morals? I'll tell you: nothing but a rag!" He sat back in his recliner, breathed in deeply, and then exhaled. "Got all worked up."

"Please, Don Tres Pasos," Ricardo spoke up, "I intend to write the lessons, but I have to get the details written first or else I'll forget. Just as Edmund here is learning and will be able to look back on your life as a guide, I'll also look back and write down those lessons that are so important. And just so you know, I was once the town notary and people told me about their private lives and I never once told another person. Edmund can vouch for that. His father came, wanting to know who helped his sons get to the United States and I didn't tell him even though he assaulted me, isn't that right, Edmund?"

"Yes, that's true."

Tres Pasos considered this. "So you're not planning on sending this to the newspapers?"

"No."

"You're not planning on making a comic book out of it?"

"No, not at all."

"You're not planning on writing one of those exposés on loan sharking?"

"Only what you want, Tres Pasos."

Tres Pasos smiled, his wrinkled face bunching together. Suddenly, the idea seemed sensible. He was already tiring after a hundred stories. Imagine if he had to tell them again; this way he'd save some breath. "All right, then," he said gruffly, as if still unsure about the undertaking, "how about a story—number three fifty-two, to be exact? And don't bother hiding outside on the patio—Tomato, get this guy a table to rest his book on!"

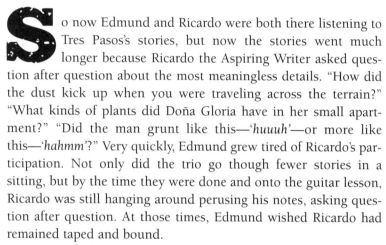

o now Edmund and Ricardo were both there listening to Tres Pasos's stories, but now the stories went much longer because Ricardo the Aspiring Writer asked question after question about the most meaningless details. "How did the dust kick up when you were traveling across the terrain?" "What kinds of plants did Doña Gloria have in her small apartment?" "Did the man grunt like this—'*huuuh*'—or more like this—'*hahmm*'?" Very quickly, Edmund grew tired of Ricardo's participation. Not only did the trio go though fewer stories in a sitting, but by the time they were done and onto the guitar lesson, Ricardo was still hanging around perusing his notes, asking question after question. At those times, Edmund wished Ricardo had remained taped and bound.

It was obvious that Tres Pasos enjoyed the idea of having a scribe. He likened the situation to the drug traffickers who hired songwriters to document their exploits. "And me, well, I'll have my own book!" He indulged Ricardo's every whim. He even gave him a small room in the back of the house where Ricardo could write in peace. The most discouraging, though, was when Tres Pasos jokingly said to Edmund, "And what's your role here?"

"I'm—uh—"

"Because you know, with Ricardo writing down the stories, it doesn't really make it necessary for you to hang around. Now my wisdom will be spread indefinitely."

"But then I don't get guitar lessons or the guitar," Edmund said, growing despondent.

"What if I just gave you the guitar and told you to scram?"

"But—" Edmund's mouth dropped open slightly. Tres Pasos laughed and looked at Tomato, who just lifted his head and grunted. "I'm just joking. We had a deal, isn't that right?"

Edmund and Ricardo listened together for several more weeks, the stories slowing to two a day and then finally one. Ricardo asked so many questions that Edmund hardly cared how the story ended or what the moral was, just that it would end. And when it came to guitar instruction, Tres Pasos paid scant attention to Edmund's progress. He'd tell Edmund to practice a chord progression, a scale, or a song, and as soon as the boy commenced playing, turn his attentions to Ricardo.

One day Edmund was playing—beautifully, he thought—his eyes closed, his fingers moving lithely across the strings, and he heard the room grow quiet. He thought maybe his performance had so moved Ricardo and Tres Pasos that they'd been struck silent. When he finished he opened his eyes and found the old man asleep in his chair. He looked around for Ricardo, and then heard his voice in the other room reciting parts of the manuscript. He touched Tres Pasos on the shoulder and said, "What did you think?"

The old man stirred, opened his mouth and made chewing noises.

"Tres Pasos, I'm done, what did you think?"

"Oh," he murmured, obviously still dazed, "that was very good."

"I think I'm ready now," Edmund said quietly, holding his breath.

"Yes," Tres Pasos said, smacking his lips and emitting a sleepy moan.

Edmund decided to try something. "Don't you think you've told me enough stories?"

"Yes, you're right."

"Don't you think I'm ready to bring the guitar home with me?"

"Yes, yes, take the guitar home with me."

"No, with *me*. I'm going to take the guitar home."

"Yes, yes."

That was confirmation enough for Edmund. He picked up the guitar and quickly and as quietly as possible tiptoed out of the house, opening the door ever so slowly, and closing it just as carefully. He could still hear Ricardo reciting the story in the back room; "And so Tres Pasos said to his son, 'You are nothing to me, nothing at all. You are dead to me as if you had never been! And that was the last he ever saw of him . . . ' "

Edmund stopped dead in the middle of the patio when he heard Tomato's voice. "And just where do you think you're going, little boy?"

Edmund turned around and found Tomato sitting in a plastic lawn chair, rolling a cigarette. "Home."

"Not with that you aren't."

"Yeah, huh, Tres Pasos gave me his permission."

Tomato laughed malignantly, his face coloring, his nose even redder. "I know that he didn't. You want to know why?" He paused to lick the paper. "Because he told me from the beginning that you didn't have an ounce of talent and that you'd never be worthy enough to take home that cherished guitar of his."

Edmund was quiet. He tried to think of something to say in retaliation, but nothing came to mind except something regarding Tomato's bulbous nose, insults to which the man was already immune.

"Did he really say that?"

Tomato sniffed and smiled. He began rolling the paper. "His exact words. And just the other day he told me something similar. I think he said, 'Not even a deaf man could play so badly.' "

Edmund carefully placed the guitar against the patio fence. The guitar made a hollow thump. He wanted to say something mean, but all he could do was stare at the rust-colored tile floor. He noticed the grout, clean and white. He saw a trail of ants. He saw the shadow of the plant, the sunlight streaming through the roof. Nothing that inspired insults.

He walked out the gate, determined never to return to Tres Pasos's.

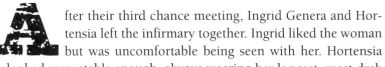
A fter their third chance meeting, Ingrid Genera and Hortensia left the infirmary together. Ingrid liked the woman but was uncomfortable being seen with her. Hortensia looked respectable enough, always wearing her longest, most drab dress. She wore less makeup, though still a considerable amount, fearing Filastro would awake and not find her attractive. They headed in the same direction, talking continuously, but Ingrid kept her head down and walked a few steps ahead or a few steps behind, nothing too noticeable, but just enough that she could distance herself if need be.

Hortensia, of course, was not oblivious to Ingrid's behavior, nor did she blame her. She decided, however, to have a little fun with the girl. "How long have you been dating Edmund?" she asked.

"What?" Ingrid exclaimed. "Oh! We're not dating. We're just friends, that's all." She felt her response too revealing, and not in the way she intended. "I think he likes me," she followed, more calmly, "but he's just a little kid."

"How old are you?"

"Fourteen."

"Well, that's about his age, no?"

Ingrid hesitated. "Yes, but—"

"But what? Because he's small, because he has nothing but peach fuzz on his lip? Let me tell you, that should be your last complaint, and take it from a woman who knows."

Ingrid's face flushed.

Hortensia noticed and smiled despite herself. "You may like the guys who are good at sports or the ones who dress cool and act tough. I did, too, but it's the ones you least expect who are the best lovers, who treat you right, and maybe you're too young to understand that—"

Ingrid wasn't. Just the other night Rafa had convinced her to kiss him. It wasn't her first kiss, but it was the first with a boy sticking his tongue in her mouth. "What are you doing?" she said, pushing him away. "I'm just showing you how it's done," he said, trying to kiss her again. She let him try, wondering if the need to gag was the fault of her own inexperience. In the end she felt as if she'd made out with a horse.

Thus Hortensia's words resonated more than she expected, but the mistress continued anyway, perhaps going further than necessary. "And, Edmund, oh, let me tell you, I heard from a friend of mine, a cousin of a friend, I should say—not a woman like me, mind you, but a respectable girl—and she said that Edmund may be small with his clothes on, but, my, was he—"

"I don't want to hear about that!" Ingrid said.

"OK, OK, I understand. No one wants to hear about the boy she has a crush on dating other girls."

"I told you, we're just friends! I feel bad for him, *that's all*, if you want to know the truth!"

Hortensia refrained, noticing how flustered the girl had become. "Yes, of course. OK."

After a moment of silence, Ingrid asked, "Who was this girl?"

Hortensia was about tell her to forget it when Ingrid asked, "It wasn't Laura, was it?"

Hortensia paused. "Yes . . . it was, actually."

"I knew it! Laura always likes the guys who like me, which is why she went on that date with Edmund the other day. Do you really think they did more?"

Hortensia thought for a moment, wanting to further Edmund's case, not wreck it. She decided on prudence. "Oh, you know, we women lie about our exploits just as much as men. I wouldn't worry about it."

Ingrid nodded, but her stomach felt queasy. "I'm going this way," she said to Hortensia.

"OK, I'll see you. Probably again at the infirmary, eh?"

*   *   *

Ingrid couldn't understand what was bothering her. She visited Edmund at the infirmary because they were friends, nothing more, but why did she feel nervous right before she was about to see him? "Probably because I'm not supposed to see him," she told herself. Plus, she had to visit him at a clinic surrounded by sick people, and that didn't help her nerves. But then why did Hortensia's words affect her? Why did she even care about Laura? "Because Laura's a bitch, that's why. Well, she can have Edmund." But that made her feel worse. "Edmund is my friend," she reasoned, "and I don't want mean girls hanging around him . . . that's all." She felt a little better.

She was almost at her door when something Edmund said earlier popped into her head and she began to laugh. They'd been sitting at the edge of Filastro's bed and Edmund lifted the sheet and began tickling his father's feet.

"What are you doing?" she asked, somewhat alarmed.

"What does it look like I'm doing?"

"Tickling his feet."

"Yup, that's what I'm doing."

"Why?"

"Because this is how I always used to wake him up before. He's real ticklish."

"Does the doctor know you do that?"

"Yeah, I told him I was going to do it, and you know what the doctor said? He said, 'That's as good an idea as any.' And he scribbled something in his notebook. And then later the head nurse came over and said, 'Because of you, the doctor has prescribed feet tickling every hour.' So I guess the nurses have to do it when I'm not here!"

Ingrid had laughed and there at her door she imagined Edmund tickling his father's feet and laughed again. She suddenly grew self-conscious and limited herself to an inward smile. Walking inside she heard her mother on the phone. She set her keys on the end table and sat down on the couch, listening to the conversation. Her mother's voice was bubbly.

"So all our papers are in order, you're sure? . . . OK, OK . . . I know I'm being paranoid, but I just can't believe it's happening after so many years! Were the flights expensive? Oh my God, I wish I was there with you right now, my love. Soon, soon . . . I can't believe it, our dream, husband, our dream! When do we leave?"

Ingrid's heart sank. She lay down on the couch and rested her head on the cushioned arm, her hair falling over the side. When Doña Celeste hung up the phone, she entered the front room and found her daughter.

"That was your father. You won't believe the news!"

"I don't want to go," Ingrid said, staring at a knothole in the ceiling rafters.

ilastro finally emerged from his coma. When he regained consciousness, he was too weak to call for help. He saw he was at the clinic, but that was all. He fell asleep again, and didn't stir until he felt a tickling sensation on the bottoms of his feet. He thought for a moment that he was dreaming, that he was back in his own bed and Edmund was trying to rouse him for work. Then he started awake and found his son at the edge of the bed moving his fingers up and down the soles of his feet.

Edmund looked up and saw his father's eyes. His mouth dropped. "It worked! It worked! I woke you!"

Filastro tried to speak but his mouth was too dry. "Water," he managed to say.

"What?" Edmund asked, coming closer.

"Water?"

"What?" he said placing his ear close to Filastro's mouth.

Filastro moved him back and weakly raised his hand to his lips as if he held an imaginary cup. Edmund understood and rushed to get the head nurse. The nurses rushed over and soon the doctor was at Filastro's side. "Oh, look at you! As awake as the day you came to see me with your boy, Edmund, here. You heeded my advice, obviously. This boy is as dedicated as a canine, visited every day, talked to you until the neighboring patients decided to go home for peace and quiet—what—what was that?" He leaned in as Filastro whispered.

"Water."

"What was that?"

Filastro gasped for air. He tried to swallow. "Water," he said again.

Edmund suddenly remembered, "He told me he needs water!"

"Get the patient some water," the doctor told the nurse.

Filastro tried to speak again. "My—my—woman?"

"Your—uh—well, someone . . . has come by . . ."

"My wife. Where is my wife?" He found Edmund's face. "Where is your mamá, mijo?"

Edmund rushed home as quickly as he could.

*   *   *

Constanza's health had improved, but not much. She slept late and woke only to watch television. She cooked little and ate even less. She cleaned the house, dusting, mopping the floor, cleaning the kitchen appliances and pans, more to have something to do than out of necessity. Every day Edmund came home and pleaded with her to visit Filastro, but she merely replied, "I'm too tired, mijo. I shouldn't go to the clinic when I'm not feeling well."

"But I don't understand," he'd say. "Why aren't you getting better? You are his wife. You need to be there for him. What if he wakes up and you're not there?"

She shook her head, "Ay, mijo, I'm too tired, just tired, that's all. Let me be."

So Edmund kept away from the house, hanging out either at the infirmary or in the central plaza. He often watched the musicians play songs, following along on an imaginary guitar. They'd call him over and lend him a real one to play, but only during the slow afternoons because once he got hold of the guitar he was hard pressed to relinquish it. The plaza musicians were impressed with his rapid improvement. "My God, boy, did you make a deal with the devil or what?" And Edmund would smile widely, wondering (and worrying) if Tres Pasos qualified as the devil.

When Edmund returned home each night, his mother was already asleep. He made as much noise as possible attempting to wake her, but she didn't stir. Constanza knew he was angry with her, but she felt powerless to give in, to explain, to do anything, for that matter. The thought of seeing Filastro made her want to scream . . . with hate? with anger, sadness? She didn't know. He had driven her children away, and now what was left? Only before, with her children by her side, there for her to protect, could she face him day in and day out, year after year. The thought of facing him alone filled her with terror. She didn't visit her husband at the infirmary because when she had seen him near death on the doctor's bed, she felt the urge to take his pillow and smother the remaining life out of him.

These were her thoughts, over and over, and these were the same thoughts occupying her mind when Edmund rushed in the door and exclaimed, "He's awake! You have to go to him, Mamá, he needs you! He asked for you!"

Constanza felt her breath quicken and her heart begin to pound. She set down the bag of rice she was about to pour into the pan and shut off the stove. She walked into her bedroom and grabbed her purse. She wore the same clothes she slept in, the same clothes she wore every day.

Edmund was aware of this. "Mamá, aren't you going to change? Comb your hair, maybe?"

"Come on, let's go."

They walked to the clinic in silence, Edmund struggling to keep up. She stared straight ahead, not acknowledging greetings from neighbors and acquaintances, not even from one shopkeeper who called out, "Haven't seen you in a while, Doña Constanza." Edmund raised his hands in a gesture of surprise and said, "Excuse her, she's not feeling herself. With my father sick and all."

When they arrived at the clinic Constanza walked straight in, past the front desk, the receptionist calling after her, "Excuse me, but who are you here to visit?" Edmund again excused his mother and said, "She's here to pick up Filastro Agustín." He watched his mother walk by the row of beds, directly toward his father's as if she knew beforehand where it was. His mother slowed and looked at Filastro, who appeared to be asleep.

From the edge of his bed Constanza said his name and he opened his eyes.

Filastro breathed in deeply, feeling his chest swell. He examined her face, immediately wanting her closer, feeling as if he hadn't seen her in years.

"My woman," he said, his mouth parched.

She stepped forward and placed her hand on his forehead. He exhaled, feeling relief for the first time since he had woken to that nightmare. How he had needed her during those interminable, torturous days.

Constanza leaned in close to his ear and whispered steadily, "Filastro Agustín, you are my husband, the father of my children, but now they are all gone, including your daughters. Only Edmund is here and if it weren't for him I'd take this pillow under your head and suffocate you so that you would never cause me pain again. Listen to me, husband. I hate you. I hate you. I fear you and we will never again live under the same roof."

With that she left the clinic as quickly as she'd come. Edmund watched her leave, too shocked to say anything.

The police came when they heard Filastro had awoken from his coma. They questioned him and he answered to the best of his ability. The events weren't entirely clear in his mind. He remembered being arrested, riding around with Captain Esteban, and then the shootout, his compadres lying dead on the ground, and finally, the woman who shot him in the knee. Everything afterward was a blur. He was astonished to hear that he had disappeared for three weeks: it felt like three years.

"You're sure it was only three weeks?" he asked.

"Yes."

"You're sure."

"Yes, I'm sure. Now, why do you think this woman saved you? She did a crude job of bandaging your wound, but fixed you up nonetheless. Any insight?"

Filastro had none. He had wished for death, he knew that. He had told the woman, or so he thought, to kill him, to put him out of his misery, but she merely repeated over and over, her voice eerily calm, "I ask you, are you an innocent man?" And he had screamed, "Yes, yes, yes, I have done nothing to you, nothing at all! Why do you torture me like this?" The woman would hit him or spit in his face, and then find some new way of torturing him, usually calling in the gangs of children—he didn't know how many; every day their appearance differed. Now he doubted they even existed. Everything but the horror was unclear. He remembered the last time the woman's face leaned in close and asked him, "Are you an innocent man?" He changed his answer, telling her, "I am not innocent! Definitely not! I am guilty!" And she smiled and pulled a rubber mallet from under her long skirt. Her arm swinging toward him, that was the last thing he remembered.

The police officer continued, "So this same woman killed Gaspar, Mendigo, and Jerry, *and* Capitán Esteban, you say?"

Filastro nodded and felt his eyes tear up. He wanted to feel sorry for his compadres, but he couldn't; he only felt his own pain.

"If we drove you around Retorno, could you show us where she lived?"

Filastro shook his head, and then murmured, "In hell."

"What was that?"

"Nothing."

*   *   *

On his third day awake he was allowed to go home. He had to sign some papers, promise to pay the debt incurred, and was lent a wheelchair. He could hardly walk. His knee couldn't take any pressure and standing up caused the blood to rush to his head. He'd almost crushed Edmund when the boy tried helping him step into his shoes. "I got you," Edmund said, his face beet-red from the strain of keeping his father upright.

A nurse finished helping Filastro dress and supported him as he was transferred from the bed to the wheelchair. "You will have someone to help you at home, right?" she asked him.

Edmund answered. "Yes, my mamá will be there, thank you."

The ride home wasn't easy. Edmund struggled, pushing the wheelchair over the cobblestones and up the inclines to the sidewalk. Once on the sidewalk the going was even slower as pedestrians could only press up against the wall or lean against a parked car in order to let them pass. Still, Edmund called out, "Move it! We have an injured person!" He stopped when he clipped a man's heel and the man turned around and told Edmund he'd throw him in the street if he did it again.

"That's no way to talk to someone pushing a wheelchair," a woman said to the man.

Edmund held his chin up, agreeing that he deserved some sort of immunity.

The man ignored them and peered down at Filastro. "I heard about what happened," he snarled. "It should have been you dead in a ditch rather than Big Gaspar. His wife is my cousin. She can't even eat."

"Well, trauma affects people in various ways," Edmund said, remembering the doctor's words. "My mamá can't eat, either."

Filastro didn't even look up. His hands were folded in his lap and he stared at them as if counting the wrinkles in his knuckles.

They continued on their way home, receiving curious glances and looks of disgust. Edmund continued to hold his head high as he pushed Filastro, glad that his father seemed oblivious to the goings-on around him. "What are you looking at?" Edmund sneered at a dull-witted man he knew for a fact to be harmless.

"Whaaaat happened to Don Filastro?"

"He was left for dead by a pack of thieves."

"Thaaaat's not what I—I heard."

"So why do you ask, then? Get out of the way."

The man giggled.

Edmund left the wheelchair and was about to give the idiot a piece of his mind and show the rest of the street that he wasn't taking it from just anyone, when his father lifted his head and said, "Mijo, let's get home."

They arrived at their door without any further confrontations. Entering the house, they found it empty. Every table and counter had been scrubbed clean, the floors sparkled; it smelled like bleach. The room where they all had slept was bare, nothing but mattresses stripped of sheets and blankets. Only two of the eight beds were made. A note lay on the one with baseball-themed sheets. Edmund grabbed it and read,

Edmund,

There is a lot of food in the refrigerator. When you need more tell me and I'll give you some money from what your siblings are sending home. I'm at your tía Lupe's. I know you are mad at me, but please try and understand. I'm sorry you are in the middle, but you were always my little monkey! I love you with all of my heart,

Mamá

P.S. Ricardo came by. He is writing this (for no charge). He wants to know where you've been. Tres Pasos does too.

Edmund looked up from the note. He was going to lie to Filastro, tell him that Mamá would be home soon, that she just had some errands to run, but his father didn't seem to care what was written. He wheeled himself over to the bed, and, holding the blanket and headboard, pulled himself out of the wheelchair and fell face-first into the pillow. He moaned in pain as he turned himself over. Soon he was asleep.

dmund headed to his tía Lupe's house to find out what was going on. "It makes no sense," he said to himself. "She hasn't spoken to her sister in twenty-something years and now she's living there! What's going on?" He arrived and rapped on the door as if in a great hurry. "Hello!" he yelled when no one came. Finally Jorge el Gato opened the door, and before Edmund had an opportunity to step inside, said, "Let's go for a walk, OK?"

"No, I want to talk to my mamá right now! She can't just abandon my papá like that when he needs her most. I need her, too. Who's going to cook, clean, help take care of my papá?"

"Come on, lower your voice. I'll explain."

"You? You hate Papá. You're probably happy that he's lying in bed with no one but me to watch over him!"

"Edmund, quiet, just listen to me." He began walking and Edmund had no choice but to follow along. "Look, our mothers have made up after all these years. Our entire lives they've never spoken, but finally Constanza understood that Filastro had come between her and her sister and she was able to let go of her anger. With all your brothers and sisters gone, who's left?" Edmund pointed emphatically to himself. "Yes, you; she does have you, but imagine what her life must be like—almost twenty-five years of taking care of children and now they're all gone. It's just her and Filastro—"

"And me! Why do they act like I'm gone, too? *All* her children! Well, I'm still here and it's not fair. I didn't take off for the United States, I didn't run away, and this is the thanks I get!"

"Edmund, imagine how hard it must be for your mamá that she would leave her youngest son at home. She's not herself and that's why she came to my mother, to recover, to start mending her wounds. Can't you understand that? Your mamá has not had an easy time, Edmund. You know; you've been there."

Edmund paused, considering this. "Something's just not right," he said. "A man's wife is his wife, and his wife should be by her husband's side when he gets left for dead."

Edmund left Jorge el Gato's side without returning to his tía Lupe's house. He no longer wanted to see his mother. He thought about going home to check on Filastro, but he couldn't face him without providing some sort of rationale for his mother's absence. He thought of the doctor's words from years ago, the ones that had saved him many a beating. "You don't want to affect your children's psychological states! You never know when they'll turn on you!" Apparently the same went for wives.

"Ah!" Edmund yelled aloud, growing more frustrated as he walked aimlessly along. His feet carried him toward the central plaza. "Here, all I want is to practice my guitar for Ingrid," he thought. "I know it's getting closer, she talks to me more and more, but once things start getting good, something bad like this happens. Why am I the one to take care of my papá? Why am I the one who has to make up excuses for my mamá? And I don't even have the guitar yet!"

These grumblings led him to recall how he broke the guitar in the first place. This reminded him of Hortensia and he was suddenly struck with an idea. "She's the only one who came to see him. Maybe she would help take care of him!"

He rushed to Disco Chido, the club of ill repute, and went around back. He hurried down the alley as quickly as possible; it was growing dark and the shadows cast by trash bags and discarded furniture appeared all too ominous. He approached what he thought was her window and cried out, "Hortensia! Hortensia!"

After five minutes of calling her name and waiting, someone opened his shutters and screamed, "She's inside the club, you damn kid!"

"Oh you go shut up!" he yelled back. He sighed and walked back down the alley. He stood in front of the entrance to Disco Chido, his hands in his pockets, wondering whether he should enter or not. Finally, he decided to go in.

dmund walked up the stairs and was surprised to walk right into the club without encountering any opposition. A fat bouncer wearing a shirt that looked as if it would have fit Edmund just sat there and languidly nodded his head when Edmund passed. This gave him courage. Maybe he was finally looking older, the events of the past weeks having given him the mature edge he needed to enter clubs and bars. His wishful thinking was short-lived.

"Hey, Maura Elena!" the bartender yelled as he dried the shot glasses, "Look what just blew in! Doesn't he look like that guy in the commercials with the cookies?"

Maura Elena, one of the fat whores at the bar, turned around and started laughing, her large mouth wide open.

Edmund knew just the commercial. He scowled and said caustically, "Oh, why, just because I have red hair?"

"No, do you have red hair?" the bartender leaned over the counter. "Come into the light, let me see."

Edmund remained where he was. "I'm looking for someone," he said.

"Well, how about a drink on the house, a soda? Didn't mean to hurt your feelings—don't look so sad, boy—the guy in the commercials is a good-looking kid. It's just funny seeing you here in Disco Chido."

Edmund thought for a moment. "You weren't talking about the elf with the green clothes?"

"The elf? No, there was no elf in the commercial."

Edmund's countenance brightened. He decided to drop the subject, but Maura Elena had risen from her stool and come over to him. She was now running her fingers through his hair. "You know who you look like?" she said, cooing in a most unflattering way.

"I look like Edmund," he said, annoyed.

"No, no," she continued touching his hair, making it stand straight up. "You look like—"

"I know who he looks like," said a drunk at the far end of the bar. "Your average twerp!" He laughed, knocking a "tap tap ta-tap" on the bar top.

"Don't listen to him," the fat woman said, her hand not having left Edmund's hair. "No, you look just like—"

Someone behind them said, "I agree with Don Pepe, he does look like a twerp, the kind who doesn't know how to play the guitar."

Edmund cringed, recognizing the voice. He turned around and saw three men playing cards, one of them Tomato.

"Shut up, Tomato," Edmund said.

Tomato got up from the table, his chair tipping back but not falling. "Say it again, you little rooster, and I'll smash you against the floor!"

Immediately, everyone was up in arms, calling for tranquility, appalled by Tomato's behavior, including his card-playing friends. The bartender called the bouncer and instructed him to keep an eye on Tomato. "He's in one of his moods," he said. "Goddamn, who picks on a child? Only you, Tomato!"

"He's not a child, he's just puny!" Tomato retorted, sitting back down to his cards, his face fixed in an icy glare.

Edmund finally removed the woman's hand from his hair and asked for Hortensia.

"I'm right here, Edmund."

He looked up and saw Hortensia's kind, if not overly made-up, face. She had quite a bit of rouge on her cheeks. Edmund was so relieved to see her that he found himself on the verge of tears. "Can I talk to you?" he muttered.

"Come to the back," she said, taking hold of his hand.

"I know who he looks like!" Edmund heard the fat whore say finally. "He looks just like Hortensia's man, Filastro Agustín—something in the eyes!"

* * *

Hortensia agreed to help Edmund care for Filastro. The next morning she was at the house, her makeup smudged, appearing to have slept little. She cooked breakfast, helped Filastro rise in bed, and changed his bandages. Filastro didn't say a word the entire time. He ate his food in silence, picking at it, taking bites and chewing the food until there couldn't possibly be anything left to chew. Hortensia was patient and after a few attempts to engage him in conversation, she desisted, content just to be there.

Edmund watched Hortensia, always close by in case she needed help. When she propped Filastro up against the headboard, Edmund was there with an extra pillow. When she brought in the eggs, beans, and tortillas, Edmund carried in the utensils. When she tried talking to Filastro—telling him how much she missed him, how scared she'd been when he went missing, how she'd cried all night after seeing him in a coma—Edmund sat right next to her, smiling, knowing these words must be good to hear. "Better than your own wife telling you she's too tired to take care of you," he thought to himself. But suddenly he missed his mother so much that he became nauseous and excused himself from the bedroom.

After Hortensia left, Edmund walked out to the backyard. He picked up Cross-Eyes and hugged him until the little dog yelped. He set the dog down and tried petting him behind the ears, but Cross-Eyes, probably fearing another suffocating hug, limped away, dragging his hind legs.

Edmund sat in the dirt, his arms resting on his knees and his head bowed. "At least it can't get any worse, right, Cross-Eyes?" That was when he heard a knock on the door. He dusted himself off and rushed to answer it. Through the metal screen he saw Ingrid Genera, one hand on her hip, the other nervously playing with a ringlet of hair.

ow long until you leave?" Edmund asked, unable to truly comprehend what she'd just told him.

"Two weeks."

"Why can't you leave later, like after you finish school?"

She shrugged. "That's a long ways off. I just started high school here."

Ingrid and her mother were leaving for the United States to be with Ingrid's father. He was a truck driver in California. He had a green card, and was able to come back to La Prudencia for a month every year. Doña Celeste and Ingrid had applied for visas countless times and been unsuccessful, but finally they'd been approved. They would fly from Guadalajara to San Francisco as easily as if going for vacation. But they would be staying for good. Ingrid would finish high school there in a place called San José.

Edmund was speechless. He stared numbly at the button on her shirt.

"Are you OK, Edmund?"

He shook his head. "Don't leave," he whispered, almost in a whimper.

"I have to."

A long moment of silence ensued. Finally, Ingrid said, "I better go, I have to tell other people, too."

If Edmund had felt bad before, his one solace—that she had come to tell him, specifically him, that she was leaving—was now gone. He suddenly became upset. "So that's why you came and told me?"

"What do you mean?"

"Just on your rounds, going to each of your friends and saying, 'I'm leaving, wish me luck, goodbye.' Who are you going to next? Pedro's, then Carlos's, then José Vásquez's—"

"Edmund, stop—" she pleaded.

He continued, "Then Pancho's, then a few girlfriends', and then, of course, Rafa's—be sure and save him for last. 'Oh, I came to see you first, Edmund, well, because you live just around the corner; you're—' "

"Edmund, stop it! Why are you being this way?"

"Why? Why? Isn't it obvious?"

"I'm sorry! What do you want me to say? I don't want to leave, either. This is hard for me. I'm sorry that you feel bad that you're not the only one I've come to tell, but we're just friends—good friends, right? We have fun hanging out and I'm going to miss you, but Edmund, it's just—"

"It's just what? You don't love me, you'll never love me, and it doesn't matter that I've practiced and practiced playing and singing for you and only you, I even got a job so that I could buy a guitar, but I got fired, and then I was forced to beg help from Tres Pasos and he screwed me over and now I'm left with no time at all, and you'll never hear me play, you'll never get a chance to know how much I love you—"

"Edmund, please, stop it, you tell me that all the time, I know you want to play me a song, but just stop. I don't want to hurt you." Tears came to her eyes. "I'm sorry. But try and understand how hard it is for me—"

"No! It is not hard for you! It's hard for me! It's not hard for you, just me . . ." He stopped because he didn't want to cry; also, because his neighbor, Doña María, the same neighbor whose bags he carried, came over and said, "Oh, hello, Edmund, can I bug your mother for some starch? I'm all out and my husband needs his pants for an outing tonight."

"I have to go," Ingrid said, placing her hand on Edmund's forearm. She turned and walked away before he could say anything. He watched her, his heart never having experienced such anguish.

"Did I interrupt something?" Doña María asked, still awaiting the response to her request.

Edmund looked squarely at her dumb face and said, "What did you say?"

"Can I have some starch? My husband needs his pants for—"

"No, I don't have any damn starch!" Edmund yelled.

Doña María started back. "¡Ay, Dios mío! Well, I see who you're taking after!" With that she turned and walked to the neighbor across the street.

As Edmund entered the house, he could hear her talking about him. "Yes, you wouldn't believe it! The apple doesn't fall far from the tree! Good thing he's so puny, otherwise he'd be brutalizing people as well as insulting them!"

"To hell with you and your damn starch!" he screamed across the street, tears steaming down his face. He was glad they couldn't see him behind the screen. He began to sob there in the doorway, slumping to the ground. He was now in the position he'd been before Ingrid arrived: head bowed, arms resting on his knees. He noticed Cross-Eyes peeking through the back screen. "Ah, it got worse!" he cried out.

"Mijo," he heard, the voice hoarse.

Edmund stood, wiped his eyes, and entered the sleep- and sick-laden bedroom. The sun had just begun to set, but the room was already dark. He felt for the lamp switch but Filastro told him to leave it.

"Darkness is better," he said in a gravelly whisper.

"Why?"

"I don't have to look at anything."

There was silence.

"Do you have to go to the bathroom?"

"No. Edmund, what were you yelling about?"

"Nothing."

"I heard you crying."

"So?"

"Tell me why."

"I can't."

Filastro began coughing. Edmund went to the kitchen and returned with water. His father drank it thirstily. He set the empty glass down and said, "Your mother was right to leave me."

"No she wasn't, Papá, she should be here."

"No, no. They were all right to leave. I deserve this."

Edmund remained silent, unable to think straight. He still couldn't believe Ingrid was leaving.

Hortensia showed up not too long after and cooked dinner, the clanging pots and her footsteps the only sounds in the silent house. While they were eating, Jorge el Gato arrived with his popsicle cart. He jingled his bell and Edmund emerged, still chewing on a piece of chicken.

he's leaving, Jorge, she's going for good," Edmund said, finding himself once again overcome with emotion.

"Who is?"

"Who? What do you mean, who? Ingrid, she's going to the United States, a place called San José, and not the one close to Autlán, either, but the one close to Wyoming or Nebraska or wherever! They have papers and everything. God, I wish her father had crashed his stupid truck and died—"

"Edmund, don't say that—"

"Well, if it weren't for him, they'd stay here, her and her stupid mom who doesn't like me!"

"Calm down, there's nothing you can do now. If her family leaves, Ingrid has to go, too. Listen, there'll be other girls—"

"Stop, I don't want to hear it! That's not true and you know it. I don't want to love other girls. I just want Ingrid and she'll want me, too, after I play for her, like you said, right? Women love serenades."

Jorge el Gato sighed deeply and clenched the handle of the popsicle cart, then he removed his hands and placed them in his pockets. "Edmund, I just said that. I don't know if it's true. Yeah, women are attracted to musicians, but you can't win someone over that easily; it's not like you play the song and bam! Ingrid is yours. It's more complicated than that. Look, listen to me . . ." He stepped close to Edmund and grabbed him squarely by the shoulders. He spoke rapidly. "I don't know what I'm talking about. Everything I've told you I don't know for myself. I've read it in magazines, seen it on television, but as far as it ever working in real life, I have no idea, except that it's probably bullshit because it's never worked for me."

"But you've been with so many girls—"

"No, Edmund, I haven't, not one," Jorge removed his hands from Edmund's shoulders and looked down at his custom-made shoe. "Every girl looks at my clubfoot and can't see anything else. No one wants to be with a cripple. Even though they don't say it, I know what's going through their minds."

"But—but—you said you made out with Georgina and Lucía and Betty and what about—"

Jorge el Gato shook his head, his face downcast. "None of them. They're just girls who were friendly to me when I sold them popsicles. Whenever I tried talking to them about things other than popsicle flavors they just nodded their heads and said, 'OK, bye, popsicle seller, thank you very much.' "

"But—but—why did you lie to me?" Edmund asked in a whimper. Now he *knew* everything was falling out from under him. "Why did you pretend like you were some great lover? I thought I was learning from an expert!"

"I'm sorry, I just wanted to be thought of as that, and you believed me, and I wanted to believe it, too, so I kept going and going and then it was too late to tell you the truth."

"But, Jorge, I never would have fallen for Ingrid or tried to make her love me if it hadn't been for you telling me all those things. I thought, 'If Jorge can do it with his clubfoot then maybe I can do it even though everyone thinks I'm a little kid.' I wouldn't have even tried. Damn, I'm so embarrassed!"

"But why would you be embarrassed?"

"Because—" he stopped, not wanting to explain.

Jorge el Gato was silent, thinking. He wanted to say the right thing, lift Edmund's sprits, and yet he didn't want to lie, give him false hope. "Look, it seems like it wasn't all for nothing," he began, choosing his words carefully. "Aren't you two friends? Being friends with a pretty girl is something. I don't even have that. She came to visit you in the infirmary, she invited you over for hot chocolate— those are all good things. Who knows, maybe my advice never worked for myself, but it went pretty far for you. Becoming friends is the first step toward something more."

"How do you know that?" Edmund asked, raising one eyebrow.

"I don't, but it just makes sense, though, right? Maybe if she weren't leaving, you would stay friends for a long time, and then, you never know what she might need. Maybe she'd tire of macho guys like Rafa and need someone who . . ."

"Who plays the guitar?"

"Uh . . . yes, maybe . . . after a while, who knows?"

The door of Edmund's heart had been reopened, and a ray of light peeped through. Once again he was thinking of the song he had to perform for Ingrid. "She has to hear it," he thought to himself. "She has to!"

"Are you OK now?" Jorge asked, realizing he'd given Edmund more hope than was his intention.

"I need to get a guitar!" Edmund exclaimed.

After Edmund explained to his half brother why he'd stopped going to Tres Pasos, Jorge el Gato began hatching a plan. He wanted to make it up to Edmund. "Maybe it's a good thing he's not easily discouraged," he reconsidered afterward. There was still a chance. Not to win Ingrid over, but to feel satisfied, to feel as if he did everything possible in his pursuit. Only then would he be able to let her go.

"Edmund has to do this and I will help him," he said to himself, pushing his cart faster over the bumpy street.

dmund carried a folded piece of paper in his pocket; on it he was to compile ways of earning money quickly. He would stop at nothing, he told himself. Unfortunately he had to stop at just that. His list, like his earlier attempts at employment, was unpromising. Number one, and his only entry thus far, was: "Find out where my mom is hiding the money my brothers and sisters send home and take enough for a guitar." He scratched that out and decided to go ask her directly.

When he arrived at his tía Lupe's house, the door was wide open so he walked right in. He found his mother and aunt eating pan dulce, drinking cinnamon tea, and laughing. Constanza's face looked relaxed, almost serene. Edmund eyed her suspiciously, resisting the urge to blurt out how miserably they were faring at home.

"Hello, mijito, my little Edmund," his mother said.

"Oh Edmundito," his tía Lupe followed, "would you like some sweet bread?"

Their cooing reminded him of Agnes and Alfonsa. "No, I'm fine, I'm not hungry. I've gotten used to cold tortillas in the morning, and so has my papá. So I'm fine, thank you."

Constanza rose from the table and walked toward Edmund, who stepped an equal amount of steps back. "Stay," he told her. "I didn't come to forgive you for abandoning me and my papá, I just wanted to ask about—"

"Edmund, please, don't. I didn't abandon you. I want you to come live with us here. I left your papá, not you. You must understand that."

Edmund held his chin up. "Well, good thing God doesn't allow that. You are his wife and just like you said in front of the priest, through sickness and health, good times and bad times, you will be—"

Constanza smiled sadly, glancing at her sister. "No, mijo, that never happened. Don't you know? Of course you don't. Your father never went to church. He hates priests. You think he'd get married in front of one? We only had a civil marriage. How he convinced me, I don't know. My parents just about died over it, but Filastro told me it was the only way he'd get married. It was only later that I realized why—so he could continue his womanizing ways and not feel the eyes of God on him. Even men like him fear damnation."

Edmund mulled over this new information. Unable to think of anything else to say, he blurted out, "But Papá needs you!"

"Of course he does. He always has, but he should have thought about that before he—" she stopped.

Edmund saw that his mother's eyes were red and watery. He softened, realizing that a simple plea wasn't going to do the trick. "OK, OK," he said quietly. "Don't cry, OK? What if "—he thought for a moment—"what if he came and begged you on his knees?"

"What if what?"

"Would you take him back?"

"No."

"What if he showed you that he had changed completely and promised never to hit you again . . . *and* he came and begged on his knees?"

She shook her head and smiled meekly, biting the corner of her bottom lip. "He'll never change."

"What if he—"

"Edmund, stop it. He'll never change. Just look who's taking care of him now—that woman from Disco Chido."

Edmund's face flushed. "Who told you that?"

"Ay, mijo, everyone loves to talk. If Filastro didn't do me in, the neighbors always finished the job. What's better than telling your comadre that a whore is taking care of your husband?"

"But that wasn't him! I'm the one who got her. He didn't ask her, I did. I needed help; I couldn't care for him alone, and she—she— she's not a whore like you think. She's his friend and mine too."

Constanza shook her head. "Edmund, mijo, come stay here with your tía Lupe. She's offered, and you can sleep in Jorge's room. Wouldn't that be fun? Leave your father to his women—"

"What if she stopped coming and he promised never to talk to another woman again, and he never went to bars either or played cards, and didn't find new compadres to hang out with, and he showed you that he wanted to be with you and only you and that he had changed . . . *and* he came here and begged on his knees, would you then?"

"Edmund, come here." She opened her arms to embrace him. He hesitated, wanting to hug her, but unable to give in. "Please, please," she implored. "Please!"

At this last insistence, he stepped toward her. She grabbed him in her arms and held him. "Mijo, I love you, you know that, please try to understand. I can't go back—"

His mother's embrace felt so warm; he wanted to stay in her arms. He wanted to forgive her for abandoning them. But he had to try once more. "What if—"

"Listen," she said, cutting him off, her voice solemn. "The only way I would ever, ever, *ever* take him back is if he went to the United States, to Texas, Wyoming, Nebraska, and got down on his knees and begged Abel, Ezekiel, Tomy, Gandolfo, Agnes, and Alfonsa their forgiveness. If he showed them that he was a changed man and they believed it, forgave him his past, then I would, too. Only then."

Edmund backed away, smiling.

"Why are you smiling?" she asked, somewhat perplexed, thinking she had presented him with an insurmountable obstacle.

"So you'll take him back, then!"

Just then Jorge el Gato entered the house and strummed what sounded like a guitar chord. "Guess what I got?" he called out. He entered the kitchen and stopped abruptly upon seeing Edmund. "Ah, man, brother-cousin, it was supposed to be a surprise!"

Edmund's mouth dropped. He was speechless. What was Jorge el Gato doing with Tres Pasos's son's guitar?

"Whose is that?" he finally managed to say.

Jorge el Gato placed it in his hands. "Yours."

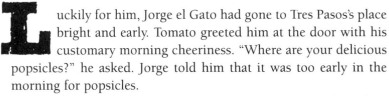

Luckily for him, Jorge el Gato had gone to Tres Pasos's place bright and early. Tomato greeted him at the door with his customary morning cheeriness. "Where are your delicious popsicles?" he asked. Jorge told him that it was too early in the morning for popsicles.

"Not for me!" Tomato responded. "I can eat them for breakfast, especially the purple kind. Now what do I owe this pleasure, my friend, how can I help you? Come, come, let's chat in front of the television; a very good program is on. Of course, you'll have my attention, but a good show is always nice to have on in the background. Isn't that right? Don't you agree?"

When they were settled in the living room Jorge el Gato asked if it'd be possible to speak with Tres Pasos.

"Well, that might be arranged. It's early for him, but let me see." He walked to the back of the house and emerged pushing an old man in a wheelchair. "He was up!" Tomato cried out.

"Quiet, Tomato, damn it," the old man grumbled, "I'm up, but it's too early for all your sunshine!" He turned to Jorge. "Good day, son, you'd like to speak to me? Well, go on, you caught me on the right morning. I've been awake for hours—can't sleep for nothing anymore. Used to be—ah, forget it, anyway, how can I help you?"

Jorge el Gato explained that he was Edmund's half brother, cousin, and best friend, and he understood that Edmund and Tres Pasos had a deal involving stories, music lessons, and a guitar. "The thing is the girl he wants to play for is leaving for the United States for good and he fears all his efforts will be in vain—"

Tres Pasos stopped him. "Do you know why Edmund left me? For the life of me I can't figure it out. I thought he was enjoying the stories and I felt good knowing that I was passing them on to a worthy soul."

"Uh—I think he said something about someone else writing the stories down—"

Tres Pasos grimaced. "Ah! That goddamned Ricardo. That's over with! He was over here pretending like he was interested in wisdom when all he wanted was to write garbage. We had a difference of opinion, I'll tell you that much, and Tomato here, he took care of the rest."

They both turned to Tomato, who was playing the drums on his thighs in tune to the commercial jingle.

"So that's it!" Tres Pasos exclaimed, "He left me after all my stories just because that sissy with high pretensions moved in on him?"

"Uh—yes, that and—I guess Tomato said something to him as well, that he would never be good enough for your son's guitar, that you had told Tomato that he had no talent, and—"

Tres Pasos turned to his assistant. "Tomato! Did you tell him that?"

"What?" he said, his eyes attempting a look of innocence. Then he hung his head and said, "I'm so sorry. Every morning I wake up and regret what I said—I do, I really do! Why I said it, I don't know!"

Tres Pasos frowned. "Well, damn him to hell. I ought to fire you, Tomato! You and your moods!"

Tomato jerked his head up and down, "Me and my moods!"

"All right, then, well, that's too bad, I really liked the kid. Now tell me, Jorge el Gato, I heard you say your name was—come to think of it, I think Edmund spoke about you, if I recall—how can I make it up to him?"

"Up to him?"

"Yeah, I'd like to repair what damage I've done."

"Damage? Uh—well, I think he's fine, he just wants a guitar to play for her."

"Tomato! Go get the guitar."

The assistant leapt from his chair and rushed to get the instrument. He returned holding it by the neck, extending it toward Tres

Pasos. The old man indicated with his head to give it to Jorge el Gato. Jorge took the guitar in his hands, holding it gently, not believing it was going to be this easy. "That's it?"

"That's it. Take it to him. Tell him to sing his heart out to that pretty little girlfriend of his and come back and tell me about it. And tell him he still has about a hundred more stories to listen to!"

*   *   *

When Jorge el Gato told his half brother how he'd obtained the guitar, Edmund was overjoyed to learn that Tres Pasos hadn't made those horrible comments. Whether he wanted to admit it or not, they had shaken his confidence.

"What do you think happened to Ricardo?" Edmund asked.

Jorge el Gato shrugged, "Who knows? It seems like Tres Pasos is good to those he likes, but if he turns against you, watch out."

Edmund returned home in much better spirits. He now had a guitar, which he proudly showed to Filastro, who merely blinked his eyes and said hoarsely, "That's good, mijo."

"Do you want me to play for you?"

"No, no, Edmund, I don't feel much like hearing music right now."

Edmund left the room and practiced in the kitchen. When Hortensia came over and cooked the midday meal, he greeted her coldly and then walked outside to play his guitar. He ignored her when she came to bring him a plate of food. When she left he didn't return her good-bye, pretending to be in the middle of a song.

Edmund heard his father call him from the bedroom. He leaned the guitar against the wall and pulled the curtain aside. "Yes?"

"You saw your mamá this morning?"

Edmund nodded. "How do you know?"

"Hortensia said you were ignoring her. I just assumed. What did your mamá say?"

The next morning Filastro rose from his bed and walked several steps to the window. His knee was in great pain, and he had to drag his leg along, but the rush of blood to his head wasn't as severe. He opened the shutters and looked outside, relieved to feel the fresh air in his nostrils. He walked toward the front room, holding bed corners and dressers for support. He tried putting weight on his right leg; it felt as if someone had taken a hammer to it. He tried again, his forehead perspiring. This time the pain wasn't as bad. He limped along, grabbing hold of the door frame. He moved the curtain aside and stepped out of the bedroom for the first time since arriving home. He called out for his son.

Edmund had been sitting at the kitchen table ever so lightly practicing his chord positions. Hearing his name called louder than usual, not knowing Filastro was merely closer, Edmund set the guitar down and sped around the corner as fast as he could. Wearing only socks, he skidded across the linoleum floor, left, then right, then—crash! right into his delicately balanced father.

Filastro tried grabbing for the door frame but started to fall onto his lame leg, which immediately gave way. He tumbled to the floor, shooting pain throughout his body, mostly his knee. He cried out. Edmund did too. "Papá! Ay!" He remained hunched over Filastro, still holding his father's shirt, which he had grabbed onto in hopes of preventing his fall.

"I'm sorry, Papá, I'm so sorry! What are you doing up?"

Filastro tried to catch his breath, his chest heaving up and down. He turned on his side and grabbed hold of a table, hoisting himself to his left knee, his right leg extended. The pain of the impact subsided somewhat. He raised himself to his feet, all his weight on his left leg, his breathing still labored.

"Papá, are you OK?"

"Yes, I'm fine. I'm fine," Filastro said, shaking his head. "Let me go back and lie down."

Only later, lying in bed, his heart finally calm, did Filastro reflect on the incident. He realized he'd felt no anger, none whatsoever. He fell, got up, that was it. He didn't blame Edmund for running around the house sliding across the floor like a little child, careless as ever. The Filastro of old would have wanted to beat someone, if not for his pain, then for his embarrassment. "I have changed," he said to himself over and over. Then he wondered, "What have I become?"

He had already admitted that he missed Constanza, his children, his compadres; he missed his life as it was before. But he knew for sure that he didn't miss himself. How did I have the energy, he wondered. Just the thought of walking around town exhausted him, let alone going about drinking and carousing. Even hitting Constanza or his children; all that seemed like such an impossible effort. Anger and rage required energy, of which he had so little left. Not even enough to say, "Damn it, Edmund, be more careful!" He could only raise himself from the floor and go back to bed. The realization of this scared him, but fear was relative; he knew that now.

He called to Edmund, who was still in the kitchen playing the guitar. "Come as fast as you can!" he called out, his voice aching from the strain.

Hearing this, Edmund set down the guitar and tiptoed around the corner, afraid of tackling his father once again. He peeked his head into the bedroom. "Yes, Papá?"

"Bring your guitar, mijo. Play for me."

"Are you sure?" Edmund asked, the excitement in his voice palpable.

"Yes! First come here, come close to me. Give me your hand!"

Edmund walked closer and hesitantly extended his hand. Filastro held it affectionately to his bristled cheek. "Mijo, I am lucky to have you."

Edmund stepped back, alarmed, his hand still clutched to Filastro's face. "What happened to you? What's wrong?"

"Nothing is wrong with me. Yes, my knee is gone, and I can barely walk around, my woman has left and so have my children, but something has come over me, Edmund, something great. I can see your confused expression, and I don't expect you to under-stand, but I'm changed! I woke from that coma a different beast— where is my anger, my rage, my desire to drink myself into dark-ness? Oh, if my compadres could hear me now, they wouldn't believe it! But Edmund, believe me!"

Edmund pushed out his bottom lip, stunned.

"I could cry right now," his father continued, "I haven't cried in years!"

"No, please don't cry."

"It's OK, son. A sissy isn't a bad thing. It's what I always tried not to be, that's true, but it is OK to *feel*, do you understand that?"

"No, I don't!" Edmund cried, exasperated, fearing his father had lost his mind.

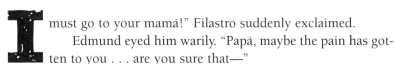
I must go to your mamá!" Filastro suddenly exclaimed.

Edmund eyed him warily. "Papá, maybe the pain has gotten to you . . . are you sure that—"

"I've never been more sure of anything in my life! Come, help me get into this wheelchair—no, I will walk! I can walk slowly, but I want to be standing when I'm there!"

Edmund had to leave the room to gather his thoughts. What had happened to his father? Had he gone crazy? Maybe when he fell he hit his head!

When Edmund walked back into the bedroom, Filastro was lying on the bed with his eyes closed. His hair disheveled, his face sunken and pale, but calm all the same. Hearing Edmund, Filastro opened his eyes. "Maybe," he said quietly, "I should wait. What if this feeling should leave me?"

"That sounds good. Wait and see," Edmund said, relieved they weren't going directly to his tía Lupe's.

"Mijo, try me."

"What do you mean?"

Filastro stared blankly at the ceiling. "Tell me something horrible, something that before would've made me tear apart the room with anger."

"Like what? You always tore the room apart."

"Like—uh—news, maybe, from your brothers?"

Edmund hesitated. "Are you sure? Why do you want to test it?"

"Because then I'll know. All will be as it was before."

"But it can't be as it was before, otherwise Mamá will never come back."

"Just test me. Oh, I know, why did your sisters leave?"
Edmund thought for a second, pursing his lips. He decided to
be safe rather than sorry. "Because they didn't want you beating
them anymore . . . I think."
"What do you mean, you think? Is that the reason? If it is, then
it's as it should be. See, Edmund, I'm fine—"
Edmund exhaled. He pushed further. "And Agnes is pregnant."
Filastro turned to his son, his eyes wide. "You mean I'll be a
grandfather!"
Edmund nodded his head warily, "And—"
"Who is the father?"
"I don't know . . ." Now Edmund was as curious as Filastro.
How far would his tolerance go? "Uh, I mean, she doesn't know,
either . . ." He watched his father's face for any change in expres-
sion. It remained calm. Edmund pushed further. "It could be any
number of guys . . ."
Filastro sighed, "My grandson will be a bastard like me."
"Uh, sure," Edmund said, exhaling deeply. "He has changed
completely," he marveled to himself.

The following day Filastro woke determined to visit Constanza.
He had Hortensia help him into the shower and then dress him, all
the while telling her that he needed to show his wife he'd changed,
and only then would his conscience begin to clear. "It will be a
long road, I have no doubts about that," he said, more animated
than she had ever seen him, "but it must begin!" She was quiet,
her face strained.
When Filastro was shaved, dressed, his hair combed, and his
teeth brushed, he looked like the new man he was professing to be.
"You look different, Papá," Edmund said, as he stared at his
father's reflection in the mirror.
Filastro turned around, his brow lifted. "In a good way?"
"Yeah, good."
Hortensia declined to accompany them even though Filastro
pleaded with her to come. "Don't you see, she needs to know that

you're not a woman of ill repute, that you're part of my life, a dear friend—"

"But Filastro, I *am* a woman of ill repute."

"In one form, yes, but you're part of our family now."

"No, I'm not. I'm here only because I care for you. I don't expect anything in return. Now, don't be silly, if I go, your wife won't be able to see beyond me. That's how women are, I know."

Filastro accepted this. He kissed her on the cheek and sat down in his wheelchair. He'd decided not to walk, the adrenaline of the previous day having waned. Edmund struggled at first, pushing the wheelchair over the cobbled streets, but once moving, the road was smoother. They were silent almost the entire distance to his tía Lupe's house. It wasn't until a block away that Filastro asked, "Is this a good idea, mijo?"

"I don't know, Papá."

"I'm nervous."

"So am I."

When they arrived, Edmund knocked and returned to his position behind the wheelchair.

His tía Lupe opened the door, and upon seeing Filastro's face, immediately closed it. Edmund knocked again. This time Jorge el Gato came to the door, and without opening the metal screen said, "Edmund, you should not have brought him here."

"He wants to apologize."

"To who?" Jorge asked. "Me? My mother? Or yours?"

"Just mine," Edmund said.

Jorge el Gato snorted. "Go away," he said, and shut the door.

The next day they went again, this time not so sharply dressed, as Hortensia hadn't shown up and wouldn't show again. They received the same response. They went every day for the next two weeks. After the first couple of attempts, Jorge el Gato stopped answering the door; the front window curtain would move, but nothing more. Edmund was discouraged, but Filastro was unfazed.

"No, mijo, it should be this way. She will come eventually."

Meantime, Edmund continued practicing his guitar, Ingrid Genera's looming departure never far from his mind. They saw each other every day, or rather Edmund saw Ingrid every day. He patiently sat on the curb across from her house and waited until she left with her mother on errands. He followed them to the stores and made no pretense of hiding.

Ingrid's mother, Doña Celeste, paid him no mind. In fact, now that they were leaving, she had no problems with Filastro Agustín's son. "Oh, look at him following you. His heart must be aching so, knowing you are leaving!" And Ingrid would turn back and find Edmund staring at her with the saddest eyes she could ever have imagined. Sad enough that one time she began to cry herself. Her mother, mistaking it for Ingrid's reluctance to leave, scolded her, "Mija, this is going to be a great change for you. You'll meet new friends and have so many more opportunities than here . . ." But Edmund saw the tears and felt at once exhilarated and miserable. He returned to practice his song. He would sing it and she would stay, he was sure; he couldn't imagine otherwise.

Filastro encouraged him, saying once, lifting his head from the pillow. "My God, mijo, when did you get so good?"

* * *

Ingrid and Doña Celeste were supposed to leave at 8:00 Saturday morning. Edmund thought this was too early for a romantic song, so he decided the serenade must take place the preceding night.

But just to make sure, he visited his tía Lupe's house to ask Jorge el Gato's opinion.

The curtain moved aside, but this time the door opened shortly afterward. "You came alone," Jorge said.

"Yes, I need your advice. Can we let the other thing rest?"

"OK."

"What I feared is happening today, or actually, early tomorrow morning, too early for a song, so should I do it tonight?" It was too painful to name specifics.

Fortunately, Jorge el Gato knew what Edmund was talking about. "Sure, that sounds better," he said. "The night is more romantic. What time are you going?"

"Ten. I don't want to go too late because then she might not wake up."

Reassured with a second opinion, Edmund turned to leave. Jorge called after him, "Brother-cousin, do you want me to come . . . for support?"

Edmund shook his head. "No, I have to do this by myself."

"OK, good luck." Jorge el Gato paused, then said, "Edmund, no matter what happens, you're ten times the Don Juan I am, I mean it."

"Really?"

"Really."

*   *   *

At 9:45 Edmund entered the bedroom to tell Filastro he was leaving for a little while. His father was asleep. He grabbed his guitar and quietly shut the door behind him. He walked toward Ingrid's house, his heart pounding. He strummed the guitar lightly, hoping to calm his nerves. People were sitting outside their homes visiting with neighbors, young men were listening to music on truck stereos, children were playing in the streets. Edmund suddenly realized he would most likely have an audience. "Why did they have to leave on a weekend?" he muttered to himself. "I should come back later!" But he pressed forward, unable to turn back, fearing he wouldn't be able to make himself return.

He arrived at Ingrid's house and saw the lights on, plenty of chatter and movement inside. Apparently they had visitors. More people arrived and Edmund heard shouts of "Comadre, you've come to say goodbye!" or "We'll miss you!" He decided to sit on the curb across the street, a location in which he had grown comfortable. He waited, his fingers tapping the base of the guitar.

Half an hour later, Edmund heard someone call his name. He looked up to see Ricardo the Former Notary.

"What are you doing sitting here?"

Edmund nodded his head in the direction of Ingrid's house. "She's leaving tomorrow."

Ricardo's face gravened in an exaggerated manner. "Leaving?"

"Yeah, for good."

Ricardo sat down next to Edmund, a little too close for comfort. Edmund scooted over. He could smell alcohol.

"You stopped going to Tres Pasos?" Ricardo asked.

"Yeah, once you came it stopped begin fun," Edmund said coldly.

Ricardo nodded his head, the grave expression not having left his face. "Yes, and now I'm gone, too. They sure worked me over— took my book, ripped it to shreds. I have it all in my head, but I'm too depressed right now to write."

"Why'd they do that?"

"Ah, because, I wasn't writing it how the old fart wanted me to."

"How were you writing it?"

"I was making it more interesting, more literary, you see, and of course a man like Tres Pasos, and *especially* someone like Tomato, wouldn't understand that. I tried varying the perspectives. Sometimes I told the story from the victim's point of view, other times from a child's, a whore's, or his various love interests. One chapter I even told it in the voice of Tres Pasos's long-dead mother. One device I used, of which I'm rather proud, was a cactus to narrate a few poetic passages. *But* he couldn't see the validity of it, and frankly, I refuse to compromise my artistic integrity for the sake of a thug like that—"

Edmund cut him off. "Ricardo, that's all very interesting, but I'm really nervous, and with you being here talking, I can't concentrate and it's making me real shaky. Look at my hands—" He lifted his left hand and made it shake.

Ricardo nodded his head and pulled a flask from his breast pocket. "Yes, I'm sorry. I'll leave now. No one wants me around, not even you, my good friend Edmund. My father the other day told me, 'Son, you are what I would call worthless.' Well, now it's your turn to spurn me!"

Edmund waited for him to stand up, but Ricardo remained sitting as if expecting Edmund to recant and tell him to stay. An awkward silence ensued, broken only when a mariachi group came around the corner tuning their instruments. Rafa was at the head, a cocksure look on his face.

They stood in front of the house and Rafa said, "Ready!" The mariachi group commenced playing, the trumpeters moving a distance away so as not to overpower the guitars and vocals. One trumpeter moved right next to Edmund, drowning out the other musicians. When the horns quieted, though, Edmund could hear Rafa's voice. Much to his dismay, his adversary sang more than competently.

Shocked by the sudden arrival, Edmund didn't realize his grand effort had been thwarted. It was Ricardo who brought it to his attention. "Man, he stole your idea! What a son of a bitch! What are you going to do?"

Edmund stared dumbly ahead. "I don't know."

When the song ended, everyone inside the house clapped loudly and Edmund heard cries of, "Oh, how romantic! I wish I was in love like that again!" "What a keeper!" "Come in, son, and bring the mariachis with you!" Rafa and the mariachi group entered the house singing, "*I hope that you go beautifully, I hope that your worries end . . .*"

Edmund hung his head, not knowing what to do. He stared at Ingrid's window in a daze, the mariachi music sounding as if it were coming from a car radio blocks away. He left Ricardo's side, holding the guitar under his arm, wanting to just set it by the side of the road and never look at it again. Ricardo called after him, "Where are you going?"

"Home!" he cried, still walking away.

"But Edmund, wait—wait! You can't give up that easy!"

"Why not?" he said, stopping but not turning around. "How can I compare with an entire mariachi group?"

"You can! I'm sure of it; I've heard you play. Anybody can hire a mariachi group. What's special about that? But you, Edmund, you've been practicing for her! Come back! You can't give up! You have tenacity, remember!"

Edmund shook his head and mumbled, "No, not anymore, I'm too tired. Nothing matters anymore." He walked away, his eyes staring at the moonlit cobblestones. He didn't look up until he reached home.

When he walked in the door, Filastro called out his name. Edmund entered the bedroom and found his father sitting up in bed, sipping tea.

"Look," he said, a proud expression on his face, "I limped to the kitchen and did it all myself. Where did you go, mijo?"

With that Edmund began to cry.

"What's happened?"

Edmund told him about going to play for Ingrid, the good-bye gathering, and Rafa's accursed mariachi ensemble.

Filastro's response was unequivocal. "You must go back!"

"I can't! She'll leave and I'll never see her again. I can't do it and plus, what's the use?"

"Of course you can do it. You've gotten this good—all that practicing—for her! Well, you must see this to its end or else you'll regret it. Trust me, you don't want to find yourself like me, alone in a little bed, your mamá refusing to see me. I had my chances, too many to count, and I let them all pass me by. What I would do to get your mamá back, but I've done too little too late. I would do anything, anything at all, but it seems there's nothing."

Edmund's head shot up. "You'd do anything?"

"Anything."

"Well, Mamá did say that she'd take you back if—"

"If what? Tell me!" Filastro almost spilled his tea. He set it down on the bedside table.

"If you went to the United States and begged all of my brothers and sisters their forgiveness and showed them that you were a changed man."

"She said that?"

"Yes, I swear it. She said only then would she take you back."

"But I'm in no state to go."

"That's why I didn't tell you. I didn't want you to be discouraged." Another idea suddenly struck Edmund, one that gave him heart. "Maybe not now, but what about later? And I can go too. We'll go together and then I can see Ingrid again. Yes! That's it! Even if she leaves, I can follow her, right? Right? Promise me that we'll go. And I'll be with Ingrid and you'll go ask my brothers and sisters for forgiveness!"

"Oh, I don't know. That seems impossible! That's why she said it. She knew I couldn't ever do it! I've never left Jalisco, let alone gone all the way to the United States, and in my condition—I'll never walk the same again!"

"But you said you'd do anything," Edmund implored.

"I did, I did, but sometimes anything is too much. I just wanted to inspire you, mijo, to go back and sing your song for that girl. You've practiced and you sound good. You've always been my little guitarrista!"

"But what about going to the United States?"

"Not now, not now, maybe with time. But now you must go play."

"Promise me you'll go!"

"Maybe—"

"No, promise me—"

Filastro sighed, seeing the excitement in Edmund's face. "OK, OK, yes, I promise . . . we'll try. Now go!"

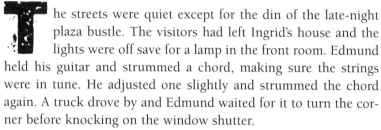

The streets were quiet except for the din of the late-night plaza bustle. The visitors had left Ingrid's house and the lights were off save for a lamp in the front room. Edmund held his guitar and strummed a chord, making sure the strings were in tune. He adjusted one slightly and strummed the chord again. A truck drove by and Edmund waited for it to turn the corner before knocking on the window shutter.

He stepped backward, his breath quickening. He stretched his fingers, attempting to loosen up. He closed his eyes and began plucking the song's introduction.

He heard the windows creak open, then the shutters swing out, but he didn't open his eyes. He began to sing:

Today begins my sadness
You are still going
Packed in your bags is my happiness
You still want to go
How I loved you, no one will love you like I do

He heard a door open, but to his right. Ingrid's was to his left. He heard a woman say quietly, "He sounds just like Chalino Sánchez." He shut his eyes tighter, fighting the urge to open them.

I'll be little more than nothing without you
I will be like the sun shut off
My light and my heat go at your side
If you leave and forget me, I know it well that . . .

Edmund now heard window shutters squeak open behind him. He continued strumming the guitar, but his mind had suddenly gone blank. For the life of him, he couldn't remember the words. He felt his fingers slip off the fret; he tried tightening his grip. A man's voice called out, "Keep going, sounds good!" He wanted to turn around; he felt as if the whole neighborhood had opened its doors. He continued playing, his eyes shut, imagining Ingrid's face before him. He sang the first verse again—he knew that repeated itself somewhere—then he began making up his own lyrics.

That day behind the church
You said I didn't love you
But I did then and I still do
More than ever.

What will I do without you?
Only you give my life purpose

Now the lyrics stopped corresponding to the music; he didn't care, he wanted to tell her everything.

Ingrid, how everyone admires your beauty
But me, I admire your bowlegs even though I call you bowlegs
sometimes as if it were a bad thing
And how one time you called me a troll
And it felt like I would die, but that's OK because then you said I
played the guitar good
And I was filled with joy just like the day you came and visited me
In the hospital where I was all alone
Every song I play for you, every chord and note
Carries your name

Someone called out, "Sing the real lyrics, idiot!" This made him open his eyes. He turned around, his brow furrowed, his fingers plucking the chorus notes as if programmed. A woman cried, "Let him sing it how he wants to! It's a serenade, can't you see?"

Now that his eyes were open, Edmund felt the courage to face Ingrid's window. He slowly turned and saw her flowery pink nightgown pulled tightly around her large stomach . . . her round breasts . . . his eyes continued upward until he saw Doña Celeste pressed against the window frame, eyeing him with a look of disapproval. Ingrid was nowhere in sight.

"Ah, I should've at least waited for her to appear," he thought to himself, a feeling of dread in his chest. He stopped strumming the guitar. He heard clapping behind him and someone called out, "He's the next Benni Terraza! I bet you! Tell me he's not!"

He waited for Doña Celeste to speak. She reached for the shutters, paused before closing them, and said, "That was nice, little boy, it really was. I never would've guessed. But she's asleep. Now go away! We have to leave early tomorrow!"

Edmund loosened his grip on the guitar. He looked down at the ground, unsure of what to do. He could start singing again, he thought, this time louder, hoping to wake her. But the sound of the fastened shutters disheartened him. "How could this be it?" he asked himself. "She didn't even hear me."

He turned away, looking down the street in the direction of his home. It seemed a thousand miles away. He realized he would never come to her door again, he would never see her face; she'd be gone from his life. How was it possible to love her so, merely for this, walking home alone, a song played but not heard by the only one who mattered? He wanted to cry, but his shock was too strong. "She'll never be mine," he said over and over in his head, "She'll never know how much I loved her, how—"

"Edmund!" he heard. He thought he'd imagined it and continued walking. "Edmund!" he heard again. He stopped, but didn't turn, still not trusting his ears.

"Ingrid, get back in here and get to sleep!" he heard Doña Celeste cry out. The door slammed and Edmund spun around. Ingrid was running toward him, her bare feet slapping delicately against the cobbled street. She wore a thin nightgown, and apparently had had time to grab a jacket. It must've been one of her father's because it was three times her size. Her cheeks were flushed and she was breathing heavily. A few steps away from him she came to a stop.

"I heard you," she said, "I heard you and it was beautiful. It was so beautiful, Edmund, thank you, thank you. No one will ever play like that for me again, no one could play so beautifully."

Her mother was standing at the door, crying out, "Get in here, girl! Now!"

Ingrid pushed up the long jacket sleeve, revealing a note in her hand. "Here," she said, handing it to Edmund. "Take it. It's my address in the United States. Write to me, OK?"

"Ingrid, mija, get over here before I drag you inside," her mother called out, her voice shrill and livid.

Ingrid turned around and waved to her mother. "OK," she said meekly. She turned back to Edmund and looked him in the eyes. "Edmund," she whispered. "I'll miss you so much." She leaned forward and kissed his cheek, close enough to his mouth that he felt her lips graze his as she backed away.

With that she turned and ran toward her house, only her head and skinny legs sticking out of the large jacket. Doña Celeste stood in the doorway ready to scold her daughter. Edmund remained unmoving, clenching the note in his right hand.

He watched her until she arrived at her door. He waited for Ingrid Genera to turn one last time, but she didn't.

THE SCOUNDREL AND THE OPTIMIST

PART

197

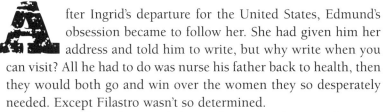

fter Ingrid's departure for the United States, Edmund's obsession became to follow her. She had given him her address and told him to write, but why write when you can visit? All he had to do was nurse his father back to health, then they would both go and win over the women they so desperately needed. Except Filastro wasn't so determined.

"Mijo, with my knee and all, maybe it's not the best idea."

"But Papá, you said! You said you'd do anything to win back Mamá."

"I did say that, and I meant it, it's just I'm no longer so young. Crossing the border is for adventurous youths, their whole lives ahead of them."

"You promised."

"I know I did, but that was to get you to serenade that girl so you wouldn't have regrets."

"And I did, and now I'll regret not going to California just as you will regret not going, too. Are you changed like you say? Shouldn't Abel, Ezekiel, Tomy, Gandolfo, Agnes, and Alfonsa see that you have?"

"Of course I'm changed. And I do want your brothers and sisters to forgive me, but maybe your mamá will come around, realize she's asked the impossible. Let's try to visit her."

So they walked to Tía Lupe's house, Filastro limping badly, almost hopping, holding onto Edmund's shoulder for support. They both knocked on the door and stepped back to wait for the answer that never came. "Five knocks," they said to one another, "and then we'll go home." But the only response was the curtain moved aside and Jorge el Gato or Tía Lupe calling out, "It's them again!"

"What if I called your brothers and sisters?" Filastro asked Edmund while walking home. "Would that be enough? Do you think they could hear it in my voice?"

Edmund considered this a worthy try. He traveled alone to his aunt's house, where his mother received him with open arms. "Oh, my little Edmund, look, I think you might be growing—is that a mustache I see? When will you come and stay with your mamacita?" He resisted all temptation. "Constanza, I'd like to call Abel. Talk to him about some stuff. Can I have his number?"

"Edmund, call me *Mamá*, and don't lie to me. I know your father put you up to this. He thinks that if he bullies them into forgiving him, he'll get me back, but I won't buy it. Plus, I don't have your brothers' numbers. They only call me."

It was now up to Edmund to cook three meals a day, clean the house, help his father dress and undress, do the shopping, pay the rent and bills—all, of course, financed by Constanza, who gave him a portion of the money his brothers and sisters sent monthly. He often thought of going to Hortensia and asking her to return, but Filastro always dissuaded him. "No, mijo, it's not right. We shouldn't take advantage of her. Your cooking is getting better."

Every day Filastro and Edmund exercised, first traveling to Constanza, and then upon being rejected, walking around town. Filastro did so with difficulty. His leg had healed crooked, the knee not corresponding with the thigh, forcing him to walk in an exaggerated manner, as if he were constantly going to topple over. Many a time Edmund reached out to prevent Filastro's fall, only for his father to wave him off, saying, "I'm fine, I'm fine, it's just how I walk!" Filastro's forehead was always sweaty, his face in a fixed grimace, primarily from the pain, but from the embarrassment, too. "Let them stare, don't pay them any mind," he told Edmund more than once. And stare folks did, and smirk, and mock, and several times, bereaved relatives of his three compadres said things like "Should have been you! You were the worst of them!" Edmund was ready to charge, but Filastro would place his hand on his son's shoulder and calm him. "It's OK, it's OK."

The Filastro of old was gone. Edmund could not deny it, but he was the only one who knew.

One morning, as Filastro and Edmund walked around the plaza, Jorge el Gato watched the hapless pair as he sat on a bench taking a break from his popsicle route. He saw Filastro's exaggerated limp and was reminded of his own hobbling trials. When he was younger, he and his mother would visit a healer and the old man or woman would brutalize his foot, leaving it in worse shape than before. For days afterward he would walk as if about to fall over. People had two reactions: they either laughed or pretended not to notice. Filastro's gait elicited the same two responses. He almost felt sorry for his father, but stopped when he saw Filastro dig in his pocket for some change and give it to Hipólito the Beggar with a nod of his head.

"What an unbelievable crock of shit!" Jorge el Gato said to himself, looking around to see if anyone else had seen this ludicrous display. "He's a phony if I ever saw one." And he was not alone: everyone thought the same upon witnessing the new Filastro Agustín—his strained, perspiring face nodding hello in response to their glares. No one believed that a man could change, let alone such a drunken brute. Regardless of what he'd been through—to hell and back, even—would he be capable of such a conversion? But that's exactly where he'd been . . . he woke up in the middle of the night remembering his compadres' cries for help, the woman's face, the wicked children, his interminable imprisonment. Not even Edmund could bring him to talk about what had happened during those three weeks.

Edmund couldn't help but wonder, though. It was Tres Pasos who was finally able to shed some light on the situation.

H e had gone back to the old loan shark soon after Ingrid's departure. He needed distraction and Tres Pasos had plenty of that, wasting no time in the resumption of his stories. One day, however, Edmund asked Tres Pasos if he wouldn't mind listening to a story of his own.

"What? But you're just a kid, you must wait before you start imparting wisdom!"

"Yes, I know, I don't have any wisdom attached to this story. It's not even really a story, it's something that's been happening . . . recently . . . last night, for instance. And I was wondering if you could help me find the lesson."

Tres Pasos frowned, thought for a moment, then agreed.

So Edmund began telling Tres Pasos about his father's former ways, how he beat his wife and children and quite a few others, except him on account of his size. He was a drunk, an unfaithful husband, a gambler, a frequenter of places of ill repute, and an abusive father in every respect—

"Sounds like we'd have gotten along in my younger days!" Tres Pasos chipped in.

Edmund agreed and proceeded to explain that his father was one of the men who disappeared with Captain Esteban in Retorno, and that he was the only survivor, but barely. He returned comatose, his leg crooked. When he woke, however, he was a different man. He missed his children, his wife, but they had deserted him—

"Except you?"

"Yes, except me."

His father had changed, Edmund truly believed it, and even though no one could accept it, knowing his temperament before, all one had to do was spend five minutes with him and the difference was evident. "The thing is . . ." Edmund paused, "I don't know if this is a good thing."

"Why do you say that?" Tres Pasos inquired. "Surely he must be easier to deal with."

"Because every night he has nightmares, waking ones, I think, because he sits up in bed. I hear and wake up, too. I ask him if he's all right. He always says, 'Mijo, I'm not an innocent man,' and I tell him, 'I know that, you are definitely not,' and he asks, 'Do you hate me?' and I tell him no, of course not. But then he asks 'Does Abel hate me?' and I tell him, 'I think so.' He goes down the line, Ezekiel, Tomy, Gandolfo, my sisters, asking the same question, 'Do they hate me?' And I'm pretty sure they all do. He asks finally, 'But why?' And I've given him various reasons, but mostly I just say, 'Because they were afraid of you.' His only response is, 'Do I deserve to die?' and I don't know what to tell him. The first time I said, 'No, you don't,' and he said, 'Yes, I do!' So the next time I told him, 'Yes, you do,' and he screamed, 'No, I don't!' So then I just said, 'Maybe you do, maybe you don't,' and he screamed, 'But I am afraid, I am afraid, I am afraid!' And I asked him, 'Of what?' And he said, 'Myself, can't you understand that? Myself!' But I don't understand so I tell him, 'No, I don't know what you mean, but maybe if you explain it . . .' He falls back to sleep after that."

Tres Pasos leaned back in his chair and crossed his feeble arms. He stared off into space, his lips moving, muttering to himself. Edmund thought he saw tears in the old man's eyes, but then he dismissed this idea because Tres Pasos must know thousands of stories like this—bad men turned good, only to then suffer nightmares.

"So you think it's a bad thing," Tres Pasos began slowly, his voice raspy, "because your father now lives in constant fear of death?"

"No, he said of *himself.*"

"Of himself, of death; it's the same thing. Why would we care about anything, let alone ourselves, if death—our own, others'—wasn't looming around the corner, waiting? Man is born ingrained with the fear of his end; it's why we have instincts solely for our preservation. But man doesn't merely survive, he lives: he loves, he desires, and once he knows loss he never forgets it. Everyone lives in fear, but most learn to cope. They put off the awful reality until old age, when they must accept their own transience. But sometimes death smacks you in the face and no matter how hard you try to forget, to cope, it lingers, staring at you from every dark corner, telling you, 'Your end will come. Not now, but it will come.' And the idea of the end, one's complete and utter expiration, is always too soon. Your father understands this now. Whatever happened, death became a reality. As it once became for me . . ." He stopped and breathed deeply.

"Let me tell you something, Edmund. I was going to save this story for another time, tell you in all its detail, but you might as well hear it now. Baltazar, my youngest son, died not that long ago, ten years, maybe. He alone I thought would escape death's grasp on my offspring. But it took him, too, and it was his parting that finally woke me to my grim existence. He was in the passenger seat, the two of us returning from an errand in the neighboring town, when I drove off the road, overcompensated the wheel and flipped the car. My son was killed on impact. I will never forget what his dead body felt like in my hands. I know the pain your father goes through, Edmund—tortured by death—why didn't it take me? How I've suffered. But in the end, I emerged a different man . . . I lost the energy, the will, to do harm. I'm not all good, but nor am I all bad, as perhaps I once was. Now my loan sharking exists on my reputation from long ago—you think Tomato inspires fear? No, the man I was does . . ." Tres Pasos paused for a moment, again staring off into space. Edmund waited. "Your father will be fine," the old man continued. "The nightmares will pass, maybe even a touch of his past self will return, maybe it will return tenfold—in which case he will be denying death despite his better judgment— but all you can do is hope."

"Hope for what?"

"That more good comes of it than bad."

"How will I know?"

"Time will tell."

Several nights later Filastro woke up screaming. Edmund turned on the lights and found Filastro sprawled on the floor, his screams quieting into sobs. Edmund rushed to his side. "Come here, Papá, it's all right, let's get to bed, no use fearing death at this time of the night."

"No, leave me, leave me be. I can stand on my own!" Filastro cried out, waving his son off. He tried to repress his cries, but made only choked blubbering noises. He rose from the floor hopping on his good leg, grabbing the bed frame for support. He sat on the edge of the mattress and wiped his eyes. He began rubbing his face vigorously and then stopped, leaving his hands over his nose and eyes.

After a while he said, "Get your guitar, mijo, play something for me."

Edmund hurried into the next room, grabbed his guitar, and began lightly strumming a song that Tres Pasos had recently taught him, a mellifluous tune about lilacs in a meadow and lovers who come to pick them, which ends suggesting the lovers were ghosts who'd killed one another in a jealous rage. He merely strummed the chords, however, leaving the lyrics to the imagination.

"Ah!" Filastro cried out, his hands still pressed to his face, "What's become of me?"

Edmund stopped playing and thought of imparting his and Tres Pasos's discussion regarding death, but Filastro continued before he had a chance. He spoke quickly, his words desperate. "Edmund, we must go to the United States. I have to see my sons and daughters again; they must see me. We will go to Wyoming and Nebraska and Texas and wherever else they are and I'll show them I've changed, that I'm not the man they knew. I'll beg their forgiveness, and if they're willing, bring them to their mother. Whether she accepts me back or not, I must do this. We will go as soon as I am able!"

Filastro's words made Edmund's heart pound. Ingrid Genera's face flashed through his mind. He saw her tearful eyes; he felt her lips as they grazed his cheek. He imagined their reunion and thought of nothing else until he'd fallen back to sleep.

First there was the question of money. Traveling to the United States cost a significant amount. Edmund suggested asking his mother for his siblings' remittances, but Filastro wouldn't hear of it. "It would take away from the point."

"How?"

"I must do this on my own. To show her I've changed. I'm not a moocher."

"What's a moocher?"

"Someone who uses other people's money with no intention of paying it back."

Edmund considered this. "But then we're moochers."

"How's that?"

"Mamá gives us money for rent, food, bills, and stuff. From the money my brothers send."

"Oh . . . yes . . . but we have to live, and you're her son, after all."

"That's what she says. She said if it was just you, she wouldn't—" Edmund caught himself. "Ah, never mind."

He then suggested asking Tres Pasos for the money. "He's the one who helped all my brothers and sisters leave; he loans money. Remember how you used to want to find out who helped them? Well, he's the one. But you wouldn't have been able to do much. He's just a little old man."

"I've heard of him," Filastro responded. "Talk about a feared person! If I'd known, I would've swallowed my pride and let well enough alone."

"But he's changed. He's nice now, at least to me. It's his assistant who's an asshole."

"How do you know so much about him?"

Edmund explained his dealings with the loan shark, even admitting that some of the stories he'd told him at the infirmary weren't from television but were in fact Tres Pasos's. It was an irrelevant point, as Filastro had no recollection of any of Edmund's stories.

"So you could ask him for money?" Filastro asked.

"That wouldn't be mooching?"

"No, because a man like that you must pay back, and on time, or else."

Edmund considered this for a few moments. "How will we earn enough to return the money?"

Filastro looked up at his son, lost in thought. "One step at a time," he said. "We'll figure it out when we get there, like everyone else."

Edmund informed his mother that they were planning to go to the United States. Constanza shook her head slowly, disbelieving. "My son, don't . . . I can hear your papá talking through you. He put you up to this, am I right? Ay,"—she sighed—"he will stop at nothing." She turned to her sister, "Can you believe this?"

Tía Lupe scoffed and shook her head, "I believe it. He'll talk a good line, my sister; don't buy it."

"It doesn't matter," Edmund said a little perturbed at his aunt's involvement. "We're going. I told him what you said about taking him back only if he went to Nebraska, Wyoming, and Texas and begged each of my brothers and sisters for forgiveness. Well, we're not only going to do that, but we're going to bring them home . . . so that you won't be alone anymore."

"Alone?" she rejoined, almost exasperated, "I'm not alone. I have my sister, my nephew, and I could have you too if you came and lived here with us! Please, Edmund, come and stay here instead of entertaining your father's wild ideas." She turned to her sister again, her brow raised.

Tía Lupe scoffed and shook her head just as she had before.

Edmund frowned, preferring the sisters when their only communication was relaying messages through him. "Like I said, you don't have to believe me. We're going, we'll bring everyone home, and we'll start over as a family."

Tía Lupe chuckled. "What about the whore who's been taking care of you? Is she part of this family?"

"For your information, her name is Hortensia, and she's no longer helping us because she didn't want people talking bad about my papá. Other than me, she's the only one who knows that he's changed. But she must have known it before because she loved him enough to come every day to the infirmary, and she cried all the time, too. Maybe he was right to serenade her. She's been a better wife than you have, Amá."

Constanza's face tightened and grew stern. "Edmund, I don't need to tell you what kind of wife I've been." She spoke, her mouth barely opening. "Now get this crazy idea out of your mind. Let him go alone on this fool's errand. I'm telling you I will never again belong to him."

"But you said—"

"Yes, I did say it, but only because I knew it wouldn't ever happen."

"We're going to go."

"Then let your papá go alone, mijo, you are too—" she stopped and placed the back of her hand on her forehead.

"Too what? Too small, is that it?"

She shook her head. "No, that's not it at all."

After visiting his mother, Edmund traveled to Tres Pasos's and found Tomato alone in the front room watching television. The assistant heard him enter and scowled. "Leave! Now!" Tres Pasos had said that ignoring Tomato was the best way to handle his moods, so Edmund entered the seating area and arranged himself on a plastic lawn chair.

"Where's Tres Pasos?"

"Asleep. Now shut up. I'm trying to watch my show!"

"But he never sleeps in the afternoons."

"He's not feeling well, now shh!"

Edmund was quiet for a few minutes, watching Tomato intently. When a commercial came on, he said, "Don't get upset, but can I ask you something very personal?"

The assistant turned slowly in his chair until his entire body faced Edmund, as if readying himself to pounce in anger. Edmund noticed this and said, "Never mind."

"No, ask!" Tomato demanded.

So he asked: "Did you get made fun of a lot when you were little?"

Tomato's face colored, his look of contempt turning into one of surprise. "What makes you say that?"

"Because sometimes when people make fun of me on account I'm so small or because I have red hair I get so angry that I want to hate all the world . . . and I just thought maybe you felt the same way."

Tomato squinted his eyes, but his body relaxed noticeably. "No, I didn't get made fun of," he said in a gentle whisper. "But . . . if you want to know the truth, I—"

"Tomato!" Tres Pasos called from the back room. "Is that Edmund I hear? I thought I told you to wake me up! I promised him my best story."

Tomato hung his head and sighed deeply. "I was just going to say," he said through clenched teeth, "that growing up, no one ever listened to me unless I made them." He rose from the recliner and disappeared into the back of the house. He emerged pushing Tres Pasos in the wheelchair, helped the old man into the recliner, and returned to his customary seat, where he stared gloomily into space.

I should have told my best stories earlier," Tres Pasos told Edmund, "because I have to be honest with you; I'm tiring. Don't have the same enthusiasm as I did before. I guess old age does that to you. And now here I am at my last one, and I feel like skipping it. I won't, because it's important, probably the most important, but I'll make it short."

Edmund was relieved. Even with several weeks' respite, he was tiring of Tres Pasos's stories as well. He thought to suggest for future reference cutting the stories down to two hundred, a hundred even. Many of them were interesting to hear, but sometimes you have to remove a few for the listener's sake, and apparently, the teller's too. Especially when, as in Edmund's case, more pressing matters were at hand.

"When you're done can I ask a favor?" Edmund asked, hoping the favor would come first, so he could get it off his chest.

"That sounds reasonable, but after. Now, here goes, the last and the best—"

The best story in Tres Pasos's collection answered what Edmund had wondered ever since first hearing the loan shark's name: why was he called Tres Pasos? Edmund had meant to ask him the day of his sisters' departure, but after his altercation with Tomato, Tres Pasos's intervention, and their subsequent deal, it slipped his mind. From then on, whenever he remembered to ask, Tres Pasos would invariably be in the middle of a story, and he knew the old man didn't like interruptions. When the story was finished, Edmund's thoughts would be elsewhere. Once during a rare early morning guitar session, while Tres Pasos was in the bathroom, he used the opportunity to ask Tomato about his boss's nickname, but Tomato was in such an exuberant mood that he discussed his own nickname, his brothers' and sisters' nicknames, his neighbors', his favorite nicknames of all time—in short, everybody's nickname except Tres Pasos's. After a while Edmund abandoned his inquiry, and for the most part stopped thinking about it altogether.

But now Edmund was thrilled to hear he would finally learn the nickname's true source.

"Well," began Tres Pasos, "this I leave for last because it's what's on everyone's mind and yet they never ask. And if they did I wouldn't tell them. But you've listened to my life's stories, so I think it's appropriate you hear the truth behind my nickname. What do you think about that?"

"Sounds good!" Edmund exclaimed, trying not to let the favor he needed to ask interfere with his enjoyment of this sure to be staggering story.

Tres Pasos even asked Tomato to leave the room and close the door behind him. Tomato complied, but showed his disappointment by slamming the door. "Even he doesn't know," Tres Pasos said. "You're going to be the first person in thirty-five years to know the truth. OK, my real name is Baltazar, same as my father and my now dead son. I got my nickname because when I was learning to walk I would get up, walk three steps, and then fall. I'd get up, sure as I could, then walk three more only to fall again and again and again! So my papá called out, 'Look at little Three Steps!' Suffice to say, the name stuck."

Edmund waited for more.

Tres Pasos began to chuckle. "You thought it'd be better, huh? You thought being number one it would blow you away. Nope! Simple little story, but within that simple little story is my most important lesson—" he looked from side to side, then leaned closer—"the one lesson of all five hundred that you mustn't forget . . . you listening?"

Edmund nodded dumbly, still in shock that that was the extent of the story.

"No matter how many times you fall down you have to get up again."

They were both silent. Edmund was sure he'd heard the lesson before and not from Tres Pasos. His face must've shown his disappointment because Tres Pasos began laughing again. "Hah! What a trite lesson for my apex, don't you think? No, seriously, there's a lesson to be learned. All my life, a whole lot of events, details, surface stuff, and a bunch of wisdom, too, but you know what? Chuck it all! And don't you pay attention to anyone who claims differently, you understand?"

Edmund's mouth hung open slightly. He nodded his head to show he was digesting this final wisdom. He thought to himself that never again would he agree to listen to 500 stories. When a suitable amount of time had passed, Edmund asked what had been on his mind since arriving that afternoon.

"Can my papá and I borrow some money to go to the United States so that I can see Ingrid, and he can beg my brothers' and sisters' forgiveness, and maybe bring them home so that my mamá accepts him back into her heart?"

Without hesitating, Tres Pasos said, "I give money to men who just want to buy pointy-toed alligator-skinned boots. Of course, I'll lend you whatever you need. Just one thing."

"What's that?"

"Come back before I die. You're the only friend I got."

Four more months passed before Filastro felt well enough to consider leaving for the United States. He and Edmund continued their daily walks, but they had ceased going to Tía Lupe's. Not because of discouragement; on the contrary: they had decided upon their assignment and now only needed to wait. Filastro grew healthier, putting back some of the weight he'd lost so drastically. His limp improved, but there was no concealing his crooked leg and awkward lean, his head moving up and down, up and down.

Edmund never stopped thinking of Ingrid Genera. He replayed the events of their relationship over and over, especially the last good-bye. He kept her address in the top drawer underneath his pajamas and T-shirts. He removed it periodically and carefully unfolded the page, examining Ingrid's handwriting and the address "560 Willow Creek Road #3R, San José, CA," wondering what Willow Creek looked like, what 3R meant, and what kind of town was San José? What would she be doing at that moment? What kind of friends had she made? Was she happy, or miserable, as he was? Did she miss him as he missed her? He avoided dwelling on these questions for too long because he found they had a tendency to torment him. Instead, he focused on the trip to the north and their imminent meeting. "Of course she misses me," he told himself. "It's impossible that I should miss her so much and she not miss me at all."

He even started earning money performing songs in the plaza. It started when one of Ingrid's neighbors recognized him from the night of the serenade. Noting the guitar over his shoulder, the woman asked if he'd play the song again. He willingly obliged and was given ten pesos in return. Someone else requested another song, and a small crowd surrounded him, calling out requests, handing him money. People said that even Benni Terraza couldn't play the guitar as well. He soon made enough to buy a pad of paper, envelopes, a nice pen, and plenty of stamps. He wrote to Ingrid whenever the inspiration hit him.

At first his letters were short, having nothing else to say except, "Dear Ingrid, How are you? I'm good. I miss you." And remembering the options given him by Ricardo the Notary, he wrote either "Warmest regards" or "Sincerely yours." Later when he'd exhausted the variations of "How are you? I'm good," he asked Jorge el Gato for ideas. When their conversations did not concern Filastro, their friendship was as strong as ever, and Edmund seemed to forget that Jorge had told him he had lied about his woman-seducing way. He still considered his brother-cousin's advice first-rate.

"Well, she probably misses La Prudencia, and you're here, so tell her about things happening around town. Remind her of home and you'll remind her of you."

So Edmund wrote about the plaza goings-on, the street beggars, the taco truck gossip, the band lineup at Disco Órale, and anything else he could think of. He waited every day for her response, but to no avail. He came up with various reasons why, finally deciding that it must be very expensive to send letters from the United States to La Prudencia, and that maybe she didn't have a job as he did.

One morning Filastro woke before dawn with a feeling of vigor he hadn't experienced since youth. He went to the window and watched the sunrise. When Edmund opened his eyes, he turned to his son and announced, "We'll go tomorrow. Pack whatever you're going to bring!"

All day was spent getting the house together, giving leftovers to dogs in the nearby alley and pigs down the street, shutting off the utilities, unplugging appliances, and leaving a note for Don Pepe, the landlord, should he come by, notifying him that they would pay the rent upon returning. Edmund took Cross-Eyes to Jorge el Gato and asked if he wouldn't mind caring for the dog

while he was away. Jorge agreed, but attempted one last time to dissuade him from going. Edmund would hear none of it. "I have to
see Ingrid again," he said. "The song was only the beginning!"

"Do you even know how far away California is from Nebraska
or Wyoming?"

"No, but we'll figure it out once we get there. It can't be that
far, right?"

Filastro and Edmund made arrangements with Tres Pasos and
Tomato for the following morning's transport van. They would
take that to Guadalajara, meet up with other travelers, and then
take a bus to the border.

When the father and son left, Tres Pasos turned to Tomato and
said, "Did you notice that man's limp?"

Tomato nodded and said, "Wouldn't be surprised if they refused
to take him."

Tres Pasos agreed. "On the other hand, I'd be surprised if they
didn't take his money."

"Not his money," Tomato retorted. "Our money."

Tres Pasos snorted. "You mean my money."

"Yes, that's right, yours."

"Ah, no use being pessimistic. He's with Edmund. The boy will
take care of him."

That evening Filastro and Edmund traveled one last time to visit
Constanza. Filastro dressed up in his best clothes, placed a dime-
sized amount of pomade in his hair, and made sure not one hair in
his mustache was out of place. He looked at himself in the mirror
as he fixed his shirt collar and sighed. "I look like the same man;
no wonder she won't talk to me."

Edmund, staring at the same reflection, responded, "No, Papá,
you don't look like the same man."

They headed over, walking slowly, both of them fearing a last
and final rejection.

Constanza had heard from Jorge el Gato that Filastro and
Edmund were leaving the next morning. She assumed they would

come by one last time. In front of the door she sat on a plastic chair, watching the evening strollers, moving her legs to avoid a passing dog or a running child. She saw two shadowy figures approach, the setting sun behind them. She recognized her son's skiplike walk and his head seemingly too large for his puny body.

The man next to him walked slowly, his head moving up and down with each labored step.

Ever since Edmund first mentioned it, she greatly doubted they would actually leave, but upon seeing their faces she knew they were going. She had wanted to dissuade them, to tell them that it wasn't necessary, that she would come back to live with them, that she would tell Abel, Ezekiel, Tomy, Gandolfo, Agnes, and Alfonsa that their father had changed and that they need not go. But somehow she knew this wouldn't have mattered. The look in their eyes told her they were gone already. She cried as they walked away, wanting to call after them, but she remained silent save for her muffled cries. Her sister came outside and comforted her, asked if he had insulted her, but all she could do was wave her away and cry. She watched until she could no longer see them, telling herself over and over, "It's not too late, it's not too late."

When Filastro and Edmund were far enough away, they turned to one another, eyeing the other's reaction. Finally, Edmund said, "At least she talked to us, huh?"

"Yes, that was a good sign," his father muttered.

Now they waited, bags in hand, outside of Tres Pasos's house for the van to arrive. It was approaching 9:00 and Tomato had been bustling about in his early-morning good humor. He even made Edmund a sack lunch and told him that he should "hurry home soon!" Seeing the bulbous-nosed man so cheery actually made Edmund feel he'd miss him. In fact, he felt he was going to miss everything. He said good-bye to his house, to his street, to the neighbors he passed on the way. "Going on a trip!" he told them.

They nodded in understanding, warily eyeing Filastro as he struggled with his backpack full of clothes, toiletries, and assortment of food items.

Three other young men arrived and stood with them. They were short, dark, and appeared to be brothers, as they shared the same underbite, giving them a baboonlike profile. They waited in silence and Edmund's attempts to converse were met with mumbled one-word answers. He left them to their silence, and, turning to his father, noticed that he too wished for quiet. The van came and they piled in. Edmund asked Tomato if Tres Pasos was going to come out and say goodbye. Tomato laughed somewhat sinisterly, and said, "Get in, this isn't a merry-go-round! Remember, you owe us." Edmund looked at his father's watch and nodded his head in recognition of the late morning hour.

The van took off without ceremony. They'd driven little more than a block when Edmund called out, "Stop!" The driver turned around and said, "What are you talking about? We're running late already! This isn't a tour bus!" The three silent brothers nodded their heads in agreement and Filastro asked, "What is it, mijo?"

"It's Jorge el Gato!" Edmund opened the van door and stepped onto the street. Jorge was waiting on the sidewalk, Cross-Eyes tied to the cart next to him. He held out several popsicles. "Take these for the road!"

Edmund ran up to him. "I'll be back soon to tell you all about it!" They shook hands and embraced. The van horn honked repeatedly and Filastro beckoned Edmund to hurry, a look of concern on his face.

"Be careful!" Jorge el Gato called after him. He met Filastro's eyes through the open door. The father and son stared at each other momentarily. Filastro nodded his head in acknowledgment. "Let's go!" Edmund said to the driver. The door slammed shut, and the van drove off, the tires peeling out to make up lost time. Jorge el Gato watched the vehicle until it disappeared, then turned and called out, "Popsicles, ice cream, treats for the kiddies!"

Once settled, Edmund turned to admire the scenery. In the window reflection he saw a figure in the front passenger seat. Hunched over, never once turning around, the person must've wished to remain unnoticed. From his vantage point, however, Edmund could see him quite clearly. He leaned over, looking past the three brothers, and thought he recognized the person's jacket and the brim of wire-framed glasses. He leaned his head over even more. That was when his suspicions were confirmed.

"Ricardo! Is that you?"

Ricardo the Former Notary relaxed his tense shoulders, realizing the futility of hiding or pretending to be somebody else for the several-hour ride. The van had picked him up at a different location owing to his poor relations with Tres Pasos and Tomato. Different loan sharks, apparently same smuggling contacts. He'd seen Edmund and his father waiting for the van and cursed the probability: of all days to leave, they were leaving today, too!

Ricardo sighed and turned around. "Hey, Edmund."

"Are you going to the United States as well?"

"That's the plan."

"But I thought you said a Man of Letters has no place washing dishes in Wyoming."

Ricardo nodded his head in recollection. "Yes, I did say that, but sometimes fathers have a way of ruining their sons' lives." Ricardo glanced at Filastro, who was staring out the window, lost in thought. He didn't recognize the young man as the notary whose typewriter he had threatened to smash; perhaps he didn't even remember. Ricardo clearly still felt strongly about the incident.

"What did your papá do?" Edmund asked.

"He took all my books and sold them," Ricardo exclaimed, his voice breaking slightly. Saying the misdeed aloud appeared to bring back the emotion.

"Really?"

Ricardo shook his head, "Well, no, not exactly. He took my books and threatened to do so if I didn't get a job and earn my keep. He said that he'd never heard of a son who was more of a burden to his family than me."

"That's too bad," Edmund said.

Ricardo gave further vent to his feelings, not once feeling self-conscious divulging such intimate details from one side of the van to the other. In the middle row the three brothers sat unmoving. Finally, Ricardo stopped and asked Edmund the purpose of his trip, and, by the way, how things had ended up with the girl.

"She left . . . but I got her address, at least," Edmund said, feeling for the folded paper in his pocket.

The van made three stops, picking up more passengers. After the first two stops they were packed in tightly, and Edmund could no longer see Ricardo in the front seat. At the third stop, the driver asked Edmund if he wouldn't mind sitting on his father's lap to make room for someone else. Edmund said he would mind. So then the driver commanded that he sit on his father's lap. "I'll drop you off right here and then what would you do?" Filastro tried to placate the man and said that it would be all right for an hour or so. Edmund was humiliated. "No one else has to sit on anyone's lap. Why do I get picked?" he lamented to himself.

Arriving in Guadalajara, Edmund had to wait until people piled out to differentiate the scenery. For the last hour he'd stared at nothing but the back of heads and perspiring, grimacing faces. He'd never been to a city before, and his first impressions were none too favorable. They stood in the middle of a dusty lot with broken buses and shells of cars surrounding them. A few food stands, a tire lot, and a crafts vendor were the only businesses in the vicinity. "This is where you wanted to live?" Edmund asked Ricardo when they were reunited outside.

"Well, the university is probably not like this . . ." he said, turning in all directions. He was also disappointed. Noticing their crestfallen expressions, Filastro informed them they were on the outskirts of the city between Tlaquepaque and the bus station. This made them feel better, and though they were disappointed to hear they wouldn't be traveling to the city center, Edmund said, "That's fine; from what it sounds like, the United States and Nebraska and San José are like ten times better."

Several more vans full of passengers arrived, followed by a large bus that was to transport them to the border. The driver who'd scolded Edmund instructed his passengers on what to do upon arriving at their northernmost destination. Edmund hoped Filastro was listening, as he was too excited to pay attention. All he heard were the driver's last words, "You'll be looking for a man with a glass eye and zigzagged sideburns."

"What's his name?" someone asked.

"Don Homobono."

Edmund heard that, too. He chortled and nudged Ricardo's arm. The driver looked for the laugh's perpetrator, glared at Edmund, and said, "I wouldn't give him any attitude, little boy. I'm your favorite uncle compared to Don Homobono."

Edmund was about to tell him he didn't have a favorite uncle when Filastro tapped his elbow and indicated for him to be quiet.

They boarded the large bus. To Edmund's relief there were plenty of seats. He jumped into one closest to the window and immediately began pushing buttons, playing with the armrests, and trying to work his footrest, which was broken. Filastro sat next to him, and Ricardo sat across the aisle, also desiring a window seat. When Edmund tired of his seat amusements, he turned to Filastro and asked, "Why are you so quiet?"

Filastro chuckled. "Just nervous, I guess."

Edmund hadn't thought to be nervous. All his brothers—even his sisters, Agnes being pregnant—had made the trip without problems, and they had traveled alone. He was with their father. He assumed their journey would go just as smoothly. And it did for the next fourteen hours driving through state after state. Every checkpoint they were stopped, the driver handed the inspector his chauffeur's documents, and the bus was waved on. They had a number of bathroom breaks, the latrine on the bus being broken. They were allowed fifteen minutes to stretch their legs, use the restroom, or buy a drink and food from the roadside vendors. The driver told the passengers, "After fifteen minutes we'll leave you, even if I see you running in my rearview mirror! Is that understood?"

Edmund turned to Filastro and asked, "Man, Papá, why is he treating us like that? We paid good money!"

"I guess at this point we don't have much say-so."

"We can tell him to be nicer."

"And he'll tell us to walk to the border."

"I'd ask for my money back, and with the money we have with us, I'd find—"

"Shhh!" his father said, almost placing his hand over Edmund's mouth. "Don't mention anything about that, mijo. Do you have yours secure?" He felt for his bundles sewn into his sleeves and pants. Edmund felt for his and smiled, "Still there."

Filastro slept much of the way, snoring lightly, his mouth ajar. Periodically Edmund would see something of interest outside and nudge him awake. Filastro would groggily examine what Edmund pointed to (if he didn't miss it completely)—a nice car, a grazing herd, a large mountain, a reservoir, a coyote, some buzzards pecking at a dead cow or dog or donkey. "Oh, look at that," he'd say, and then fall back to sleep. Edmund was too excited for sleep; he couldn't relax even when darkness fell and the landscape was no longer visible out the window. He'd never sat in one place for so long.

Every fifteen minutes he looked over at Ricardo, who was either asleep or writing in his notebook. "What are you writing?" Edmund called out. Several people told him to hush. The passenger next to Ricardo looked at him as if he were a bug in his beer. "How many times you going to call across the aisle?" he grumbled. "It's late. Get some sleep."

Ricardo wrote something in his notebook, tore out the page, and handed it to the man, who begrudgingly handed it to Edmund. It read, "As a descriptive exercise, I'm writing about all I've seen out the window."

Edmund nodded his head, wishing Ricardo would allow him to read these descriptive exercises. Then he fell asleep and didn't wake until the bus stopped early the next morning.

"Everybody wake up and get out! Wake up!" the driver called out.

Edmund woke up, yawned, and stretched, more than a little disoriented. Upon regaining his wits he exclaimed, "We're almost there! Hand me my bag, Papá!"

Filastro had been awake for several hours watching the sunrise. He went back and forth wondering whether or not his sons and daughters would accept him. Maybe they'd refuse to see him as their mother had done. Maybe they'd see the change in him immediately and graciously invite him into their homes. He'd begin oldest to youngest, Abel the hardest to convince, his twin daughters the easiest. For sure he'd apologize to Tomy's wife, Paty, as he distinctly remembered calling her every variation of whore that came to mind. He thought again and again, "Maybe we should just turn back." But as the landscape changed—factory towns in the middle of desert, more signs in English, arrows pointing to Texas and Arizona—he decided they'd come this far, so they might as well keep going.

The passengers slowly filed out. He handed Edmund his bag and grabbed his own, slinging it onto his back. He limped down the row, holding onto the seats for support. Sitting for so long had made his joints feel glued together. His knee no longer hurt as badly; it was his muscles and bones that ached without reprieve.

Edmund helped him down the bus steps and once outside they both stretched their arms wide and shook out their legs. Filastro even rolled his head back and forth as he saw some people doing. They were once again on the outskirts of a city, a mixture of junked cars, billboards, and seedy eating establishments. Ricardo approached Filastro and Edmund and asked, "So, is this where we wait for Don What's-His-Face?"

Filastro nodded unsurely.

Edmund smiled inside thinking of what's-his-face's name.

One of the three silent brothers finally spoke. "No, we're supposed to wait over there, at La Finca, that restaurant or bar thing," and he indicated the direction with a flick of his head. "Right? You are all with Don Homobono, no?"

Edmund started to laugh and Filastro nudged him.

"What?"

"Control yourself."

"But I can't get over it. Who would name their child Homobono? Have you heard of that name?"

"Yeah, I had a friend named Homobono when I was little. Now, come on."

Edmund walked alongside the three brothers with the identical underbite. He asked them the purpose of their journey and they ignored him. He assumed they hadn't heard, so he asked again.

"To work," one said.

"Yeah, work," followed another.

The third brother nodded.

"Well that's good. I hear there's plenty up there. My brothers all got work, my sisters, too, and they send a lot of money home. I mean not a lot lot, but a good amount. We're going to bring them back, actually. You see, my mamá told my papá that she wouldn't take him back unless he went to the United States and asked all his children to forgive him. Yeah, he was real hard to deal with before, but—"

"Edmund!" Filastro said. "Help me, let me have your shoulder."

The three brothers turned to look at the father and son. Filastro noticed their eyes on his limp and felt the need to say, "Ay, knee got stiff sitting all that time!"

They looked at him each with the same wary expression.

They arrived at La Finca and a short fat man standing at the door whispered to them, "You want a whore, you want a little fuck before you go, how about some mescal or marijuana? Yeah, you want some of that, I know it—"

No one responded except Edmund, who asked, "We're looking for Don Homobono, do you know him?"

With a flick of his head the short fat man indicated to enter. "He's probably dancing like always."

Edmund glanced at Ricardo, who was writing furiously in his black book. Edmund edged closer and whispered, "What are you writing? Isn't it hard to write and walk?"

Ricardo sighed and said, "My great idea. Every Man of Letters needs one—I have it!"

Edmund waited. "Well, what is it?"

"I'm not going to jinx myself like last time. I'm still smarting from the wounds Tomato dealt me."

La Finca was dark, but surprisingly crowded for such an early hour. People sat at round tables and ate posole and birria or drank coffee, which the waitress, if asked, topped off with rum. The juke-box was blasting and a handsome couple was dancing. The woman was tall and skinny, with long black hair underneath a cowboy hat. She wore a shirt that was little more than a bra. Noticing her scanty attire, the three brothers suddenly became animated, turning to one another and smiling shyly. The dancing man was also tall and wore a cowboy hat. He danced like a chicken, flapping his arms ups and down. Occasionally he'd stop mid-flap and pause for two or three seconds, a move his partner apparently loved because she wiggled around him when he did so. Following their fourteen-hour bus ride, Ricardo, Filastro, Edmund, and the three brothers were awestruck. So much so that they didn't notice the dancing man's zigzagged sideburns or his glass eye, which occasionally picked up the gleam of the strobe light.

When the song stopped, the man bowed to his partner, and walked toward the group of men carrying backpacks. He held up his arms in salutation and said, "You must be my next transport! Welcome to La Finca, I'm Don Homo—homo—bonoooo!"

Edmund began laughing hysterically, thinking the pronounce-ment was meant as a joke to enliven the group. The others remained silent, however. Filastro nudged his son. Ricardo nudged his friend. Edmund got the clue and quieted. But too late, for the man glared at him with his one good eye, his glass eye seemingly trans-

fixed on the boy's ear. After a tense moment, Don Homobono beckoned them to follow. Single-file, they passed the bar, the tables, the
dance floor, the women of ill repute in repose, and into a dimly
lighted hallway.

Filastro was reminded of his outing with Captain Esteban.
How many back rooms had they visited? The memory made him
break into a cold sweat.

CHAPTER 61

I—I just love da—dancing!" Don Homobono said. "It relieves me of all stress. Now to business. You owe me half the money now, the other half upon arrival. If—if you don—do not arrive, well, then I have my share, and you have ah—at least a li—little to help you upon your return. There are no guarantees, here, you un—understand that?"

Everyone nodded, except Edmund, who couldn't help staring at the man's glass eye; it was green and his good eye was black. He wondered why he didn't get the same color.

"Now," continued the man, his voice louder. He was looking at Edmund still fixated on the glass eye. "I—I don't like ta—taking small children. They slow the trip down considerably, and if something should happen, the—they rarely survive by—by themselves—"

Edmund nodded his head, still not listening. But then his father turned in his direction and spoke.

"He's not a child, Don Homobono, he's fourteen. He's quite strong, even though he looks so small."

Don Homobono looked at Edmund in disbelief. "You're fourteen?"

"Yeah, why?"

Don Homobono looked at the three brothers. "He's fourteen! Hah!"

The three brothers smiled nervously and Don Homobono laughed heartily. "Poor kid!"

Edmund was about to retaliate, having a number of good insults at his disposal, when Filastro placed his hand firmly on his shoulder. He pursed his lips and remained silent.

Everyone stole to his respective corner and removed wads of cash from various hiding places, tops of hats, linings of pants, soles of shoes; everyone, that is, except for Ricardo the Former Notary, who removed an orange leather billfold. Wetting his fingers with saliva he counted ten one hundred dollar bills. "There you go," he said confidently. Don Homobono smiled, "I tha—thank you."

When all the money was collected, Don Homobono laid out the trip itinerary: they would travel by van to Trigomil, where they'd connect with others and board a tractor-trailer carrying electronics into Arizona. Once across they'd be met by a man, who, "ha—happens to be my—my father," Don Homobono said with an air of pride, "and his name is also Homobono."

Edmund pretended to cough to mask his snort. "Excuse me," he said.

Don Homobono Jr. frowned, his glass eye open wide. He continued, "Once you're pick—picked up, you'll be taken to safe houses in different locations. From there, you'll arrange passage to your intended destination. Is everything clear? If anything should happen along the way—if you should be caught by immigration, for one—then I'm in no way responsible. It hap—happens every day and every day people try again. So I warn you against ratting me out, or any of my associates. Your inconvenience will soon—soon be our pain, which will soon be your pain . . . tenfold, if you know what I mean. D—do I make myself clear? This is the Homobono way."

Everyone nodded his head in agreement. Edmund couldn't help but smile.

"Wha—what, little boy, may—may I ask, d—do you find so—so funny?" Don Homobono fixed his one good eye on Edmund. "You stand there smiling like an idiot. What is it?"

"Nothing," Edmund mumbled, looking down at the ground.

They gathered outside and met several more passengers. A young woman showed up in a short skirt, a white blouse, and high-heeled shoes. She held a purse, nothing more. Two young men were also waiting, stone-faced and solemn. Both had elaborate tattoos of eagles on their necks. Edmund was about to inquire as to their significance when he noticed another tattoo just below the eagle that said, "Go Screw Your Mother." Large leather suitcases rested at their feet. They appeared heavy, but when Edmund passed by—admiring the tattoos—he accidentally bumped a suitcase, almost knocking it over. "There must be hardly anything in it," he thought.

Don Homobono paid no attention to the two young men, but said to the girl, "Señorita, who—who the he—hell told you this was a disco outing?"

Her eyes opened wide in astonishment. "What are you talking about, sir?"

"I'm talking about your high-heeled shoes and your little skirt. What do you think you're about to do, cross the dance floor?"

"My cousins said it was going to be easy. They said it was no problem at all. So I wanted to look nice for my arrival. When do you think that'll be, in an hour or so?"

Don Homobono laughed and the two tattooed men laughed as well. "Hah! C—country types—I love it! They tell each other nothing but lies just so th—their family and friends think they've made it big. 'Oh, yes, the trip was like a walk around the placita!' Hah! No, mija, go—go inside La Finca; talk to a woman named Berta. She'll give you some shoes, at least."

The girl began to cry, still confused. Would it *not* take an hour, maybe two? She walked inside the restaurant, emerging several minutes later wearing a long-sleeved T-shirt, jeans much too big for her, and shabby tennis shoes. Don Homobono gave his approval and told her she'd thank him later. Edmund, noticing the girl's frazzled state, approached her. "Don't worry, it's going to be easy enough, and once we're there, you'll be able to put on your nice clothes."

She smiled. "Thanks."

"What's your name?"

"Panchita, and yours?"

"Edmund. Why are you going to the United States?"

"My boyfriend is there. I wanted to look nice for him. How long do you think it takes to get to Nebraska?"

"Couple hours, probably. We're going there, too. It's one of our stops."

"Why are you going?"

"This girl I love is in California. Her name's Ingrid Genera."

"You look young. How do you know she's the one?"

"Yeah, well, I look younger than I am. I just know. She gave me her address."

"Oh . . ." she paused. "I wish my boyfriend would come for me rather than me having to go for him."

"Yeah?"

"Who knows whether he even wants me to come. He doesn't know. He thinks I saved the money for an addition on the house he's building for his parents."

"I'm sure he wants you to come."

Panchita half-smiled.

Don Homobono opened his cell phone, held it to his ear for three seconds, then closed it. He called the group together and said that he'd just been notified the van was on its way.

Doesn't your hand hurt?"

Edmund inched his way over to Ricardo, still writing furiously in his notebook.

His mouth pursed tightly, Ricardo's eyes followed his hand as it crossed the page. "I have no time!" he whispered.

Edmund left him alone and waited in silence. The van pulled up with a skid, enveloping everyone in dust. When the cloud cleared, Edmund examined the vehicle; it wasn't what he was expecting. The driver stepped out and opened the back doors. There were no windows, no seats either. Don Homobono instructed them to enter. They did so warily, eyeing one another. Ricardo even ceased writing. Only the two tattooed men jumped in without hesitation. "There aren't arm rests," Edmund said to break the tension. He heard several snickers, which satisfied him.

"I—I'll be in front," Don Homobono said gruffly, smoothing out his zigzagged sideburns with his thumbs. He closed the doors with a slam, leaving them in darkness. Only a small beam of light trickled through. Ricardo groaned and put away his notebook. Edmund's eyes adjusted to the darkness and soon he was able to make out faces. He stared at Panchita, who he thought was smiling at him. He moved his eyes to Ricardo, then to the three brothers. Edmund couldn't see the two tattooed men, as they were on his side of the van, but he was glad of it: they made him nervous. Why have a tattoo that says "Go Screw Your Mother"? He wasn't about to ask.

Finally he turned to his father and found him staring at the roof interior, his mouth slightly ajar, breathing deeply. Edmund assumed he was trying to sleep.

Before long, the van had taken off. He had no idea whether they were going fast or slowly.

* * *

Filastro imagined their arrival in Nebraska. Edmund had some-how found Abel's address; the others' they hoped to get from him. He pictured Abel's face livid, afraid. How would he show him he'd come in peace, not a shred of malice in his heart? Maybe he and Edmund would compose a note. Edmund would deliver it and he'd wait at a nearby restaurant, not a bar, and have something to drink, a soda or just water. With any luck, Abel and Edmund would show up.

"I'm a changed man," he would say.

"I don't believe you. You look the same to me. Why have you come, to drag me back?"

"No, I've come to ask your forgiveness."

"Well, I forgive you, now go."

"No, mijo, listen, I don't drink anymore—look, I have a soda! I don't have the energy even to swat a fly. Please, I'm not the man you knew."

"OK, and so what? You think I'm just going to jump into your arms?"

"I don't know what to expect. I needed for you to know, that's all."

And then Abel would grow quiet, lose his hostility. He'd give him the rest of his siblings' addresses. Would he come with them? Would he promise to join them later? Filastro couldn't know.

Then he'd leave to find Ezekiel, then Tomy and his wife, Gandolfo, the twins. He imagined them all living within a few blocks of one another. He knew that one was in Texas, a few in Nebraska, and Tomy was in Wyoming, but in his thoughts these might as well have been street names. The journey was now, the trip across the border, hours and hours imagining the same thing, agonizing over it. They were still in Mexico. How much longer would it take?

They drove all day, the back of the van growing hotter and hotter. Edmund's shirt was drenched. His father had been asleep for a long time and he worried that he'd passed out. He shook his arm to wake him, just to make sure. Filastro kept his eyes closed, but nodded his head as if understanding his son's intention. Ricardo began to mumble unintelligibly. Edmund thought he might be praying. Panchita told him to be quiet; he was making her nervous. But Ricardo continued mumbling louder and louder. One of the two tattooed men kicked Ricardo's leg and told him to shut up, but he continued, seemingly delirious.

"I want to get out!" Ricardo yelled suddenly. "I want to get out!"

"Shut up, so do we all," one of the men said.

"No, you don't understand. I want to get out!"

Edmund tried raising himself to see if he could calm Ricardo, but he felt so light-headed that he had to sit back down. Edmund reached in his bag and found his water bottle. He drank it thirstily, then handed it to his father. Between the two of them it was gone in a matter of gulps, but they felt better. Ricardo continued yelling. One of the men said, "Throw some water on him."

"We don't have enough," Edmund said. "We've already finished off one bottle. Don't you have any water?"

The man opened a zipper and reached his hand inside. He pulled out a container.

"I want to get out! I'm not made for this!" Ricardo cried out. Then he mumbled, "I'm a Man of Letters . . ."

"What's he talking about?" Panchita asked.

"He was the town notary," Edmund responded.

The same man said, "I don't care what he is. He needs to shut up. We're all in the same boat." His tattooed friend chuckled. The man leaned over and poured water on Ricardo's head. Immediately he woke from his delirium, shaking his head, wiping the water from his face. "You've drenched me! What'd you do that for?"

"Just shut up," the man said.

"What? Why did you do that?" Ricardo said, his voice shrill. "I don't understand! Why would you do that?" He felt around him. "Holy shit! You drenched my book, too! The ink is going to blur— you—you—why did you do that? Edmund, why did he do that?"

"You were going crazy, saying things. He had to wake you."

Ricardo quieted and leaned his head back. He either fell asleep or passed out. Everyone was silent, relieved that the screaming had ended.

ight fell and they were in complete darkness. The heat and mugginess remained, however, and they were all relieved when the van finally stopped with a violent skid. Edmund along with everyone else watched the doors, anxiously awaiting the relief their opening would bring. The suspense was unbearable. Edmund heard a moan; he thought it was Panchita, but then it came again; this time he thought it was Ricardo. Now it was his turn to cry out, "Open, open! It's hot in here!"

Edmund felt for Filastro's hand and squeezed it. Filastro squeezed his hand in return. He too yelled hoarsely, "Come on!"

Then someone said, "All of you, shut up if you want to stay alive." It came from one of the tattooed men.

"What do you mean?" Panchita cried out.

There was a light rap on the outside of the van.

"Shh!" came from one of the men.

Everyone was silent, including Ricardo.

"Now I want everyone to listen to me," said the man sternly. "These doors are going to open and I don't want one of you to move. Not an inch! We'll instruct you to step out of the van, one by one—"

"And who are you?" Edmund cried.

"Shut up! You'll take all the money that you have hidden in your pants, hats, shoes, and remove it. We also want all valuables that you might have in your backpacks."

"You're robbing us?" Ricardo whimpered.

"Yes, what do you think? Now you shut up. I've heard enough from you. And no one think of running—"

The van door creaked, then opened slowly. Fresh air rushed in. It felt as if they had been doused with water. So great was the relief that everyone momentarily forgot they were being robbed. Suddenly, though, they were cold and their sweat-drenched shirts were now causing them to shiver. The temperature outside was freezing, cold enough, at least, that the men who opened the doors were wearing thick jackets. They also carried guns.

The two men in the back stepped out carrying their suitcases. They opened the luggage and revealed what Edmund had suspected: the bags were empty except for several containers of water. The man who'd spoken in the van beckoned the three brothers to exit first. They wore the same frightened expression, looking at one another as if unsure of what to do, hoping the others had an answer.

"No, no, no use thinking of a way out of this. Empty your pockets or we'll strip you and find it ourselves."

The brothers stepped down slowly and reached into their hats and pant legs and removed wads of bills. They handed over the money, which was then dropped into the suitcases. One of the men rummaged through their bags, but little of value was found; only a necklace that was bitten into and discarded. One of the brothers bent down to pick it up and was kicked in his ass, then pushed to the ground. Another robber brandished a gun and instructed them to sit down, hands over their heads.

The same routine was repeated with Panchita, except the man groped her and laughed. She began crying only when they looked through her purse and dumped its entire contents into the suitcase. Edmund saw a whole bunch of jewelry and makeup. The man handed the purse back to her and said, "You're lucky we don't take more." This got a rise out of the others.

Filastro and Edmund were called next. Filastro struggled, his body stiff from the long ride. He couldn't straighten out either leg. The men were too impatient. They grabbed his arms and dragged him out of the van. Filastro groaned. Edmund cried, "Hey watch it! He's hurt!" A hand grabbed his arm and pulled him out as well. He glared at the men with the tattoos. "Now I know why it says 'Go Screw Your Mother.'"

The men laughed and one slapped Edmund over the head. "You talk big for such a little kid. Now put your damn money in the suitcase."

"I don't have any," Edmund responded unthinkingly.

"Yes, you do, I know you do. You want me to take your clothes and search them myself?"

"No," Filastro said. Edmund looked up at him, his father's face more tired than scared. "He's my son. I have all our money." He reached into his pant leg, felt around, and removed the wad of bills. Believing him, the men pushed Filastro and Edmund toward the others.

Next came Ricardo, remarkably stoic as he pulled out his orange leather billfold and emptied his bag. "Oh, so now you've grown a sack of balls?" one of the tattooed men teased. They pushed Ricardo toward the others and kicked him in the ass for a laugh. The men zipped up the suitcases and carried them to a truck parked directly in front of the van. "They must've cut the van off to stop it," Edmund thought. He wondered where Don Homobono had disappeared.

Ricardo sat next to Edmund and whispered, "Are you OK?"

"No, of course not!" he whispered loudly.

"Shh! Listen, I have an idea."

"What?"

"Do you remember Tres Pasos's ninety-sixth best story?"

"Sort of . . . remind me."

"The one where he's alone in a room with a group of men threatening to kill him?"

"The one where he uses his skills as a ventriloquist?"

"No, that was ninety-three. The one where he decides to— here, just watch."

Ricardo stood up. Edmund grabbed for him, now remembering story ninety-six in its entirety.

In story ninety-six, Tres Pasos turned the tables on a group of men attempting to rob and kill him. Five scoundrels surrounded him, the ringleader holding a gun to his head, demanding he cough up where he'd stashed his money. On a whim, knowing his options were limited, Tres Pasos asked the man where *his* money was stashed and not only that, but "get it quick or else hell will have to be paid!" Seeing the look of confusion on the man's face, he continued improvising. "Tell me right now, goddamn it, or I'll have one of these four men, one of whom is *actually* under my pay—it could be either of them—fill you full of bullet holes." In the end, confusion and suspicion reigned, the robbers ended up shooting one another, and Tres Pasos snuck out with his life.

Ricardo would've had better luck with the ventriloquist trick. Dumb valor having replaced his delirium, he stood and said to the desert highwaymen, "All right, goddamn it, now I want everyone to listen to me or else!"

Edmund looked up in fear, knowing what was coming; the others in the group looked up in confusion. They still had their hands raised, except for Ricardo, who now walked forward with his right hand in his pocket, forming a sharp bulge. Edmund assumed it was the notebook or pen; he hoped the men didn't assume the same. The robbers were silent, and Ricardo must've thought he had them at that moment of confusion when Tres Pasos so deftly turned the tables. His courage abandoned him, however, when he noticed in the distance the dark outline of a man face forward on the ground. He paused, losing his train of thought as he focused on a glimmer of light emitted from a small glass sphere several inches from the man's face.

He realized the man was Don Homobono; the glass sphere was his eye. Ricardo was no longer so sure of his plan.

"What the fuck do you think you're doing?" one of the robbers demanded.

He couldn't look away from the glass eye. "Uh—uh—listen here!" he attempted, "I—want—everyone to—"

And then he was hit in the back of the head and knocked unconscious.

When Ricardo woke he found the blurred forms of Filastro and Edmund sitting in front of a small fire. It was still dark. He raised his head and felt dizzy. "Who lit the fire?" he asked drowsily.

"The robbers did," Panchita said. His head had been resting in her lap. He looked at her, finding it difficult to focus.

She handed him his glasses. "They were going to take them but I begged them not to because then you'd be blind and sure to get lost."

Ricardo squinted as he fixed the glasses on his nose. "Thanks," he said, looking around him. "What happened to the three brothers?"

"The robbers said that we're five miles from the border in that direction or we could go three miles in the other direction to the closest town and start over. They said if we left soon, we'd make it to Arizona by sunrise and before the heat. So the three brothers took off for the border. We told the robbers that we couldn't leave you or else you'd be dead, so they lit a fire and wished us better luck next time. Then they drove off."

Ricardo tried to rise, but fell over and dry heaved. "Ah, I can't move," he moaned.

"That's all right," Panchita said, "We'll go back to the town together. I can't make it walking. I think I'm just going to go home. I'll go with you to the town, OK?"

Ricardo nodded. When the nausea passed, he raised his head and found Filastro and Edmund still staring numbly at the fire. He wondered why they were so silent.

* * *

Edmund saw in his father's face that he wanted to go back. Filastro was exhausted and his body ached. He hardly cared that they'd been robbed, their coyote killed, all their efforts thwarted. All he wanted was to sleep, stretch his legs, and try winning Constanza back another way. But Edmund could think only of Ingrid. He had already been on the road two days, sat on a bus for fourteen hours, sat huddled in a suffocating windowless van for who knows how long. In his mind, visiting Ingrid was merely a matter of walking that five miles into Arizona.

"Let's go, Papá," he said upon hearing which direction to go.

"No, mijo, let's wait. I can't. My legs feel like wood."

"Let's go with them, Papá," he said when the three silent brothers took off without so much as a good-bye.

"No, Edmund, let's wait for your friend to wake up. What was he thinking, by the way?"

Edmund shrugged. "I don't know."

"He was being brave," Panchita said, stroking Ricardo's hair.

Edmund and Filastro looked at each other, eyebrows raised. The former notary had obviously impressed someone.

"Well, so we can cross when he wakes up?" Edmund asked.

"We'll see, mijo."

And they sat in silence, Edmund thinking of Ingrid and how he couldn't imagine coming this far only to turn back. If Filastro thought of anything other than his exhaustion, it was of Constanza. He remembered her eyes when they left. She would want him to turn back, if not for his sake, then for their son's.

dmund's persistence won out. When the fire began to die, Ricardo and Panchita decided to leave. They stood up, Ricardo leaning on Panchita for support, and began walking. They assumed Filastro and Edmund would follow. Struggling to rise, Filastro reached for his son's shoulder, but Edmund remained seated.

"I thought you wanted to win Mamá back," Edmund mumbled.

"I do, but with time. I can't do it this way."

"But she said it was the only way. We have to go and bring my brothers and sisters back to her or else we'll both be alone."

"I know, but maybe not forever—" he paused. "Mijo, I'm too old to walk so far."

"It's just five miles and then we're there."

"No, five miles to the border and then who knows how much more until reaching safety."

"Maybe there'll be a town just on the other side."

"And maybe there won't be."

"Papá, please, we've made it this far. We'll be fine. I'll help you. I feel good. We have some money, half of what we started with. If we return to La Prudencia, how will we pay back Tres Pasos, but if we keep going maybe we could use this to help save or something . . ."

Filastro sighed heavily. He looked at Panchita and Ricardo waiting ten yards away, wondering what the two could be discussing.

"We've talked about this for months. This is what we wanted to do. We'll be fine—" Edmund paused before saying quietly, "If you turn back, I'll go by myself, I swear it."

Filastro didn't have the strength to argue. Edmund couldn't be dissuaded, and what difference did it make anyway, whether north or south, five miles or three, the outlook was bleak. He languidly gestured to Ricardo and Panchita, "Go," he said. "We're going the other way."

"Are you sure?" Ricardo called out, thinking he had missed something in the darkness. Were they not in as bad shape as he was? He pushed up his glasses on his nose. "They're going to try crossing," Panchita whispered. Ricardo fished in his bag, removed a water bottle, and tossed it at them. The bottle hit the ground and skipped close to Edmund's feet. Edmund grabbed it and looked up at his father. "We're going?"

"Yeah, now, before too much time passes."

Edmund jumped up excitedly. He waved to Ricardo and Panchita, a smile on his face. "Good luck!" he called after them. The fire was now dead. Instinctively, Filastro kicked dirt on top, and then, looking around at the rocks and dry brush, realized the futility of the gesture. "What would burn that's not already scorched day in and day out?" he said to himself. His apprehension came back, clenching his chest, making his body feel even weaker. But Edmund was already walking ahead.

Two hours later they saw the sun rising to their right and knew they were heading north. This would have been comforting if the light hadn't also illuminated the extent of their isolation. For as far as they could see, there was nothing but cactuses, dry brush, and rocks. Filastro kept pace with Edmund despite his limp and the pain in his legs. The air was still bitterly cold and the prospect of the sun's heat was welcome. They both had donned all the clothes in their bags. Now they slowly began peeling off layers. By the time the sun was fully above the horizon, they wore one layer of clothing and were sweating. "It's going to be hot, huh?" Edmund said.

"Uh-huh," Filastro grunted.

Neither of them mentioned the fact that they should have reached the border by now.

"Maybe we haven't gone five miles because my papá is limping," Edmund thought.

"We're lost," Filastro said to himself. "We've gone at least seven miles."

Finally Edmund voiced his concern. "Where's the border?"

"I don't know," gasped Filastro. "Let's stop for a moment. I have to sit. Just for a second."

They found a rock to sit on, the surface still cold from the long night.

"What does the border look like?" Edmund asked.

Filastro shrugged, trying to catch his breath.

Edmund imagined a long stone fence like the ones surrounding everyone's ranch outside of La Prudencia. He looked around him. "Plenty of rocks for a big fence out here," he thought to himself. He asked Filastro, "Is there like a big fence or something?"

Filastro had no idea. "Maybe."

"Do you think we'll have any trouble climbing it?"

"I'd like to find it first," Filastro said. "Come on, I'm ready. Let's go."

They began walking. Edmund kept spotting lizards, little ones. He fought the urge to lunge after them until he saw a big lizard that cured his urges. "My God!" he cried. "Look how big that thing is! Do you know what kind of lizard that is?"

Filastro noticed and said, "Watch out for snakes, too."

The thought of snakes made Edmund jumpy. He would have preferred to imagine himself and his father completely alone with the rocks and brush. Every dead branch made him scoot out of the way into the path of something else resembling a snake, which would in turn make him jump the other way.

"Calm down, Edmund," Filastro scolded him. "Just focus on what's in front of you."

They ate the last of their food in the shade of a clump of cactuses. Edmund chewed his crackers slowly, wondering if his father was going to say something about the lack of provisions. When he didn't, he assumed they'd be all right. "If he's not worrying about it, then I'm not going to," Edmund said to reassure himself. But Filastro could hardly stomach his crackers, such was his concern.

They walked on, Filastro's limp becoming worse. He knew he wouldn't be able to go much further unless they rested for several hours. They had hardly slept the night before, though they had slept plenty on the bus ride. The sun was getting stronger, taking their energy with each step.

Edmund's exhaustion was so great that he no longer cared about snakes or large lizards in his path. His mouth hung open and he continually had to wipe the sweat from his forehead to keep it out of his eyes. He looked in vain for a stone fence.

The sun was almost directly above them when they came across a small wooden shack in front of a row of mesquite trees. It leaned to one side and many of the side boards were missing. Still, Filastro considered it a godsend. "Thank you, Lord!" he cried out.

Edmund turned to him, not thinking they would stop just yet, and certainly not in that crumbling shack. "What?" he asked.

"We have to stay there, mijo, at least until night falls. I'm too tired to go on."

Hearing the desperation in his father's voice, Edmund nodded his head. "OK, but . . . what is it? Does anybody live there?"

"No, it's abandoned—probably just an old watershed."

They approached slowly, the entrance to the side. Filastro peeked in the doorway, Edmund close behind, ready to run if there were any snakes. It was empty. They sat down, Filastro practically collapsing. It seemed just as hot in the shack and continued to grow hotter as the day progressed. Filastro slept, but Edmund was too uncomfortable. From time to time he peeked his head out the door, as if there might be something of passing interest. Only the blinding sun greeted him. He felt it penetrating his exposed skin and pulled back into the shade. He was glad they'd decided to stop.

He found a stray red ant, and, having nothing better to do, began blowing on it. The ant fell on its back, its legs moving furiously. He felt bad for flipping it over, so he scoured the ground for a stick or dried weed, but found nothing useful. He thought of venturing outside to look for a small stick or cactus needle, but one step in the sun was enough to dissuade him. He decided to forgo the danger of it biting him and use his finger. When he returned, though, the ant was gone. He looked all over, wondering where it could have disappeared. Filastro finally grumbled for him to sit still.

He rested on his elbows, worrying that the ant might reappear seeking vengeance. Soon he felt his eyelids grow heavy. He rested his head on the dirt and fell asleep.

When they woke it was already dark. They stumbled outside, more than a little disoriented. They began walking, each of them assuming the other was certain of their direction. After half an hour, Edmund could tell Filastro was struggling to keep up. He slowed down, but even then Filastro's breathing continued growing louder and more nasal; he stopped every hundred feet to rub his knee or to stretch his legs. Edmund felt a twinge of regret for having made his father push northward. "I couldn't have known it was going to be so far," he said to console himself. "The robbers said five miles—" and then he sighed, thinking, "What did they care whether it was five or fifty?"

The bright moon made clear their surroundings, but Edmund was no longer interested in the desert landscape, nor was he worried about snakes or lizards. As he walked, he allowed his mind to wander. He imagined telling Ingrid about his adventure; how they'd been robbed, their coyote killed, how they had crossed the border in the middle of the night; and now here he was standing in front of her, having traveled such distances because he loved her so. Over and over again he imagined Ingrid's face as she opened her door: sometimes full of passion, happiness, or delight, sometimes shocked only to recover and be full of passion, happiness, or delight. Then a thought entered his mind of which he couldn't rid himself. When the door opened, her face displayed not delight, but shock and nervous disappointment. "Ingrid, it's me!" he said, but then none other than Rafa appeared behind her. "Big trip for a little runt!" he said and proceeded to punch him. Edmund tried to imagine himself punching back, but his imaginative efforts fell short. "Rafa's not going to be there," he reassured himself, " . . . but what if someone else is?"

"What are you talking about?" Filastro asked.

Edmund was startled from his reverie. "What?"

"You're talking to yourself. What about? Come, let's sit. We've been walking for two hours already. I need to rest." He placed his hands on his knees and coughed violently.

"Papá, are you OK?"

"Yes, yes, let me sit, let me sit," he gasped.

They found a good-sized rock on which to rest. Filastro asked Edmund to rub his knee. "I can't lean down, mijo; I'll topple over." Edmund sat cross-legged on the hard ground. As gently as possible he held his father's knee. Filastro let out a cry. "Ah! Not so hard!"

"But I didn't grab it hard."

"That hurt like hell. Lift up my pant leg. Look at it; see if it's OK."

Edmund slowly lifted up his father's pant leg, but struggled raising it past his knee as it had swollen considerably. The top of his shin was dark and discolored. He raised the pant leg some more, Filastro grimacing and clenching his teeth, and saw that the entire knee was dark—black or purple, he couldn't tell in the darkness. He rolled down the pant leg and said, "It doesn't look too good."

"I know. But I'll be fine. Let me just rest some more and then we'll take off. We should reach the border soon."

They sat in silence for several minutes. Filastro's heavy breathing kept time: inhale, exhale, one second, inhale, exhale, two seconds, then it began to slow down, more measured. Finally, he spoke, "Edmund, tell me, what were you talking to yourself about?"

Edmund recalled his thoughts of Ingrid, his imaginings of her happiness and delight, her shock and nervous disappointment, damned Rafa waiting in the wings . . . his tormented heart. And then he thought of his father's mangled knee.

"Nothing really," he said to Filastro. "Just dumb stuff to pass the time."

They walked for two more hours, progressing slowly, as Edmund now had to support Filastro. The right leg dragged between them like a burden they would've preferred to leave behind. Filastro grunted, and periodically so did Edmund, his shoulder strained from the weight of his father's arm.

"You OK?" Edmund asked when Filastro would groan especially loudly.

"Yeah," Filastro grunted back.

Then Filastro would ask, "Are you OK, mijo?"

"Yes, just fine," Edmund responded, barely able to get the words out.

The bright moon was of little use, as everything looked exactly the same. The flatness of the terrain gave them no illusions: they could see forever, and forever was nothing but cacti and mesquite trees. Occasionally Edmund thought he saw a man and would call out, "Help!" but it would be a cactus. After several erroneous sightings, Filastro told him to make sure the form moved before calling out to it. Ten minutes later Edmund cried out, "Hey, hey!"

"Where?" Filastro gasped.

Edmund pointed. They both looked closer. Yet another cactus. Edmund bowed his head and apologized. "It's OK," Filastro told him, the disappointment evident in his voice. From then on Edmund kept his mouth shut.

They had to stop again, this time for Edmund, who could no longer take Filastro's weight. "I'm too weak, Papá, I'm sorry!" he cried, on the verge of tears.

"No, mijo, not at all—you've almost been carrying me for several hours!"

They couldn't find any large rocks, so they sat on the ground, Edmund having to help lower his father, worrying how he'd get him back up again. Filastro's heart pounded. He blinked his eyes and wiped his face; everything was beginning to blur. After several minutes, Edmund stood up noticing something in the dirt. "Are those tire tracks?" Filastro kept his eyes on a clump of weeds in front of him.

Edmund followed the faint trail with his eyes. There were two sets of tracks. "It's not possible that . . ." His heart sunk, suddenly remembering his uncertainty upon leaving the shack. He saw a water bottle and some clothes a few yards away, the remains of a fire a few feet further. He scanned the landscape, squinting his eyes to make out forms in the darkness. Then he saw it. "No! No! It's not possible!" he cried.

Hearing the fear in his son's voice, Filastro's head jerked up. "What is it, mijo?"

"We're in the same place! We walked right back where we came from!"

Filastro looked around. "It could be another camp."

Edmund shook his head, continuing to stare at what had confirmed his suspicions. He pointed. "Look, it's Don Homobono."

Filastro was silent. He stared at the body, a resigned expression on his face.

"Ah!" Edmund cried in frustration. He tore at his shirt and stomped the ground. "We'll never make it! Never! Never! All this way for nothing!"

He continued until Filastro called out, "Edmund! Stop it!" His voice calmed. "We can still make it back. If we head in the direction we just came, we'll hit the shack again and then travel a little further. If we need to turn back, we can, then at least be safe for the next day."

"It's too far, we'll never make it—your knee is too bad!"

"No, we will. We'll take it slow, there's plenty of darkness left—"

"No, we can't," Edmund said, wiping tears from his face. "Let's head back to the town they said was close to here. Where Ricardo is. And from there we'll rest and decide what to do."

Filastro weighed this. After a moment he nodded, sighing, "OK, mijo, yes, that's a better idea." He leaned his head back on the ground and stared at the sky full of stars. He was conscious of his chest rising and lowering; his heavy breathing began to calm. He closed his eyes.

✳   ✳   ✳

When he woke he found Edmund rocking back and forth, his arms around his knees, his head bowed. He was sniffling, repeating to himself, "No, no, no, no . . ."

Filastro lifted his head. "Mijo, what's wrong?"

Edmund jerked up. "Papá!" he cried. "I couldn't wake you. You had passed out—I thought maybe you were—are you OK now?"

Filastro rose to his elbows. "I think. Help me to my feet."

Edmund scrambled up, grabbed underneath his father's arms, and lifted him. Filastro was able to give little of his own strength. Propping him up, Edmund scooted over to see if Filastro could stand on his own. He moved some more and Filastro held out his hand for support. "Stay close," Filastro said. "Let me have your shoulder."

He stepped forward and Edmund moved with him. They traveled ten yards before Filastro's legs gave way. Edmund reached for him, but his father's weight was too much and he fell along with him. Filastro groaned in pain. Edmund had broken his father's fall, but now he was being crushed underneath him. He had to push and slide, push and slide. He felt his shirt rise up and the scrape of rocks and dirt, the prick of a spiky weed against his bare back. Finally he was able to break free. He turned his father over, grabbed underneath his armpits, and lifted his torso, propping him up. Filastro was just a heavy, limp mass. "I can't, I can't," he kept saying. "Go on without me. You'll be able to make it."

"No, Papá, don't say that," Edmund said. They were sitting back to back, Edmund pressing against Filastro so that he stayed upright.

"Let's just rest some more," Filastro said, calming. "I'll be OK. Don't let me sleep. Talk to me—don't let me go to sleep. I need to stay awake. I'll rest and regain my strength . . . we'll make it . . . talk to me."

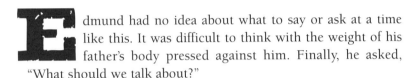
Edmund had no idea about what to say or ask at a time like this. It was difficult to think with the weight of his father's body pressed against him. Finally, he asked, "What should we talk about?"

"The girl you played the guitar for," Filastro said, "the one who left." He shifted his position, pressing harder against Edmund's back. "You love her?"

"Yes," Edmund grunted.

"That's good, mijo."

"What's good?"

"It's good that you love her. It is good to fall in love, especially at your age."

"It doesn't feel good; it's been nothing but torment. And now look at me—in the middle of the desert all because I wanted to see her again."

Filastro chuckled. "But you'll be fine. Love makes you crazy, makes you—" he paused, "just crazy."

"Were you like that—ever, like with Mamá?"

"Who, me? And your amá? Yes, I guess there was a time."

"You don't remember?"

"No, no, I do. It was a long time ago, though."

"How did you meet?"

Filastro breathed in deeply and sighed. He was quiet for a long time. "We met at a wedding," he began. "One of my cousins, I think, I don't remember whose it was. Your mother was there, too—"

"What did she look like? Beautiful?"

"Who, your mamá? Well, I—uh—you see, what happened was I started drinking early, so I don't remember what she looked like exactly, just that—uh—well, I was drinking a lot and I was dancing with every girl I could get my hands on—"

"Did you dance with Mamá?"

"No, I didn't, or at least I don't think I did. No, no, I didn't."

"Why didn't you dance with her?"

"I don't think she liked to dance."

"But Mamá loves to dance."

"Well, maybe then she didn't."

"No, she says that she loved to dance ever since she was a little girl—"

"Edmund, I don't know, then. I don't know why I didn't dance with her. The point is I was dancing and drinking and then I rolled over my ankle and fell. It was my own fault. I was spinning around too much and that's not a good idea when you're drunk. I got up and was embarrassed, so I decided to pretend that someone had tripped me so that I didn't look so stupid. So I pushed the guy closest to me and said, 'Watch it with your dance moves, you ugly goat.' The only thing was this was the bride's father. But I was already blurry-eyed, so I didn't pay attention. Everyone started yelling, 'Go home you drunk! Go home! Drunks are always ruining weddings!' I felt even more stupid and embarrassed, so of course it made me want to fight someone. But everybody kept moving away from me so that I couldn't get my hands on anyone—"

"This is the story about how you met Mamá?" Edmund asked.

"Yes, yes, let me finish. I was just swinging my arms, lunging at people, and everybody was laughing. It felt like the entire dance hall was laughing and pointing at me. I decided I was going to make as big a scene as possible. If I couldn't beat up someone, I was going to—I don't know what I had in mind—but I headed for the food table. I was going to knock it over, probably—" he chuckled, imagining himself.

"And about Mamá?"

"I'll get to that, mijo. Just before I was about to knock over the table full of food, I noticed a girl who had broken my heart. Her name was Alfonsa, like your sister. Your sister was named after her, in fact. Well, I was still in love with her and still upset that she wouldn't have me anymore. So when I saw her face, her beautiful eyes, red lips, her hair done so nicely, I sobered up some. She had this way of looking at you with her eyes half open, her mouth puckered. It made her look like the biggest bitch in the world, but everyone wanted her for that very reason, including me, even though she had called me a bastard. I decided to pretend that I was acting like this because of her. So I said, 'Alfonsa, see what's become of me! See what you've done!' She turned bright red and everybody in the dance hall turned to look at her as if she was the one to blame. Because a man who's drunk for no reason is a son of a bitch, but a man drunk because his heart is broken, well, that's understandable, especially at a wedding. So I left, stumbling out, my hand clenched to my chest—" Filastro chuckled again.

"And Mamá?" Edmund asked, wanting at least some mention of her.

"And your mamá was outside getting some fresh air with her friends. I stumbled right into them. They hadn't witnessed what I had done, thankfully. One of her friends said, 'Watch it, you drunk!' They all laughed playfully. I decided to try my luck and get a date—"

"With Mamá?" Edmund anticipated.

"No, no," Filastro sighed. "I asked the girl who had told me to watch it. 'How about we go for a drink at Beny's Place?' I said. She waved me off. So I tried my luck with the girl next to her. 'And you, beautiful thing?' She smiled flirtatiously and I knew that if I waited around long enough I'd take her home, but I didn't want to hang around. So I asked the next girl and the next and they all just shooed me away. So then I see your mamá, and she looked—"

"Did she look beautiful?"

"Well, yes, later on I saw that. At first she seemed kind of plain, but I thought her eyes were pretty . . . I think. Yes, I thought she had very pretty eyes. Then I said to her my usual line, 'I didn't ask you first because I knew a decent girl like you wouldn't have any time for a drunk like me.' Her friends decided to head inside because they were cold and tired of me. So there I was, ready to just go home and sleep, when I hear your mamá say to me, 'Hey, drunk guy, you're right, I am decent, but I'll walk with you.' She saved my night! All my embarrassment and anger went away and I took her arm in mine, and we went to the plaza. Later she told me that she felt bad for me, that I looked so sad. She wanted to cheer me up. She never went back inside, so she never heard that I was the drunk who was about to ruin the wedding." Filastro stopped and was quiet.

Edmund waited for more. "And that's it?" he asked.

"No, that's not it." Filastro leaned his head back to look at the sky. Edmund felt his father's head against his own.

o on without me, mijo," Filastro whispered.

"No, don't say that, Papá."

"I've been a son of a bitch my entire life. I deserve this fate, to die like this."

"But you've changed. You're not how you used to be."

"What does that matter, mijo? Who but you knows? And does it make up for my entire life of cheating and drinking, trying to destroy myself and everyone around me? What's a couple of months of being a decent man compared to a lifetime of shit?"

"But it'll be more than a couple of months. We'll make it across and show Abel, Ezekiel, Tomy, Gandolfo, and Agnes and Alfonsa that you've changed, that you're a good man now. Then you have the rest of your life."

"No, it'll come back."

"What will?"

"Me. I'll come back."

"But this is you, right?"

Edmund felt his father shake his head. "Who knows? I sure don't. I don't even know what happened to me. Seems to me once a shit always a shit."

"What did happen to you?"

"Lost my compadres, almost lost my life. I was tortured for weeks, and all I wanted was to live. Wanted to live so badly that I—I—mijo, I don't even know why I wanted to live—for what? I am nothing, I've always known that. A shit. Worthless. But there I was wishing just to breathe and be happy and have my life back again. But now I see that it doesn't matter. I thought I had a second chance, but death was coming for me anyway. I escaped it for no reason, no reason at all. I'll die here and there'll be no difference than if I had been killed months ago."

"But you changed."

"For what? Your mamá still hates me, your brothers and sisters will remember me as I was when they left. There's no difference . . . no one knows."

"But I know. I know you changed."

"Yes, but—"

"Doesn't it matter that I know?"

"You always knew. You never hated me."

"I didn't. I didn't hate you."

"Why? Because I didn't beat you?"

"I don't know why; I just didn't. Because you're my papá, that's why."

"But I'm father to your brothers and sisters, too."

Edmund began to cry. "I don't know why I didn't hate you, I don't know why, I just didn't." He tried to muffle his sobs.

"Don't cry, mijo, don't cry. I deserve this. It's you who doesn't. I'm sorry. I wish I had made it so that you could've seen Ingrid again—"

"No! If I hadn't wanted to see her, we would've just gone to the town and been fine, but I said I'd go without you and you felt like you had to. If it hadn't been for me—"

"Edmund, you know that's not true. I did it because I wanted to cross. I wanted to see my children, I wanted to bring them back to your mother. I wanted to change my life. You can't blame yourself. And we'll be fine. Don't cry; we'll be fine. We'll rest and head back to that town and see a doctor about my leg—we'll be OK. Stop, stop crying—"

Edmund wiped his eyes and sniffed a few times. He wiped his nose with his hand and then wiped his wet hand on the dirt. "Why did you beat them so much?"

He felt his father shrug.

"You don't know why?"

"I don't know," Filastro said, his voice hoarse. "I was just angry."

"At what?"

"Just angry. Angry that nothing ever turned out how I wanted."

"Like what?"

"Mijo, I don't know," Filastro whispered. "I wish I could tell you. I wish I could explain, but I can't explain it to myself. It's just how I was inside. Angry. And drinking helped, helped make me— it took away some of the anger. But it always came back."

"What if the anger comes for me?"

"What do you mean?"

"The anger, Papá. Sometimes I have it too."

"Not like me, mijo. You'll never be like me."

"But what if I am? What if when I get older and have a wife and children? Right now I get angry and no one seems to care because what can I do? I'm just a little kid; I can't hurt anyone."

"Edmund, I promise. You won't be like me. I promise you."

"But how can you know? What were you like at my age?"

"I don't know how I was. I don't remember. But you're not like me."

Edmund was quiet. After several minutes of silence, he leaned forward to grab a rock by his foot. He felt his father's body fall backward against him. Filastro grunted and struggled to raise himself, but his arms were too weak. To come unfolded, Edmund had to push backward with all his strength. When his own breathing calmed, he could feel and hear his father's. "I fell asleep," Filastro gasped. "Keep talking, I can't fall asleep. I'm sorry. Keep talking."

Edmund thought quickly. "OK, then, tell me what happened next with Mamá."

He felt Filastro shake his head. "No, let it remain in the past. A son shouldn't know everything."

"Why? What happened?"

Filastro allowed his breathing to calm before answering. "Nothing, just more of the same. I've always been a bastard; who doesn't know that? With your mother it was no different. I took advantage of her, as I did others. She was the first to end up pregnant. And then she wouldn't let me go. She pursued me until I had no choice but to marry."

"So you never loved her?"

"Maybe I did. Yes, I did, but only with time. It's not like it is with you, at your age. It gets more complicated when you're older. Love isn't like some song, some soap opera."

"If you never loved her, then why do you want her back?"

"Because I need her. I've been with her for more than half my life. That is a kind of love."

"I don't understand."

"Someday you will. Only these last couple of months have I thought about it. Before, never. But now I want to bring your brothers and sisters to her because your mother deserves to be happy. She deserves more than I've given her."

Edmund was quiet for a minute before asking, "Do you love Hortensia?"

"Why do you ask that?"

"Because she loves you."

"How do you know?"

"Because I can tell."

"How?"

"Because I love Ingrid. I can sometimes see it in others. She would do anything for you."

"Edmund, I don't know. I've never thought much about these things, let alone talk about them. Now, come on. Help me rise. We should get going or else the sun will catch us."

Standing up consumed what energy they had stored resting. Edmund was panting by the time he pulled his father to his feet. He had no strength left in his upper body, but seeing his father's pain and exhaustion, he gave him his shoulder to lean on anyway. He stepped ahead, focusing on the ground in front of them, knowing that if Filastro tripped it would be impossible to pull him back up again.

They walked for twenty minutes before Edmund stopped suddenly, grabbing hold of his father so that momentum didn't propel him forward.

"What is it?" Filastro murmured.

"Are we sure we're heading in the right direction?"

"I don't know," he said, his voice barely audible. "Aren't we heading in the same direction we started in—south, no?"

"Yeah, but how do you know we're going south? When we sat down to rest I got turned around. And the robbers just pointed—maybe it's south, southwest, east? We can't make another mistake."

Filastro said nothing for a long time. He was breathing heavily. "Mijo, I don't know," he said finally.

They walked on. Edmund saw a glimmer of light in the distance. He thought it could be the town, but maybe it was just the moonlight. As they walked, he felt more and more of his father's weight. He adjusted his father's arm so that it rested on a different part of his shoulder, and placed his other arm around Filastro's side, pulling him closer. Sweat streamed down his forehead; he couldn't wipe the drops from his eyes.

"Papá, are you OK?"

Filastro uttered no response.

Just as his body was about to collapse, Edmund spotted a large boulder ten yards ahead, tall enough that Filastro could lean against it while he rested his shoulder. "We'll stop there"— Edmund grunted—"for a little bit . . . OK, Papá?" Edmund grunted again, trying to shift the weight. He now felt as if he was carrying his father.

Anticipating relief, Edmund stepped forward too quickly and tripped over his own feet. He fell face forward, his father's body on top of him. Filastro made no sound, not even a grunt or moan. The weight crushed Edmund; he felt the body's stiffness, realizing it had been that way for a while—ten minutes, an hour? He had lost track of time. He squirmed out from underneath the body, breathing heavily, crying. Once free, he lay on the dirt, catching his breath, wondering what to do next.

Using the little strength he had left, he rose and propped up his father so that they sat back to back. His eyes closed and he opened them, but they closed again. Despite his terror, sleep overcame him.

Edmund felt the sun beating down on his face. He struggled to open his heavy eyelids, feeling the pain of the light. He looked around him, hoping he'd see something in the morning light that he hadn't noticed in the darkness. Still, nothing but desert. He felt Filastro's back against his own. He carefully shifted on the hard ground knowing that if he moved too much, his father's body would fall to the dirt. He was afraid to turn his head.

When border patrolman Lt. Percibal Ruiz arrived home from work, he found his wife sitting on the couch grading papers. She was a teacher at the elementary school and had crossed the border herself twenty years ago with her parents. She understood that his job was his job, and better her husband arrest and detain people than some of the ruffians who would fill his position the minute he resigned. Still, she asked that he not mention his work to her. Not one word.

He had tried just the other day. He told her a story he'd heard about a troupe of clowns who'd crossed the border in full gear. A colleague of his claimed he found the troupe huddled around a campfire, heating tortillas. Their faces were painted, their red noses on. They hadn't tried to run, but merely began putting on an act, falling over one another, running around with exaggerated strides, honking horns. The man and his partners were so surprised—confused was more like it—that they only caught one of them. The rest escaped, two of them in what looked like a cardboard car; they were holding cutouts and making engine noises. When the colleague and his partners asked the detainee about the clown show, the man responded with a mime act. By that time, however, the humor of the situation had worn off and they were too frustrated at having lost seven illegals. When Percibal finished telling the story, he thought his wife would at least laugh. Instead, she said, "Is that what you guys do, just sit around and make up ludicrous border-crossing stories? Well, here's one. Ana's mother and father were taken from work yesterday—deported. She's staying with an aunt now and has no idea where her parents are!"

"Who's Ana?" he asked, exasperated because no matter how many times he delineated his job from the INS, his wife still conflated the two.

"One of my students."

"Well, I'm sorry. You have to admit, though, clowns? That's funny, right?"

Apparently not. Today, however, a story weighed on him that wasn't the least bit humorous. He had found a fourteen-year old boy alongside his dead father. The boy looked younger, more like a child. The father's leg was injured badly; from what he gathered later, the injury had happened before they tried to cross and worsened during the journey. If he hadn't died, it would have to have been amputated.

He and his partner had approached and the boy didn't even look up. He just stared blankly ahead, he and his father back-to-back. Thankfully, they found him early or else the boy would've been dead as well. All through dinner he wanted to tell his wife what had happened, but could see in her face that she wasn't in the mood. "You'd think I picked them off with a rifle," he thought to himself. If he hadn't found the boy, he would have surely died. He saved a life today, as he did every day, and his wife refused to hear. They ate dinner in silence and then watched television. Usually they cuddled on the couch, but tonight he didn't feel like it.

When they were in bed his wife said to him, "What's wrong? You haven't said a word all night."

"You don't want to hear it," he mumbled. He reached to shut off the light.

"Wait. You look really bothered. Tell me."

Percibal sighed. "Today in the morning," he began, "Mitch and I came across this kid. Just a boy. He said he was fourteen, but he looked no older than Johnny. He and his father were out there, no more than a hundred yards from Fox Crossing. A mile further and they'd have hit a town either side of the border. We found them sitting back-to-back. The father was dead."

His wife was silent.

"We approached the boy and he didn't look at us, just kept staring ahead. We tried talking to him, but he didn't respond. It wasn't until later, back at the station, that we got more information from him—just his name, where he was from, but at first he was just silent. He wouldn't look at his dad. The father had a messed up leg; should've never been out there."

He was quiet and his wife began to cry. "I'm sorry," his wife said. "Is that all you wanted to tell me?"

Percibal shook his head. "No, there's more." He paused.

"What is it?" his wife said, placing her hand on his.

"The thing is, afterward I didn't feel like returning back to patrol, so I told the captain and he said it'd be all right if I just processed detainees for the rest of the day. That meant I saw the kid again. Well, he recognized me right away, and after getting some food and water he looked a little better, and he started talking to me. At first, I listened to him, smiling and nodding my head, just continuing my paperwork, feeling bad for him. I thought he just needed someone to talk to. But the kid wouldn't stop talking. I guess he thought he was in trouble, like in jail, and that he needed to convince me he'd done nothing wrong. So he started telling me about all his brothers, and how they left one by one because their father beat them, and that the father beat his mother and sisters, too, and that the sisters came here because one of them got pregnant and was afraid of what the father might do.

"After an hour or so I told him he should probably get some rest, but he just told me he wasn't tired and plus, he wasn't finished telling me what happened. So I just nodded my head, and tried to fill out the paperwork while he talked, but every now and then he'd stop and ask me, 'Do you know why I said that to so and so?' and I'd have to ask him to repeat himself. After this happened like five times, he informed me that some old man had taught him how to tell if someone is listening to your story or not. So I just set down my pen and listened to him because it was easier than half-listening. Anyway, he talked a lot about how his father was badly hurt in some accident and became a different man as a result; he no longer got angry, no longer drank, even. The mother had left by this time and now the father wanted her to return. But she told the boy she wouldn't take his father back unless the man went to the United States and apologized to every single one of his sons and daughters and begged their forgiveness.

"After telling me that this was the reason they were coming here, the kid stopped and waited for me to respond. But what could I say except, 'All right, do you want anything else to eat?' And he just said, 'No, I'd like to go to Nebraska and Wyoming and Texas to tell my brothers and sisters that our father is dead and that before he died he became a good man.' I told him that I couldn't help him, and that we had to return him to Mexico the next day. And I guess he thought I wasn't convinced of his innocence, so then he began telling me about this girl he was in love with and how he'd learned to play the guitar in order to serenade her. I guess she came here with her family not too long ago and that's another reason why he needed me to set him free, so he could go visit California.

"By now it was late afternoon and the kid was still talking. I had my break and he followed me to the door and told me that if I didn't believe he could play the guitar good, I should bring one and he'd show me. I told him I was just stepping out for a Coke in the vending machine. When I came back, he was waiting for me and he started right in telling me all that had happened up until leaving for here and then when he finished, he asked if that was enough. I said, 'Enough what?' 'Enough to go,' he said.

"I said I couldn't let him go, that there are ways, but I'd get in trouble. 'For what?' he asked me. And I told him about all the legal regulations and protocol and he just said, 'But I have to tell my brothers and sisters about our papá.' I told him sorry. He looked pissed off, but I just had to ignore him. After that he went to the corner and just sat and started telling other detainees loud enough for me to hear that I didn't know anything and that I talked funny and I must be the assistant because I didn't have any say-so . . . "

Percibal stopped and his wife waited, sensing there was more. He was lost in thought.

"What else?" she asked.

"I told the captain I'd bring the kid to the overnight detention center, where they keep the processed detainees, but instead—"

"Percibal, you didn't," she said, suddenly knowing what her husband was about to say.

"I bought him a ticket to Texas. He wanted to go to Nebraska first, but I told him Texas was closer. And then I told him all the places he wanted to go were really far from one another, but he didn't seem to care. He just kept telling me he'd already been on a fourteen-hour bus ride and who knows how long walking in the desert."

"But—but he's just a boy, how could you—all alone—"

He rose and found his pants that he'd hung in the closet. He came back with a folded piece of paper and handed it to his wife. "He wanted me to send this to his girlfriend in California. He wanted her to get it before he arrived." He scooted down on the bed and pulled the sheet over his chest. He stared up at the ceiling, thinking of the boy's face when he told him he'd let him go only if he stopped talking. He didn't even appear surprised, merely dogged. "He'll be fine," Percibal told his wife. "I'm sure of it."

She unfolded the piece of paper and read the letter.

Ingrid

I am in the United States! First I have to go to Texas and then Nebraska and then Wyoming to visit my brothers and sisters but then I will visit you in San José So maybe I'll be there like in two or three days. Will you come meet me at the bus stop because I have no idea where you live? If not that's all right I will ask around. I have your address in my head. How big a town is San José? Not to worry I will see you soon.

Warmest regards,

Edmund